GOING NOWHERE FAST
BY: SAMUEL T. YEAGER

D1516948

A SPECIAL THANKS

First and forever appreciated, the Creator, and most High, GOD. You've held fast with your protective, and loving hand and I am humbly grateful. *Thank you.*

Mother, I want to thank you for never giving up on me, even when my actions reflected I gave up on self. You mean the world to me, and I'm honored to have a mother as wonderful as you.

To my starting five, Cha'vion, La'don, Tyteanna, Scooter and lil Sam, just know your father has always loved you, even in my absence. You have always been the strength that kept me pushing forward. *Thank you.*

I would like to give a special thanks to a pillar of love, honor and respect in my family, my little brother. You've rose to the occasion and held the family down like a King should, time, and time again. Keep doing your thing. *Thank you, Charles Yeager.*

To those that held me down during the creation of this book, Big Shot, Playa Tone, Teddy Kane, Mad-G, Lil Ed, Mandy, Yung Animal, Shirleen, Mignon, Mone'e, Trina, and the whole MN D.O.C, just to name a few, *Thank you. And for those I failed to mention, thank you too.*

Inclosing, to all I will say is, we will see a brighter day, because it is *A Finer Way.*

GOING NOWHERE FAST

A TALE BY
SAMUEL T. YEAGER

After a dash of Gang Life, two teaspoons of Drug
Abuse, a gallon of Unhealthy Love, and six ounces of
the Deepest desire, to take your Family away from the
Madness in the HOOD, on top of sixty kilos of Failure,
then you would only possess, half of the Recipe of
MIKE'S LIFE...

"GOING NOWHERE FAST" is a reflection of Dis
function in its Rawest form...

So, if you're looking for Chaos and Confusion in a Tale
that's based on a True Story, "GOING NOWHERE FAST"
will give you that, and much, much more...

A Special Note to The Reader

As you dive into Mike's journey through life, embrace the changes of his mind-state. Once that's accomplished, you will give yourself a chance to see and feel the story for what it really is......

GOING NOWHERE FAST
PREFACE

Mike cracked the fortune cookie in half and slowly pulled out the fortune. Once he got a firm grip on it, using the thumb and index finger of both hands, he read it.

"KEEP CALM THE BIG ONE IS COMING".

Mike was a lost child from birth, destine to go down the wrong path of life. Growing up on the south side of Minneapolis played a small part in the life style he chose. The main force behind such a decision was his family. Every since he could remember, his family kept their hands in the fast life, pimping, running numbers, and the biggest of all, selling drugs.

Mike watched his family lose their devotion as they dug deeper into using the drugs they sold for so many years. Once he was of age, to where he understood what was going on around him, he made up his mind, that he would hit the streets and make it big. The plan, make enough money so he could take his mom away from the madness, so they could once again be a strong family.

Mike knew something was missing out of his life, and he figured it had to be true love. When it came to his father, he was never really around, so to Mike, his dad couldn't possibly love him. When it came to his mother, she wouldn't stop using when he would ask her to. So, with her love, something had to be missing.

After giving birth to such an understanding, Mike went to the streets to chase down his dream of finding that love and acceptance.

Only if he knew how fast his life was slipping away........

GOING NOWHERE FAST
CHAPTER 1

Fresh out of the County Home School, which is a detention center for minors, Mike had a plan.
He spent the last five months visualizing his fast future, and slick talking his way to an early release.

If everything went right, his girlfriend Jackie would get her own apartment, now that she was on Aid. He would then move in with her and their daughter Shonna, so they could be a family. The mission was all about working and talking things slow, until he got off probation.

Once word came down from his counselor Mr. Jones, that he would get out on his early release date, the only one Mike called and told was Jackie. He had to make sure she was around, so he could get a piece of that fine ass of hers right away.

When Mike asked Mr. Jones for a ride home, he was more than happy to do so. Even though Mike showed a great deal of growth over the five months that he was in his program, Mr. Jones still found himself worry about him.

On the ride home, Mike kept thinking how he was going to do right, keep his nose clean, and be a family man. It wasn't until they were exiting the freeway, that Mike realized for the first time, "Damn, mom moved and I don't know shit about the new spot."

As if such a thought had drained him of his energy, he leaned to his right and let his head rest on the window, as he closed his eyes.

Still dwelling on his new dilemma, Mike didn't even realize they were no longer moving.

"We're here!"

Was all Mr. Jones had to say for Mike to snap out of his zone. Before he made a move, he quickly surveyed the scene. What Mike witnessed, was all he knew, fools out and about moving fast.

Mike couldn't see the worried look on his face, but Mr. Jones sure did. "Mike, you'll be fine."

"Yeah, I know," Mike replied.

At that moment, such words of encouragement, was truly needed, because Mike found himself questioning his ability to stay focused.

"It's going to be hard, but I'll make it," he then added.

"I know you will," Mr. Jones agreed, sizing Mike up.

"Well, let me get out of here," was Mike's exiting words, as he tried to make it sound convincing.

"Alright then, take care and feel free to call, you got my office number."

Without another word said, Mike grabbed his bag and got out of the van. He stood there in the street, and didn't move until he saw his counselor turn the corner. Before he could cross the street, to get to get to his building, he saw some faces he knew, and some transactions he also knew were drug deals. "Damn, mom moved right in the zone," he thought. He just shook his head and kept on moving.

A smooth six taps on the door, like always, gave birth to a frenzy of foot movements in the house. That put a smile on his face as he pictured his oldest sister Tony, along with his little brother Sam, getting overpowered by their mom, so she could be the first to open the door and see his face.

He heard his mom say, "Is that my baby, the Lord brought by baby home". If there was one thing he hated most, it was hearing her saying things like that. He knew she was still getting her lungs dirty from time to time, with that crack smoke.

As the door came open, he masked his frown with a half cocked smile. He soon found himself drenched in hugs and kisses. His mom looked back in the house and said,

"Jackie look, my baby's home! So Girl you better come get you some of this suga!"

Mike pushed his way into the house, to see Jackie still at the table looking finer ever. Right away their eyes locked and their minds became one. The only thing on their mind was pleasing the other and they both knew it.

It was Mike that broke their connection when he started looking around the apartment. Knowing her son, his mom said, " Baby your room is in the back. All you got to do is walk straight back and it's the door you see at the end of the hallway."

With that said, Mike didn't waste any time on heading for his room. As he walked down the hall, the first door to the right opened, and his mom's boyfriend Ron, came walking out. All Mike could think when he saw him was, "why is mom fucking with this drunk loser?"

As if he could read Mike's mind, Ron looked at him and said, "I'm very good to your mother."

"Yeah right," was Mike's reply as he kept on walking.

Mike didn't realize how he had missed the bathroom and the kitchen. The only thing on his mind was getting a piece of that ass of Jackie's, as he tried to make up for the five months he spent on lock-down. As soon as he made it to his room he turned around to see the smiling face of his little sister, Tasha. With no second thought, he picked her up and gave her a hug and real big kiss.

"Mike, are you here to stay, this time?"

"Yeah, I don't got to go back."
"That's good, because I miss you."

"Well, I miss you to. So how old are you now?"
"Six."
"You're getting old."
"No I'm not."
"O.K., if you say so, but look, go get Jackie".
"O.K."
After he put his sister down and she went running down the hallway, he opened the door to his room. He was pleased to see a nicely made bed and a radio next to it. He figured that was all that was needed to complete the task of pleasing Jackie. To set the mood, he turned on the radio, only to find it already on "KMOJ." By the time he got done working the volume, he turned around to see Jackie standing there with back to the closed door. Feeling himself coming to life from seeing her, he said, "What's up, Ba?"
More than ready to feel him inside of her, Jackie simply replied, "you."
"Is that right," he asked?
"I ain't even going to answer that," she replied. "But here take this."
Jackie then walked over to Mike and handed him a small bag of light green hydro and blunt. Mike cracked a smile as he looked at her, prouder than ever. He then quickly opened the blunt and cracked it down the middle; he was more than ready to get the party started. With that out of the way, he realized he had now where to dumb the tobacco.
Jackie saw what was going on, so she figured she would help. "Do you want me to go flush it for you real quick," she asked?
Mike gave her a sharp "No." In his mind, there was no way he was about to let her out of his sight, not even for a minute. Not until he got a piece of that ass, first.

Knowing he had to act fast, before the mood was lost, Mike stepped over to the window, which was cracked a little, and he dumped the blunt in the window sill. Jackie

just looked at him and shook her head. Already know what she was thinking, Mike said, "Shit, I don't got no time to be playing games, and I ain't letting you out my sight and I mean that. Now come give me a kiss, with your fine ass."

He knew how to work her and he did it every time. That's why she was so loyal to him, and they both loved it.

When Mike finished rolling up, he ran into another problem, he didn't have a light. Even though he didn't think she would have one, he asked anyway, "Jackie, you got a light?"

Reluctantly she reached in her pocket and came out with a red Bic. She figured he wouldn't like the color, and she was right.

"What the fuck is this," Mike snapped?

Looking away, because she hated seeing him mad, Jackie was like; "Stop trippin' I took it from one of my cousins."

Stuck on some gang shit, Mike said; "Yeah that's the problem."

On the verge of snapping herself, Jackie made eye contact with Mike and was like "Anyway."

Realizing she was getting mad, Mike reluctantly took the lighter and lit the blunt. As if his tolerance was still at an all time high, like it was before he went away, he took a deep pull. After taking such a hit, he started coughing and choking, as a tear or two rolled down his cheek.

"Damn! Nigga, don't kill yourself," Jackie cried out.

Mike just looked at her with a smile on his face as he hit it again. Satisfied with the tingle in the back of his throat, he handed Jackie the blunt and told her to hit it. Even though she didn't smoke, she hit it anyway.

Once they smoked half of it, Mike put it out on the window sill. He then laid back on the bed and watched as

11

Jackie climbed on top of him. To his liking, she began to kiss him softly, while her hands quickly went to work on his belt.

It didn't take Jackie long to achieve her main goal of breaching the barrier of his pants. With a little help from Mike, she then pulled boxers and all off with one smooth swoop. Mike's joystick was exposed and it was fully alert. Jackie didn't waste no time taking complete control of it.
Mike looked down at her in wonder. With one calculated motion, Jackie slowly licked the base. She then worked her way all the way up to his firing hole. Mike's body went tense from the pleasure and she climbed on top of him and placed her hands on his chest. With both of their hearts pounding, they looked deep into each other eyes. One of Jackie's hands disappeared as she guided Mike's joystick into her wet walls of pleasure. As it penetrated, it sent both them soaring. It took the strength of then thousand men to hold them back from reaching their peak.
Back in control of herself, Jackie regained her focus, when it came to the mission at hand. With both hands back on his chest, she arched her back as far as it would go, as she rode him in the most exotic way. Every time Mike would try to grab hold, she would knock his hands off. Such actions were driving him crazy. He couldn't take it anymore, so with a burst of energy, he lifted her up and laid her on her back. It was his time to play and he was more than ready to do so.
Jackie couldn't ask for anything more and her action said just that. As she cried out, "Oh yes," as she opened her legs even wider. She then cocked and locked them. She wanted to make sure Mike had access to both hands, so he could do whatever came to mind, with them.
Mike worked her fast then slow, as he whispered dirty shit in her ear. It was her slutty replies that fed his ego, forcing him to work her even harder.

"Oh yes Daddy, hit this pussy,"
"Oh you like that," he asked?
"Yes, oh yes, Damn, I missed you".

"I missed you too, baby".
The faster Mike worked it, the harder Jackie threw it back to him. Together, they both went limp, as the five months of built up pressure was released.
Once Mike's breathing slowed down, he rolled over and grabbed the blunt. He re-lit it, and then as if he lost track during their session, he asked, "What year is it?"
Playing along, Jackie cracked a smile and replied in her most politest voice, "Well, It's June 14, 1994, and you're 17 years old. And if you need to know the time, its around one."
Mike didn't bother to hit her with a come back, he just started laughing. He was feeling better than he had for a long time, and he was loving it.
Before he took the last hit of the blunt roach, he told Jackie, "Go start the shower".
Quickly, she wrapped herself in one of the sheets and tip-toed down the hall and into the bathroom. When she came back in the room, Mike was lying on the bed, still naked. Knowing he was high, Jackie took his hand and lead the way to the shower.
By the time they washed each other up and rinsed off, Mike's joystick came back to life. Even though Jackie was behind it, she said, "You know it ain't enough room in here for that".
Still wet, Mike stepped out and Jackie followed, already knowing where they were headed. Jackie backed up to the sink, and Mike picked her up and set her there; for a quick love session.
Once they got back in the shower, there was a knock on the door. Mike said, "Who is it"?
"It's your mother, and I got some towels for you".

Reluctantly, Mike got out and walked to the door. With the door cracked, his mom handed him the two towels and said, " Jackie, what are you in there doing to my son"?

After hearing such a question, Mike and Jackie couldn't help but laugh. As she walked away, his mom too was laughing.
When Mike turned around to walk back to the shower, he realized for the first time, how small the bathroom was.   V "Damn! Ba look, I could jump in the tub from the doorway, and you know I ain't no athlete."
" Boy you crazy," Jackie replied, laughing.
" Come on now Ba, this is a bullshit ass bathroom," Mike added. " Look how close the sink is to the toilet and tub. You can wash your hands while you take a shit, now that's bad."
Together they laughed, as they took in the scene.
While Mike was cracking jokes about the bathroom, Jackie turned the water off and got out. She took one of towels from Mike and dried herself off: as Mike did the same. They then wrapped the towels around themselves and headed back to the bedroom.
With project, "please Jackie", out of the way, Mike figured it was time for him to see what his new surroundings were all about. As they got dressed, he checked his pockets. What he felt, he knew had to be money. To his surprise, he pulled out three crispy, one hundred dollar bills. Right away, he knew his mom was behind such a gift.
"Baby, do you got something for me"? He asked, already knowing she did.
No reply came, just action. Jackie reached in her pocket and pulled out two hundred and fifty dollars.
Feeling like his plans were falling into place, Mike's thoughts started flowing again. "Where's my baby at", was the first thing he asked.
"She at home, with my mom".

"Well when am I gonna to see her"? Mike followed up.

"Don't start trippin', you're gonna see her. You know I needed my time, first".

Before Mike could come back with a rebuttal, Jackie walked out of the room, sassy as ever.

It was actions such as that, that kept the flames, between them alive. Mike just stood there with a smile on his face as he shook his head slightly. " Man that girl is crazy," he thought.

Feeling pretty good, Mike got in motion to re-analyze his surroundings. He took the trip back down the hallway, and stopped when he reached the kitchen. Just like the bathroom, it too was oh so small. The ice-box was next to the sink, which was next to the stove. When he saw such a scene, the only thing he could think of, was how he had to get his family away form such bullshit.

When he made it to the living room, he saw that everyone but Ron was sitting at the dinning room table talking.

"Here baby, I got some keys for you," was the first thing his mom said when she looked up to see him.

The set to the car was the only ones he was focused on, as he took the keys from his mom. He then asked, "Mom, is your car out front? Cause I didn't see it when I came in."

"Yeah, there's probably a lot of things you didn't see," Tony cut in on some joking shit.

"You're right about that," Mike fired back. " But I'm bout to go take a look now."

" Well you be careful out there," his mom demanded.

" You already know," Mike replied, as he walked out.

Together, his mom and Tony looked at Jackie and said, " Girl go out there with him."

" What you thought I wasn't," Jackie fired back, already on her way to the door.

GOING NOWHERE FAST
CHAPTER 2

The sun was shinning bright, and it seemed that everyone that lived on the block was out and about, moving around. With Jackie at his side, Mike sat on the front steps of the building, in silence. It was time to take in everything that was going on around him, and that is what he did.

Mike noticed the few cars parked up and down the street, along with his mom's Pontiac and Ron's Caddie, which was in front of the building. Across the street he saw fiends going in and out of two houses, that were side by side. "I bet mom's been over there once or twice," he thought. "I'm home now, so I better not catch no one trying to sell my mom shit!"

To stop himself from getting mad, he knew he needed to think about something else. So he turned to Jackie and asked, "How many apartment are in this building"?

"Six. Two in the basement floor, two on the second and third."

"For real!" Mike fired back in disbelief. " From the outside, you couldn't picture six apartments fitting in this building. That's why all the shit inside is so small."

From behind Mike heard the building door open. He took a look back to see four niggas around his age, coming out. The one that seemed to be leading the pack stopped and said, "What's up, you must be Lolla's son?"

Quick and strong, Mike shot back, "That's right."

Knowing her man, Jackie gave Mike a once over, to make sure he was still cool. She knew how he could get at times, and she wasn't in the mood for such madness.

Wanting to get to know Mike, from hearing so much about him, from his mom, the leader of the pack offered his name and a little more. "Mike look, I be up in Apartment Six, and if you need anything, get at me. They call me Tee."

"Well, I see you already know my name, and I'm sure you also know I just got out".

Tee cracked a smile and said, "Yeah, you're right about that; but look, later we can get together and I'll smoke."

" Cool," Mike replied.

Instead offering a response, Tee caught up with his boys as they walked down the steps.

"So, that's who been selling my mom that shit," was the thought that ran through Mike's mind as he watched Tee walk away.

Jackie took one look at Mike and said, "chill out".

Trying to look confused, Mike was like, "what, I ain't on shit".

"Yeah right", was all she had to say and they both started laughing. It was the sound of a car system, that made Mike regain his focus. There was no car in sight, that he could place the sudden sounds of "Black Super Man" by "Above the Law", coming out of. He heard it at an all time high, and that's when he looked to his left. At the corner he spotted the source, a blue Monte, which he knew was his homie, Blast.

Mike cracked a smile when Blast turned the Monte toward his house. He jumped up and dusted himself off, and started walking to where Blast pulled up too. As Blast got out, Mike saw he wasn't alone. The Big homie, Cie, was with him.

Strictly on business, Blast asked Mike one thing, "Are you ready?"

Without giving it a second thought, Mike replied, "You best believe it".

Hearing all he needed to hear, Blast got back in the car and said, "Give us ten and ten." He then put the car in motion and pulled off.

Mike walked back to the steps to see Jackie glaring at him. He hated when she did that, because the outcome was always the same, him feeling guilty,

"What's up," she asked"?

"What's up with what?"

"If you don't know, I don't know," Jackie replied, as she looked down the street. Knowing she was being played with, and not liking it, she stood up and walked back into the building.

Trying to play tough role, Mike was like "Yeah, take your ass in the house."

After two or three minutes of him sitting there by himself, to his surprise, six of his homies rolled up on bikes. All he could think was, "Damn! Things get around fast."

Needing to know, he asked, "How did ya'll know I was out ?"

It was his homie, Joker, that cut in with, "A little bird told us." Which sent them into a frenzy of laughter.

When things calmed down Joker let it be known what was on his mind. "A Mike, you tryin' to smoke?"

"Hell Yeah," was Mike's reply as a smile appeared on his face. Joker got off his bike and sat next to mike, so he could start project; get your smoke on.

Mike noticed how the others were acting while him and Joker talked. Their eyes stayed fixed on the street, as they kept looking up and down the block. After putting two and two together, Mike realized what was going on. They were on the look-out, and Mike knew they all had good heat on them too. So, knowing he was safe, he relaxed and said, "Joker, hurry up with that blunt."

Everyone's attention shifted when they heard Blast coming up the block. He parked across the street from Mike's building; this time Cie also got out. They then walked over to the building.

The five, which were still sitting on their bikes, paid their respects to Blast and Cie. Then they regained their focus on keeping an eye out for anything funny.

For the next few minutes Mike, Joker, Blast, and Cie sat on the steps talking shit to one another as they enjoyed the smoke in the air. Ready to get back to business, Cie said, " A Mike, can we go in and talk, or something?"

"Right, right," Mike replied in a hurry, all the while getting to his feet

" Cuz, I'll ce out here," said Joker, as he watched his three homies walk in the building.

" Cool, he wont ce long," Cie replied.

When Mike and his two friends walked in, the talking in the house stopped. Everyone then watched as Mike led the way to his room. Before they reached the hallway, Blast and Cie both stopped and said, "Hi" to Mike's mom and sister, Tony.

Once they made it to the room, they sat on the bed, while Mike turned on the radio. That's when Cie said, "Damn, cuz what you been doing in here?"

As they laughed, Mike replied, "Cuz you're already knowing."

Which caused them to laugh even harder. Cie Stood up and reached in his pocket. He pulled out a fat bag of bud, which Mike knew was Hydro. He handed the bag to Blast and told him to roll one up. Then he reached in his other pocket and pulled out two ounces of crack. He threw them on the bed, as he looked at Mike and said, "Get your shit in order and get at me."

"Cuz don't even trip," was Mike's come back as he looked at the two zips.

After using the same spot that Mike had, Blast put the finishing touches on his project. Satisfied with his work, he handed the blunt and bag to Cie.

"Saturday we're having a BBQ," said Cie.

" Bet," Mike replied, happy to hear such new.

" I'll side threw to pick you up." Cie added, putting his bag away.

" Cuz what I got to get?" Mike asked.

" Here, take this to the head, and don't worry about shit," Cie ordered, as he handed Mike the blunt.

"Cool," Mike fired back

" 'ight homie we got to roll, but get at me," said Cie.

" Cuz I'm on it," Mike stated firmly, trying to let the big homie know that he was on his game.

Standing there staring at the two zips of crack on his bed, was how Jackie found him.

"Snap out of it," Jackie ordered. " And what have you got your self into?"

"Close the door, we need to talk", Mike replied, in a low tone.

Jackie closed the door and stood in front of him, as he sat on the bed. Mike tapped the spot next to him and told her to sit down. After one of those little looks and a slight pause, she found her spot on his right side. When he turned to look at her, she looked deep into his eyes and said, " Mike, baby, what are you doing?"

"Baby, I'm gonna make things right, so just ride with me on this one. All I need is a six month run and that's it. By Shonna's birthday, I'll be done. You know how bad I want to get shit right. So, are you with me?"

"Boy, stop playin'," Jackie replied, feeling that tingle from excitement. "You know I'm with you."

With that said and done, Mike started giving out instructions. " Well look baby, go get a plate and look in that small ass bathroom and see if you can find a razor or a safety pin."

Jackie got right to work; she liked doing things for her man. It gave her a sense of worth and purpose.
Mike sat there on the bed, thinking about his new fast future. Then his thoughts were interrupted by Jackie handing him what he asked for. He looked at her with amazement on his face. "Damn baby, what did you do, run and get this shit?"

She had the plate, a razor and a safety pin. She didn't care to respond; she just gave him her famous smirk. He looked over the smirk, as he placed the plate on the bed and put one of the ounces of crack on it. Then he picked up the other ball and handed it to Jackie and told her to hold it.

"What about that on the plate," she asked?

"I need you to bust that down while I run to the store real quick."

" All of it?"

" Yea," Mike replied as he walked out of the room and closed the door behind him. As he made his way to the door, he saw everyone on the couch watching T.V.

"Mom, I'm going to the store, do you need anything?"

"No, but let me give you this pager, before I forget."

"Is it on?"

"You know it is. Something told me to get it turned back on for you. It's the same number and everything. All you got to do is tum it on."

" For real, man I needed this," Mike said, smiling from ear to ear. " Thanks ma'.... I'll be back."

Before he cold make it to the door, his older sister, Tony, was hot on his tail. He looked back at her and said,

21

"Where you going?"

"With you, shit, I need a ride home to get something."

" Where you stay cause I'm on one and I don't got time to be running around town and shit."

"Two houses from your friend that was just at the house."

"Who, Blast?"

"Yeah, I think that's his name."

When they finally made it outside, Mike seen that Joker and his crew was nowhere in sight.

"Damn! I forgot all about Cuz."

"He said he'll be back later."

"Is that right?"

"Yep, that's what he told me to tell you."

" 'ight," Mike replied as he kept it moving. Before they could make it out of the yard, Mike watched as a lady walked his way. What he heard next was like music to his ears.

Once she was close enough for him to hear she asked, " Baby you know where I can get two for thirty?"

With a smile on his face, Mike told her, "If you can be cool while I run to the store, I'll do better then that. Look, just have a seat on the step and trust me, you'll be alright".

The lady did what Mike asked her, as he ran to the car. As he closed the drivers door, he saw Tony was still standing where he had the small conversation with the lady. He opened the passenger door and called out to her. "Girl, if you're coming, come the fuck on!"

Tony ran and got in. Before she could close the door, Mike had the car in motion. The ride to the store was made without a word said. They were both stuck in their own thoughts. While Tony looked straight ahead, to her self she thought, "Damn, mom is good, she knew he was back on. I just hope his shit is good cause I don't want to go home and deal with Ted and his tired ass, for nothing. Shit, I wish I had my new glass on me. I hate that mom broke hers".

When it came to Mike, he was stuck on, how he had a real good feeling on how things would wok out this time. "I couldn't even make it to the car without someone needing something. Man, I hope it's always like this. Boy, fools move over, Mike is home."

With that in mind, he let out a little laugh.

Thinking she missed something, Tony asked, "what's funny?"

Mike didn't bother to respond, he just looked at her and shook his head. Right then he realized, she heard everything that he said to shorty at the building. "Fuck! Now her and mom's gonna be on my back," he couldn't help but think.

When they pulled up to the store, Tony asked, "can you get me some Newport's?"

Without a response, Mike got out and walked into the store. Before he could get all the way inside the store, he noticed a man watching him. He brushed it off and found the aisle the plastic baggies were in. As he picked up a box, he turned to see the man coming his way.

At a whisper, he walked up and asked one thing, " You know where I can copp at around here?"

"Damn, do I got, I'm a drug dealer written on my forehead, or is these fools around here truly off the hook?" Mike thought to himself. Satisfied that the man had the look of a true friend, he gave him directions to the building.

" I know exactly where that's at."

" Well, if you walk around there and give me ten minutes, I'll take good car of you."

" Bet, I been looking for a real motha fucka' to shop wit."

"Don't even trip, I got you. Just have a seat on the steps and I'll be there."

"You gonna look out, right?"

"Yeah, don't trip."

" Well, I'll be there," was the last thing the man said as he headed for the door.

When it came to Mike, "I'm bout to make a killing," was his outburst as he walked to go pay for his shit.

As he placed the box of baggies on the counter the clerk said, "Will that be it?"

"Let me get a pack of Newport 100's and a box of blunts."

The clerk looked at Mike funny, but still got what he asked for. He then started placing the items in a small, brown paper bag.

Seeing that, Mike was like "I don't need a bag."

As the clerk rang up the items he replied, "Yes you do, and that will be $8.47."

Knowing it would piss him off, Mike handed the clerk a hundred dollar bill. Even though the clerk hated given up so much change, his greed wouldn't let him pass up on money. So, he took the hundred dollar bill with a smile and found change.

Mike got back to the car to find Tony still sitting there quietly. He handed her the Newports and put the car in motion. On the way to Tony's, the silence was interrupted by Mike's pager going off. At the same time, they looked down at it.

"Damn, I forgot I even had a pager".

"Shit, you just got it, so who got the number?"

"Didn't you hear mom say it's the same number? Damn! Girl, you almost made me miss the tum".

"How the fuck did I almost make you miss the tum"? "Man, fuck all that, where's your house"?

"Right there, with the brown Cutlass parked in front".

"Who's car is that, "Mike asked?

"It's mine, I got it from aunty."

"Well, how much you want for it right now?"

"Boy, stop playing."

"Do I look like I'm playing?"

" Well give me $300.00 for it right now."

"You ain't said shit."

"We'll see then nigga!"

"Look, get what you got to get and come on.
I got to get moving."

Mike got out and looked over the Cutlass, while Tony ran in. Right away he saw two things about the car that he liked, the white guts, and the clean body. To himself he thought, "All I got to do is get it painted black, put a tint on it and get a real good tune up, come up on some rims, and I'm good."

"Boy come on, let's go."

To Mike's surprise, when he turned around, Tony was already in the car. Determined to get back home as fast as he could, he jumped in the car and pulled off. He ran a red light, or two, as he pushed his luck to the max. Tony just sat there looking at him as she shook her head.

"Boy, you need help."

" Yes I do, so let me give you $250.00 for it."

" Give it to me right now, then."

" I got you, just kick back," was Mike's last words as he pulled up to the building. When he looked up at the steps, he couldn't believe what he saw. The lady, the man, and four more fiends were sitting on his steps.

Once Tony saw Mike's awaiting party, she said,
" What's this, a feen picnic?"

Mike walked up to the man from the store and said, "I'm glad to see you, Eighty, right?"

"Yep."

"Cool, I got you, just let me run in real quick," Mike replied, as he looked at the first lady he met. " Baby girl, walk with me."

As Mike walked into the building, the lady followed. Once in the hallway, Mike asked his new friend, "What's up with them?"

"Shit, they said they wanted to get on. So, I told them to wait for you. Them fools across the street got mad cause we wouldn't fuck wit them. But, fuck 'em, you know?"

"Look baby, go see what they want and let me know."

"Well, two got $100.00, one got $45.00 and the last one got $20.00, and she got more, but she wanted to make sure shit was right."

" Well look, I'm gonna run in real quick and put it together. So, go tell them I'll be right out."

As he walked in the house, his pager went off again, and he said, "Damn, I forgot to call that number back, shit".

He looked down to see it was the same number. Focused on taking care of his business, he ran to his room to find Jackie laying on the bed.

"Baby, where's the plate and shit," he asked?

"Look behind the radio."

When he grabbed the plate, he saw everything was broke down in pill's and halfs. He opened the box of baggies and handed them to Jackie.

"Look, I need you to put two halfs, and two pills together, three times. Then, I need a half and a pill in one bag, a half in another, and in the last one, I need a real fat pill. Hurry up and put that together for me."

" What you gonna do wit' all of that?"

"I got some fools out there waiting for me right now, so lets go."

When Mike opened his door to leave, he found his mom standing right there. Already knowing what she was on, he asked anyway, "Mom what's up?"

"You know what's up."

"Look, I'll be right back, just sit back and chill."

He made his way out the door to find his new friend and
one of the new faces. One by one, she ushered them in and
Mike took care of them. While making the exchange with
the man from the store, he heard his apartment door open.
Mike took a look back to see Jackie standing there. He
knew she was there to make sure he was alright, so he
didn't trip.

" If this is any good, I'll be back," said the man from the
store, as he left.

" Well, you'll be back then," Mike fired back smiling.

With every one else cleared out, Mike gave the half to his
new friend and she handed him the $30 bucks. He put the
twenty in his pocket and handed her ten back.

" That's for helping me out."

" From now on, I'm just fucking with you shorty."

" Well, you know where I'm at," Mike replied.

" I sure do, and I'll be back you best believe that."

"Alright, then, you be cool."

" Oh, I will and I'm gonna bring you some more money."

" Yeah you do that," Mike shot back calmly, ushering her
out the building.

Back in his room, he found the plate once again behind
the radio. With his hand in plastic baggie, he picked up a
half. He then walked to his door, and called his mom. He
knew if he didn't get her out of the way, she would stay on
his back. He wasn't in the mood for that.

" Mike, your sister said are you gonna buy her car or
what?"

"Look mom, take this and tell her to come here."

" Boy don't be trippin', look out for your sister."

"Yeah right, just tell her to come here".

As his mom was leaving, Jackie came back in the room.
With a frown on her face she asked, "Mike, what do you
want me to do with the rest of that?"

"Shit, I thought you was gonna bag it all up."

"You ain't tell me to do all that."

Before he allowed himself too get pissed, Mike took a deep breath, and said, " Cool, look baby, will you do that for me?"

Her response was a smack of the lips, which was followed by her doing what she was asked. Just when Mike was about to comment on Jackie's sign of discomfort, he heard someone walking towards his room. Knowing it was Tony, he walked into the hall to meet her.

" Damn nigga, you can let me in your funky ass room."

" Fuck the bullshit. Girl what you want for the car?"

" I want half and half, that's what I want."

" Here, take this one fifty, and I'll grab three half's for you."

Tony's eyes got big as she eyed Mike's little bankroll. When he noticed how she was looking, he said, "That don 't make sense. Look, I'll be right back."

After he finally took care of Tony, Mike walked back in the room and closed the door. Feeling a little tired, he submitted to the comfort of the bed.

Jackie looked at him and said, "I hope you know what your doing."

"Baby, I got this, don't trip," was Mike's only reply, as he slipped into the darkness of sleep.

GOING NO WHERE FAST
CHAPTER 3

Mike's slumber was interrupted by the sound of his pager going off, and someone knocking on the door. He jumped to his feet and the first thing he looked for was Jackie. Once he saw she was nowhere in sight, he looked behind the radio to see all of his work bagged up, and put in one bag. The zip he gave her to hold was resting next to it.

There was another knock on the door and Mike said, "Damn! Here I come, shit!" He looked down at his pager to see the same number. "Man, I need to see who this is that keeps paging me."

He put the bag with all of the bagged up work in it, in his pocket, While the other zip found it's resting spot under the mattress. With everything put up, he opened the door to see Tony, and she had the look in her eyes.

"What's up?" He asked.

"Them people outside want you."

"Well, what they want?"

"Boy stop playin' like you don 't know."

"Look, go tell them here I come. Can you do that"?

"It's gone cost you."

"Shit, I bet it is," Mike replied as he stepped back in the room and closed the door.

After putting up half of his bag, and grabbing the blunt Cie gave him, Mike headed for the front door. He made it to the bathroom, and his mom came out. Right away he saw that she too had that look in her eyes. In the past, he would leave until later that night or the next day, when he knew she was fucking around. He hated seeing her like that.

"Mom, where's Jackie?"

"Boy, she walked home 20 minutes ago."

"Did she tell you to tell me something?"

"She said, when you got time for her, she'll be at home. And another thing, what ever you're doing, watch yourself. Do you hear me"?

Before it could turn into a long lecture, he said, "I hear you, mom." He then walked away. When he made it to the front room, he saw Sam, Tasha, and Ron watching T.V. They looked at him, and without saying a word, he knew what the message was, "Mom's trippin' again."

Still looking at the party sitting on the couch, Mike just shook his head. That's when Tony walked in the door.

"Mike, are you going somewhere?"

"No, why"?

"Because, I might need to talk to you later."

"Yeah right, I bet you will."

"Oh yeah, before I forget, you need to go talk to Uncle Ced and his crazy ass bitch. They live down stairs in apartment one".

"Alright, I'll see what they're talking about".

Mike walked outside to find his new friend, the man from the store, and the lady that just had $20.00. He also saw the fools from across the street looking his way. His new friend was the first to see him.

"Damn, Shorty, where you been? Shit, we was about to go across the street."

"Well, I'm glad y'all didn't. Now what's up?"

"I need something for $30, she got $50, and he got $80."

"Cool, I got y'all, but step in the building."

Once in the building, Mike took care of them, and they left. His new friend made sure she was last, but she didn't leave. As Mike put his money together, he looked up to see her still standing there.

"What's up baby girl?"

"I wanted to know if you would be into doin' a lil somethin' for somethin' or we could do it on the up and up? I don't want to disrespect you in any way. I don't know what it is about you, but I really dig you."

For the first time, Mike looked her over. "She didn't look bad at all," he thought to himself. She was a red bone, like he liked, with her hair pulled into a ponytail. She was well dressed, with a small waist and she couldn't have been over 30, he figured. Trying to make sense of it all, Mike told himself, "She probably got one of them old Chi town niggas that just turned her out."

Seeing Mike was caught up in his thoughts, she figured she would clear some things up. "I get high to enjoy myself. I also like doing other things. So, what do you say?"

Mike didn't care to respond. He just started walking down the stairs, which led to the bottom floor. He got to the last step and looked back to see her right behind him. The sight of her got his dick hard. It was all about what he knew was about to happen. From the look in her eyes, Mike knew she was hot, and she needed to be cooled off.

Mike found apartment one, and knocked. His uncle opened the door, and the first thing Mike recognized, was the look in his eyes. It was the look that said, "I've been fucking around."

His uncle was like, "Oh, what's up nephew, come on in."

Mike and his new friend walked in to see a little of nothing, inside. There was a T.V. on the floor, some bags of clothes, and that was just about it. His uncle's girlfriend came out of a back room. When she saw Mike, she ran up and gave him a hug.

"Boy, how long have you been out?"

"I just got out today."

Hearing those words were disappointing, but his uncle had to ask anyway. "Well, you ain't on yet, are?"

"Come on unc, you know I mean business."

"Well nephew, give your uncle something for $10, and I'm gonna help you get some money."

"I got you, but where's the bathroom?"

His uncle pointed down the hallway and said, "It's the first door on your left."

With the directions, Mike headed for the bathroom. He didn't have to tell his new friend to come on, because she was right behind him. Once in the bathroom, with the door closed, Mike reached in his pocket and pulled out his bag. While his friend sat on the edge of the tub, he found a nice size pill. He then told her, "I'll be right back."

Mike took the ten dollars from his uncle and gave him the pill. Before he headed back to the bathroom, he let his uncle know what the mission was.

"Look unc, I got to take care of something real quick, so I'll be in the bathroom for a minute."

"Don't even trip, it's all good."

Mike walked back in the bathroom to find his friend ass whole naked. He stood there with his back to the closed door, taking her all in. "Damn, this bitch is bad," he thought. Without saying a word, she walked up to him and dropped to her knees. She undid his pants and found what she was looking for.

Mike was looking down, watching her every move. She grabbed his joystick with both hands, and licked her lips. Looking up at him, she went to work. She licked the top of his joystick, working her tongue, which seemed to be very experienced.

"Do you like that Daddy," is what she asked him over and over again?

"You know I do," was his answer every time.

He saw one of her hands disappear between her legs. When that took place, she took hold of Mike's joystick. She was soaring form the sensation of rubbing her own love box, and having all of Mike in her mouth.

"Oh yes, oh yes," were the only words that found a way to escape her. She worked with great determination to please herself, and Mike.

Feeling the pressure building up, Mike knew with the next lick, he could lose it. Not on it, because he was looking to have a little bit more fun with her, he reached down and tapped her chin.

"Not like that," he said.

She looked up at him and cracked a smile. Thankful that she was gonna feel it all up in her, she cracked a dirty smile as Mike told her to get up on the sink. She did what she was told with the utmost urgency. It seemed she couldn't keep her hands off herself, because she kept rubbing her erect nipples.

Mike found what he was looking for in his back pocket. She saw the condom and said, "Give me that, and come here."

As Mike's joystick penetrated deep into her hot zone, her body went tense. Mike then watched as her eyes rolled into the back of her head. When he saw that, he thought to himself, "I got this bitch." He cuffed her legs in his arms, and pulled her as close to him as he could, without her falling off the sink. He didn't want anything holding him back from going inside of her, as deep as he could. In mid-motion, Mike stopped and pulled out.

Startled by his sudden action, she looked at him and said, "Please don't stop."

Mike took her hand and told her to bend over and hold onto the tub. Eagerly, she bent over and spread her legs. With the joystick in hand, she forcefully pushed it back inside of her.

Mike looked down at the love juices, which were flowing, and said, "I'm about to fuck the shit out of you".

"Oh yes, give it to me!"

Mike started pounding away. As he long stroked her, she was throwing it back to him with just as much force.

"Oh yes, I want to feel it all up in me," she yelled.

"You like that, don't you? Now throw it back to me," Mike demanded.

"Oh yes, oh yes, I love it, shit!"

With one smooth move, he pulled out and slid it in her exotic tunnel of pleasure. To his surprise, it was already wet from the love juices, which were everywhere. It was still tight, like he hoped it would be, but he knew, she wasn't new to it.

"That's what I'm talking about, fuck me, please fuck me," she begged.

Knowing he had her right where he wanted her, he went to work. They were both breathing hard, both focused on reaching their peak. With one more, "Oh yes, oh yes," Mike felt her go limp. He thrust himself deep into her with all the force he could master. Then he too, went limp.

After they caught their breath, and got dressed, she handed Mike his two pills back, and said, " When I get some more money, I'll be back to get those. And thanks for such a good time." She then walked out.

Mike stood there, and said to himself, "Damn, I'm good." As soon as he walked out of the bathroom, his uncle was right there. Before he could speak, Mike handed him a pill and said, "I'll be back."

Mike made it back outside and just stood there. Even

though it was dark, people were still out, as if it was daytime. He saw the fools across the street, and some new faces, sitting on the steps next door. Tee and his boys were mingling around the front yard also.

Tee approached Mike when he spotted him standing on top of the stairs.

" Mike, what's up! You tryin' to smoke?" Tee asked.

"Yeah, we can do that."

" Well, I got to go upstairs and put it together."

Mike looked down at his pager and said, "Is there a phone up there?"

"Yep, come on," Tee replied, leading the way .

As they stepped in, Mike saw a table, a phone, and some chairs. " Damn, niggas be getting money out of this bitch," Mike thought.

Tee handed Mike the phone and went to a room in the back.

Mike looked down at his pager and called the number. On the second ring, a female answered, "Hello."

"This is Mike, did someone page?"

"Yeah, this is Kim. Damn Nigga, what took you so long to call back?"

"Shit, I ain't heard from you in a minute."

"So," Kim fired back.

" What's up, you tryin' to kick it?"

" I paged you up didn't I."

"Well, hit me tomorrow around two thirty, cause I got to go to this class from 1 :45 to 2:20. Then I'll come and get you and we'll see what we can get into".

In Mike's mind, the only thing they could do was come back to his house and fuck.

"It's on," Kim replied.

" Cool."

" And when I page you, don't take forever to call back."

"Yeah right, just page me tomorrow. I got to get off this phone".

By then, Tee was standing right there with the blunt in his mouth. "Mike, you ready," he asked?

"Yeah!"

Once outside, Mike stopped Tee when he went to light up the blunt. "Slow down, we can smoke in the car."

"Yeah, let's do that," Tee agreed with that idea.

The two of them got in Mike's mom's car and smoked. When they were finishing up, someone knocked on the passenger window. Tee rolled it down and Mike saw it was one of the fools from across the street. Along wit him, was a fool from next door.

Tee was like, "What's up?"

The one from across the street said, "Match one?"

Mike cut in, "I got it, come on, y'all can get in."

Once they got in back, next door said his name was "Ice." Then across the street, said his name was, "Dee".

As Mike reached in his Dickey shirt pocket to get his blunt, he offered his name. He figured by the looks of it, they already knew Tee.

Mike didn't blaze his until theirs were fully out. As soon as the scent of Mike's blunt was in the air, everyone got excited. The only thing everyone kept saying was, "That's that shit! Mike, do you got some more of that, can you get some more of that? I'll buy whatever your people got, right now."

" I'll see what I can do," Mike replied, loving the attention.

Halfway through the blunt, Mike saw his new friend walking up to the building. Some of Tee's homies were fucking with her, so Mike jumped out of the car. To no one in particular, Mike said, "She's with me."

She turned to see Mike, then she walked past everyone and went into the building.

When Mike walked into the building, he said,

" What's up?"

"I got two hundred dollars for you, so take care of me with your fine, high ass."

" Damn, she sucked the shit out of my dick," Mike thought, sizing her up.

As if she read his mind, she said, "This ain't for me, it's for someone else, so get your mind on business".

Mike started laughing, as he reached in his pocket and pulled out his stash. He put together four half's, along with two pills and handed it to her. With a smile on her face, she slid him the money.

"Look, I'm in for the night," said Mike, as he put his money in his pocket. " So get at me tomorrow."

"Thanks for telling me. I would have been pissed if I would of came back on a blank one."

" Naw, I wouldn't of wanted that."

" You and me both!"

Together, they walked back outside. Mike was grateful to see Tee standing at the bottom of the stairs, with his keys in his hand.

" Here Mike, I made sure that I locked all your doors."

" Good lookin' out."

" So what's up Mike, what are you about to do?"

" I'm about to go and relax, I'll get up with you tomorrow."

"Well, you know where I'm at."

Mike went in the house and went straight to his room. All he could think of was resting his tired mind. By the time his head touched the pillow, he was out.

GOING NOWHERE FAST
CHAPTER 4

Mike woke up the next morning to find he no longer had his Dickies on. Right away, he knew that was a sign his mom came in and checked on him last night. When mike found his pants nicely folded on the floor, by the radio, he quickly checked for his money. Once he pulled out his bankroll, he reached in his other pocket for his bag of work. It too was there like he'd hoped, it would still be. As he looked at his two prize possessions, there was no doubt in his mind, that the pinch went down. How much was missing from both was unknown, and it was all thanks to him getting so high. He couldn't remember how much work he had, let alone how much he sold, so knowing he was at fault, he said, "Fuck it!"

Mike mapped out the moves he needed to make for the day, in his head, as he was in the shower. "First things first, I got to go see my kids," he thought. His daughter Shonna, and his son Tod, wouldn't be a problem. When it came to his daughter Rolanda, he knew he would have to track her and her mom down. Then he wanted to slide by his old friend Pam's, to see her baby. The word on the wire was, there's a good chance he's the father of her son. There were two problems, when it came to this situation, for Mike. The first problem was she stayed on the wrong side of Lake Street, in the 30's, which is the stomping grounds for the "Anti-Mike Extremists", and anything "blue". Then it was the fact that she named her son after one of them cats.

38

Knowing all of this, Mike made mental note that he had to see Blast, before he made such a trip.

After Mike got dressed, he counted his money and his work. He had a grand and some change in cash, and $800.00 in work, not counting the ball of crack he still had under his mattress. Feeling a lot better after getting a full count on what he was working with, he was ready to move around.

On his way to the front door, he found his mom laying on the couch, watching T.V. His first words to her were, "Mom, do someone owe me something?"

She looked at him and replied, "No, and boy, wasn't no one in your stuff."

"Well, look mom, I got a few things to do today, so I'll be gone til' later."

"Baby, did you even eat?"

"I'll get something while I'm on the move."

"Well, you be careful out there, and watch yourself out there. You hear me?"

"I hear you mom, don't trip."

As Mike walked out of the building, he saw a car pulling up. He quickly counted four or five heads in the car. He closely watched as a lady got out of the passenger door, and started walking his way. When she got close enough, Mike was like, "What's up?"

She quickly shot back, "I got $300 dollars, but I need something real nice."

"Don't even trip, I got something real nice for you, so follow me."

They walked back to the building and went in. mike pulled out is bag and found eight halfs. He handed her the $400 dollars worth of work, and she handed him the money. She looked the work over, then popped the eight halfs in her mouth, where they found a resting spot under her tongue. She did her best to speak, "What do they call you?"

The first thing that came to his mind was Shorty, so he said, "Call me Shorty."

"Well, Shorty, I'll be back, so make sure you're around."

" Don't trip, I got you."

Without another word said, the lady walked out and headed back to her awaiting party. Once Mike heard them pull off, he made his way to his car. He sat there behind the wheel and decided Jackie's would be his first stop.

The trip to Jackie's was made by using nothing but side streets. That was due to the fact he had no business driving, because he didn't have a driver's license. He got out of the car and looked down at his pager. That's when he thought, "Damn! I should of gave that bitch my pager number, shit. Fuck it, I'll see her again."

Mike then made his way to Jackie's door and knocked twice. Jackie opened it and she had their daughter Shonna, in her arms. Mike took his daughter and drenched her with kisses, as he followed Jackie in. Mike played with Shonna until she passed out in his arms. As gentle as he could, Mike laid her down on her blanket, on the love seat. That's when, for the first time since he'd been there, he gave Jackie a once over. She was just laying there, with a big T-shirt on, hair everywhere. To him, it seemed she lost her ambition. He was somewhat bothered, but he still found the need to escort her to the back room.

Finished up with Jackie, Mike walked out of the room and closed the door. Just his luck, Jackie's mom was coming out the bathroom, at that very moment. As soon as she saw him, she had one thing to ask, "Are you on yet?"

Mike quickly thought, "I shouldn't tell this dirty bitch shit." He then replayed the time when he lived with them. One night, while he was asleep, she came in the room with $17 dollars. Half asleep, he gave her a pill for it. He then put the $17 dollars in his daughter's barrette can, on the dresser. She came back four more times that night, and the same thing happened. The next morning, when Mike woke up, he looked in the can, only to find a lonely $17.00.

After putting two and two together, he realized she used the same $17 dollars, over and over again. When he confronted her, all she had to say was, "You're gonna get your money on the first!"

Then it was the time she climbed through their bedroom window, because they a lock on their door. Jackie woke up late one night, when she thought she heard something. Right away, she woke Mike up and asked him, "Did you hear that?"

"No," Mike replied. Instead of falling back to sleep, he was in the mood to smoke, which had to be followed up with a nice love session.

The next morning, when he went in the closet to get his bag of work, he saw it was short. He knew who was behind it, but he didn't know how. Pissed off, Mike made the trip downstairs.

As soon as Jackie's mom saw him she said, "Boy, y'all had me in that closet for two hours last night."

That's when it hit him, "This bitch was in the closet watching me fuck the shit out of her daughter, with a mouth full of crack!"

After realizing that, he didn't even ask for the money, he just shook his head and walked away.

Jackie's mom brought Mike back to the present, when she said, "Look, let me get one for this $15 dollars."

She wasn't trying to hear he wasn't back on, because she knew better.

Reluctantly, he took care of her and got ghosted.

Mike pulled up in the alley behind Blast's building and honked his horn. As he waited for Blast to peek his head out of the door or window, he remembered about his car. He thought, "Damn!, I got to get my keys from Tony's ass."

When Mike saw Blast walk out of his back door, he parked his car.

Before Mike could get the door open good, Blast hollered down, "Cuz, come on up!"

Once Mike made it up to Blast's apartment, they went straight to his room. Mike closed door behind him, and when he turned around, his heart dropped. Blast's two big ass dogs were staring at him. One was a Pitbull and the other was Rottweiler.

Blast saw the fear in Mike's eyes and he quickly said, "Cuz, you're a'ight."

Mike slowly walked over to the chair in the corner of the room and said, "Damn Cuz!"

When the laughter came to an end, Blast asked Mike one thing and the party was on. "Cuz, you tryin' to smoke?"

"You know I am," Mike fired back.

Blast pulled out a real nice sized bad of the lightest green buds, that Mike had ever seen. From such a sight, Mike had to ask, "Cuz, let me give you two fifty for some of that?"

After Blast just looked at him, Mike said, "Come on cuz."

Blast didn't say a word, he just reached in his shoe-box and got a baggie. Mike then watched, as Blast dropped buds in it.

As they were finishing up the blunt, Mike let the real reason he was there, be known. Mike looked at Blast, and said, "Homie, I need something nice, cause I need to make a trip across Lake."

Blast smiled and said, "Don't trip, I got you."

He then reached under his pillow and came out with a 3.80.

Straight to business, Mike he checked the clip. Once he saw it was full, Mike slid it back in the gun, and put it in his waistband. With that out of the way, Mike hit the blunt one last time, and said, "Cuz, I got to get in motion."

Mike left his car parked behind Blast's, and he walked over to his sister's. He knocked on the door and Tony answered. As soon as she saw who it was, her face lit up.

"What's up bra, I was just thinking about you!"

"Girl, what you want?"

"Damn! I can't just think about my little brother?"

"Like I said, what do you want?"

"Well, I need two for thirty."

"Well, I need my keys to my car."

After they both got what they wanted, Mike walked back to his mom's car. He sat behind the wheel, thinking to himself, "I'm the fucking man." To finish off such a moment, he looked in the mirror, and smiled at himself. With the 3.80 in his lap, he put the car in motion. When he was stopped by the first stop sign he ran into, he rolled down both windows. He didn't want anything to fuck up his aim, just in case something did jump off.

Mike rolled to his next destination in complete silence. He had to go over to Pam's cousin, Keita 's house, to pick her up, so she could take him over to Pam's. The problem with this was that she lived in the heart of the neighborhood, he had no business being in.

Mike figured, while he was at Keita's, he could run across the street, to see his cousin T.Bone. As he drove, Mike hoped for a few things. One, that Keita was home, and two, that his cousin didn't have any neighborhood friends over. The truth, upon the matter, was Mike really didn't have any business hanging out with his cousin, in the first place, and he knew it.

Mike pulled in front of Keita's and parked. Before he got out of the car, he looked up and down the street. To his liking, there was no movement on the block. He figured it was due to the fact that it was still early. With the car still running, he got out and ran up to her door. When it came to the gun in his hand, he kept it pressed close to his hip.

Mike tapped the doorbell a few times real quick. He then put his back to the door, as he watched the street. When he heard someone opening the door, he turned around to see Keita's face. She looked at him and her eyes got real big. She quickly said, "Boy! What are you doing over here?"

Mike replied, "Everything's cool."

At the moment, his eyes looked down at the gun in his hand. Her eyes followed his, and she saw what was in his hand. After seeing all she needed to see, she grabbed his arm, and said, "Get in here with your crazy ass."

As Mike walked into the house he slid the gun into his pocket. Before he could explain why he was there, she said it for him.

"You want to go see Pam's baby don't you? Shit, he looks just like you."

All Mike said was, "Well, are you ready?"

Before she could answer, he took a quick peek out of the window. Once Keita felt she had his attention again she said, "give me five minutes, and I'll be ready to go. Shit, I just got off the phone with her. I was about to get on the bus and go over there." Not in the mood to talk anymore, Mike cut in and said, "Well look, I got to run to my people's house across the street, so when you're ready, walk over there and knock on the door."

Instead of walking across the street, Mike got in his car and made a U-turn. He couldn't chance leaving it over there. He needed it close by, just in case he needed to make a quick get away.

After taking the same precautions, as he took walking up to Keita's door, he got the same reaction from his cousin. The first thing T.Bone asked when they made it in the house was, "When did you get out?"

"Shit, just yesterday. You knew they couldn't hold a real one down for long. But look, do you wonna come roll with me for a while?"

"Bet, I ain't got shit else to do."

Mike looked out the window and he was glad to see Keita coming. Without warning, he turned and headed for the door. As he opened up the door, he said, "Come on Cousin, let's roll."

He then walked out of the house. With gun in hand, Mike sprinted to the car and told Keita to get in the back. She tried too, but it was locked. She told Mike and that irritated him, because he had to reach back there, to unlock it. That meant he had to take his eyes off of the block, and that was the last thing he wanted to do.

Once Keita got in the car, T.Bone still wasn't coming. Ready to get moving, Mike blew the horn. After he did it, he was mad at himself for doing such a dumb thing. He was trying to stay low-key, not call attention to himself.

T.Bone came running out, and he already knew Mike was pissed. Mike opened the passenger door for him, and before T. Bone could close the door, Mike had the car in motion. Right away, Keita told Mike to make a U-turn. He did what he was told and he sped up, as he tried to make the light before it turned red. The light turned red and Mike reluctantly slowed the car down, until they completely stopped. Mike felt so naked, sitting at his enemies infamous corner. It was like he was in the center of a big bulls-eye, and everyone in the car knew it. It was Keita that broke the silence, when she said, "Mike, you got to make a left, right here."

After seeing all he wanted to see, Mike said, "Fuck the red light." Getting pulled over was the last of his worries, so he took his turn.

For the rest of the ride to Pam's, Mike did his best to calm down. It was apparent to T.Bone and Keita, that he was on edge, so they gave him his space. The only talking was from Keita, giving him the directions to Pam's.

When they finally made it to Pam's, Keita got out and said, "Mike, I'll be right back."

Mike just looked at T.Bone, and asked, "Do you want to smoke one?"

T.Bone was taken back by such a question. He frowned at Mike, and said, "Now you already know."

Mike didn't bother to respond, he just handed T.Bone what he needed to get the party started. A moment later, he looked towards the house Keita went in, to find Pam's tall, fine red ass, standing there. She had her arms crossed, looking sexy as ever.

Moving too fast, Mike got of the car and his gun fell to the ground. He forgot that he had it on his lap. Real smooth, he picked it up it, and cuffed it, as he slid it into his pocket.

As he walked up to her, she said, "I see you're still on that bullshit."

Before she could get her last word out good, he shot back, "It's good to see you too."

He then tried to give her a hug. She just kept her arms crossed, and took a step back. Mike just looked at her with a little smile on his face. "She's still acting up," he thought. He stood there, looking deep into her eyes. To Mike, she had some of the most beautiful eyes, that he'd ever seen. It wasn't the color, it was the message within them.

She put a stop to his little moment with; "Did you come to

see my son, or what?"

"Why you giving me a hard time? You know I did."

"If I didn't give you a hard time, it wouldn't be me," was the venom, Pam spit back, as she walked in the house. She then held the door open and asked, "Are you coming in, or what?"

As soon as they walked into the front room, Pam's mom handed her the baby. Pam then handed her son to Mike, as she introduced him to her mom. Her mom took one good look at Mike, and said, " Booda do look just like him." She then laughed a little, as she walked out of the room.

GOING NO WHERE FAST
CHAPTER 5

Looking down at the little life in his arms, sent a chill up Mike's spine. After taking one look at the baby, with his curly hair, Mike's mind took him to his baby picture, on his mom's wall. "He looks just like me when I was a baby," he thought. There was no denying it, this was his baby, and he knew it.

Before he could prepare himself, his thoughts took him on one mean emotional roller-coaster. "Well, I got to do what I can to get to know him, but damn, she named him after that fool. One of the same fools that would love to put a stop to my motha fuckin' life! What the fuck am I pose to do wit' that?"

Mike couldn't keep his thoughts to himself any longer. So he asked, hoping it was a misunderstanding or something, "Pam, what's his name?"

She just looked at him and said, "You heard my mom call him Booda."

"Yeah, I heard that, but what's his real name?"

"You already know, so why do we got to go there?"

It was T.Bone that helped Mike escape such a situation, by hunking the horn.

Mike had never been so happy to hear a car horn before in his life. He handed Pam their son and said, "I'll be right back. I got to see what my cousin wants, that's him out there blowing."

When he made it outside, he saw Keita and T.Bone sitting

on the hood of his car. They were smoking, what he knew
was a Newport. He walked up to them and asked, "Do ya'll
want to get something to eat?"

Keita's "hell yeah" was faster then T.Bone's, but that was
all Mike needed to hear. As he climbed behind the wheel,
he said, "Well, go get your cousin and let's go."

Keita didn't care to reply, she just ran in to get Pam.

After seeing that stressful look on Mike's face, T.Bone
walked up to the driver's window, and said, "What's up
cousin?"

"I got another son."

Somewhat confused, T.Bone said, "That's cool, so what's
the problem?"

"Shiit, she named him after you know. So what am I pose
to do wit that?"

Instead of coming up with an answer for Mike's problem,
T.Bone took a step back, and hit his Newport. He knew
Mike was making a statement, and not asking him the
question.

T.Bone was just finishing his cigarette, when Pam and
Keita walked up. They both walked to the back to get in,
when Mike said, "Bone, let her sit up front."

Pam cut in, "That's cool, I wouldn't want the wrong
person to see me up front."

"Shit, I don't want the wrong person to see us at all," Mike
fired back.

Everyone wanted to laugh, but they knew he wasn't
joking. If the wrong person did see Mike, they were aware
that all of their lives would be in danger.

With everyone in their proper positions, Mike pulled off.
A block away from Pam's, he told T.Bone to blaze up.
Eager to fill his lungs up with smoke, T.Bone started rolling
up the window. When Mike realized what he was doing, he
said, "T.Bone, keep it down, I'll let you know when you can
roll it up." T.Bone looked at him and saw he wasn't playing,

so he rolled it back down. Realizing what Mike was on, T.Bone lit the blunt. He hit it twice and passed it to Mike, who passed it to Pam. At that very moment, Keita had a bright idea, "A Mike, play some music."

Calm as ever, his only words were, "Ain't shit cracking."

Once they made it to Lake Street, Mike cut on the radio and told T.Bone he could roll up the window. Even though he was trying to enjoy his high and relax a little, Mike still stayed on the lookout. His eyes kept darting from side to side, then back to the rear-view. His pattern was interrupted when he looked in the rear-view and found Pam looking at him shaking her head. Their eyes were locked, and Mike drove for over a block, in such a state.

Back on point, Mike looked at his pager, and saw it was a little after ten. He thought, "Man, I'm making good timing." He then looked to see where the blunt was, and he was somewhat disappointed to see Keita putting it out.

Everyone in the car was high, Pam and Keita were giggling to themselves, over nothing. T.Bone was stuck in a zone, laid back with the seat damn near in Keita's lap. When it came to Mike, he was letting his thoughts run wild. "Damn, I hope I don't run into them fools, cause I ain't with the game playing. Even thought I got a careful, I still got to be the first to let these hot one's ride."

With the last thought, came the thought of his gun, still in his pocket. He pulled it out and sat it on his lap. When Pam asked, "Where we eating at?"

Mike knew they passed Embers. He looked in the rear-view and sure enough, they just passed it . He looked in the rear-view and sure enough, they just passed it. Remaining cool, Mike didn't respond, he just pulled into S.A., which was on the next corner. After he slid the gun under the driver's seat, he pulled out his bankroll. He peeled off ten dollars, and turned around to face Pam. With bankroll in hand, flashing it, he gave Pam the ten. "Will you go pay for the gas for me? Put the whole ten in."

Without saying another word, Pam got out, and went to pay for the gas. Mike laughed, as he thought, "This girl's something else." He then got out to pump the gas. When Pam walked out of the gas station, Mike told her to come here.

She walked up to him and said, "What is it?"

"Why you tripping?"

"I'm cool," she replied, as she got back in the car.

Mike stood there stuck, until he heard something spilling. When he looked down, he saw that the gas was corning out of his tank. He fucked around, and went over close to two dollars.

After he paid for the gas he wasted, he walked back to the car. At the door, he thought, "Man, this bitch is poison!"

Once he pulled up in Ember's parking lot, he gave it a once over. He had to make sure he didn't recognize one that he knew belonged to someone that meant him no good. Satisfied that things were cool, he parked as close to the door as possible.

As soon as they stepped into Ember's Mike spotted a face he wasn't trying to see. It was one of them fools, his bitch, and two kids. Mike could tell they were leaving, because they were walking towards him. Right away, Mike's heart sped up, and his hands started getting sweaty. All he kept thinking was, "Damn, Damn, Damn!, It's on now." He felt for the spot where his gun should be, only to realize he left it under the fucking seat.

Mike's survival instincts kicked in, so he slipped his hand a bit under his shirt, as if to say, he was on point.

Mike realized out of his party, he was the first one to spot the fool. When the other three finally did, they all looked at Mike. With his "I mean business" face on, Mike kept on walking. As they passed each other, Mike and the fool made eye contact. They both knew Mike was slipping.

Mike walked up to the hostess, and before she could ask, he said, "A table for four. Away from the window."

Feeling something was missing, he turned around to see his party, all having a laugh or two with the fool. He heard a lot of street talking going on. The whole conversation consisted of "B-words" mainly, and no "C-words" whatsoever.

Mad at himself, Mike just walked over to the table, where the waitress was standing, and sat down. As she was leaving, he said, "Can you tell whoever, we're ready to order?"

She looked at Mike, then at the "new rap group," and said, "If you say so."

The fool looked at Pam and said, "I'm a ball blood, and let him know I seen you bickin' it with dude. What's up with Dog, anyway?"

Pam followed his eyes and when she saw he was looking towards Mike, she understood. He was asking her, "What's up with Mike." To try to smooth things over, she said, "He ain't on nothing."

"Well be bool, and Bone, I'm a get up with you later."

" Yep, do that," T-Bone replied.

With his elbows on the table, Mike rested his forehead in his palms. With his eyes closed, he slowly shook his head, and thought, "Mike, what the fuck are you doing?" When he shook it off, Pam was standing there looking down at him, and the other two were already sitting down.

Mike looked at Keita, and said, "Go get that from under the seat for me."

She read his face and saw this was no game. She got up and headed for the car.

Mike heard a car system, that seemed to be close. He quickly walked over to the window, to take a look. At the corner of the side street, he saw a red Caddi, stopped by a red light. When it turned green, the fool turned down Lake and rolled by real slow.

Mike cracked a little smile, and thought, "This nigga parked down the street, that was smart."

When Mike turned around, to walk back to the table, he saw that Keita was just sitting down. Boy was he glad to see her.

They all ordered the basic breakfast, and when the waitress walked away, Keita gave Mike her handbag. For the next minute or so, everyone was speechless. It was Keita that broke the silence, when she asked, "Mike, when did you say you got out?"

"Yesterday, around this time."

Pam just shook her head and said, "You need to slow yo' ass down!"

Mike didn't bother to respond to her comment, he was just glad she saw he was doing things at a fast pace. He looked over at T.Bone, and said, "Bone, do you think things need to be slowed down?"

" shiiit,I think they need to be sped up, and that's on the real."

"See baby, there you have it."

"Whatever Mike," Pam fired back, as she rolled her eyes.

When they got done eating, Mike paid for it, then they all made a dash for the car. The three of them knew, like Mike knew, hot one's don't got names on them. Mike pulled out and turned onto Lake Street. Like before, the windows came down and the radio went off. Once again, they rolled in silence, until Mike looked in the rear-view at the two in the back, and said, "I got one more run to make, then I'll take y'all where y'all need to go."

He then told T.Bone to roll up another one.

By the time they pulled into the alley behind Mike's sister's house, the windows were back up and they were smoking. Coming up the alley, Mike saw that blast and the homie,

C-Clown were hanging out in the back. Mike pulled up to them and they both jumped in the back with Keita and Pam. Mike parked behind Blast's building, and they got blowed.

Blast told C-Clown to blaze his blunt up and C-Clown said, "Cuz, someone got to match me, this one blunt won't do shit for us."

That's when Blast pulled out a fat one of his own. Mike enjoyed himself, as he and his Homies had a conversation, filled with C-words. He looked in the rear-view at blast, and said, "Cuz, ce cool and let me hit that."

"Cuz, kick cack and relax."

Halfway through the last party-stick, Mike looked down at his pager. He saw it was a little after 11:30, and that meant he had to get moving. Before Mike could speak, Blast said, "Come on C-Clown, Cuz, let's roll. Cuz got to get little."

Shocked, Mike asked, "Cuz, how did you know that?"

"Cuz, I seen you looking at your pager. Nigga. it's all good, ce cool and slide cack through later."

As they both got out, Mike said, "Y'all ce safe, and keep it cracking."

Mike pulled off and drove around the front. He parked in front of his Cutless and told T.Bone to come on. They both got out of the car, and Mike said, "Bone, I need you to drive my car to the shop so I can get a real nice tune up on it."

Surprised, T.Bone was like, "This is your Cuttie for real! when did you get this?"

"Yesterday," was the only information Mike was willing to offer.

Mike handed him the key and T.Bone got in. With a slight tum of the key, it started up. That's when Mike remembered what was wrong with the it. He said, "Damn!, tum it off and pop the hood."

T.Bone did what he was asked, and watched as Mike walked to the trunk. Mike was in luck, there was some anti-freeze in there. He filled the car up and told T.Bone, "we got to move fast."

A block from the car shop, Mike's journey came to a halt, as the stop-light turned red. The first honk didn't get his attention, but the second one did. He glanced in the rear-view to see if it was T.Bone. It was, and he was pointing to the car on Mike's passenger side. Confused, Mike turned to see his other cousin, Bee, in his Caddi, looking straight ahead. Knowing Bee didn't see him yet, Mike started honking too.

When Bee heard the consistent honking, he looked over to his left. The first thing he saw was a middle finger, then he focused on the smiling face of Mike. He quickly rolled his window down, and said, "What's up fool!"

All Mike said was, "Follow Bone, he's behind me."

As the last word rolled off his tongue, the light turned green and he pulled off.

Once at the shop, Mike got out and waited for T.Bone and Bee to park. He walked up to Be and gave him a big hug, which he followed up with a jab to Bee's rib. Before Bee could really start talking, Mike said, "Hold on cousin, let me take care of this car, then we can kick it."

On cue, T.Bone handed him the key, and he ran in. After he told the clerk what he wanted don't to his car, he gave him his pager number, the key, and $150.00 up-front. With the receipt in hand, Mike said, "Page me when it's ready," and he walked out.

"Can we smoke?" Bee asked, when Mike made it back. Mike didn't bother to reply. He just sat there for a minute, trying to figure out how he could pull it off. He knew he couldn't be just sitting around all day, on bullshit. Then it came to him. He walked to his car, and asked Pam if she knew how to drive? Keita cut in and said, "I do." He saw how Pam was acting and it pissed him off. He had no time to deal with her bullshit, so he said, "Keita, I need you to drive, and we're gonna follow y'all in the other car. Where y'all going anyway?"

"To get our hair done, downtown."

"Keita, go head and drive, but don't be on no bullshit."

"I know."

As Mike walked away, Keita called him. He turned around to see her behind the wheel, and Pam still in the back. Somewhat frustrated, he walked to the passenger window, and said, "Pam, you can get in the front now, Damn! Keita, what's up?"

"Do you got your gun?"

Mike just tapped his pocket, and walked to the passenger door of Bee's Caddi, and got in.

T.Bone and Bee stood there, looking at Mike like, what the fuck is he on? Once it hit them, then they too got in.

Before Bee could ask, Mike simply said, "Follow them, and Bone roll one up."

With that out of the way, Mike laid back in the leather seat of the Caddi. He then thought, "Shit, now I can enjoy my high, now that I'm not driving."

GOING NO WHERE FAST
CHAPTER 6

T.Bone had to literally shake Mike's shoulder to get him out of the zone he was in. Bee looked over at Mike, and said, "Damn nigga, you didn't hear him calling you?"

"He wasin't callin' me!"

"Shit, he said your name three times."

"Yeah, whatever."

Mike took the blunt from T.Bone and hit it twice before he passed it to Bee.

Shit, he was already high. The only reason he was smoking again was because he didn't like to tell people no. To him, that out weighed the fact that he only had a little over two hours to bring his high down for his class.

Bee hit the blunt for the sixth time, when T.Bone said, "Damn nigga, are you gonna pass it?"

"Nigga, shut that shit up, you been with Mike all morning, so I know you smoked already. Everyone knows Mike don't play no games when it comes to getting high."

Knowing he had a point, they all started laughing and he passed the blunt to T.Bone.

Mike cut in, and said, "If there's one thing everyone knows about me, it's I love to kick it for real. Now let me hit that."

T.Bone and Bee damn near started crying because they were laughing so hard. T.Bone then put his two cents in, "That's because you're a drug addict."

Such a comment wasn't funny to Mike, it hit too close to

home. Without warning, he turned around and snapped. "Look nigga, my mom's a drug addict, my sister is a drug addict, my dad's a drug addict, my aunt's a drug addict, along with my uncles, and a cousin or two. My grandma's even a drug addict, fool-ass nigga. I'll tell you what I am, I'm a Boss Motha Fuckin' Playa, now get that right!"

He then hit the blunt one last time, and passed it to Bee.

"Nigga, you need some help!" Said Bee, which caused them all to laugh.

When Keita pulled over, Mike figured they was at the hair shop. As he watched the two ladies get out, he said, " Bone, you got to ride with Bee, I got Something I need to handle."

He then turned to Bee, and said, "Bee, you're right, I do need some help, getting this money, so come by the building around seven. You know where it's at right?"

"Yeah, I helped your mom move in."

"Cool, if I ain't there, wait for me. It's on! I'm telling you."

Ready to get moving, he got out and headed towards the spot where his female friends were standing. Within four steps, he remembered what he was missing. With no hesitation, he turned around and ran back to Bee's car.

T.Bone was just closing the passenger door, when Mike started tapping on the window. He tapped on it so fast, it startled T.Bone. He flinched a little, then when he saw who it was, he rolled down the window, and asked, "What's up?"

"You know what's up, nigga give me my bag."

"Oh yeah, I forgot all about it."

Together, Mike and Bee said, "Yeah, I bet," and they all laughed.

With his weed in his pocket, and feeling real cool after a good laugh, Mike started walking back towards his awaiting party. Once he saw his car was still running, he decided to say his farewells from the car. He opened the driver's door, then turned to look at Pam. As confident as he could, he said, "I'll stay in touch."

As their eyes locked, they both knew he wouldn't. His false pride was to strong for him to deal with. Knowing he had a son that was named after another man, tore a chunk out of his heart, which he felt was already dying slowly.

The only way he knew how to deal with situations he couldn't physically fight, shoot, or hustle to get, was to run mentally, which was achieved by blocking out such unpleasant confrontations. At that moment, it was time for him to get to running.

He looked at them one last time, and said, "Take care."

They both replied, "Stay safe, and slow the fuck down!"

With that out of the way, he got in the car and pulled off. There was no shaking the thoughts and pain he was feeling over his son. Forced to stop due to the light turning red, he lost it. He started banging his open hands on the wheel, as he screamed over and over again, "Fuck, Fuck, Fuck!" All of the sudden, Mike felt someone watching him. He looked over to his right and saw the fear in the eyes of an old white man. When the old white man saw Mike looking his way, he refocused his stare, as he looked straight ahead.

Mike hated driving downtown, because he was so close to the police's "Big House." Under such stress, he was glad to be in that part of town. He needed somewhere to park, and fast. Like he knew he would, he saw one of the many parking ramps. He pulled up to the security box, took the ticket, and the arm went up. After finding the darkest spot, between two trucks, he parked. With the car cut off, he quickly rolled up the last blunt he had in his box.

Being one step closer to numbing his pain, he started up the car and drove off. He rolled up to the parking ramp security window, and handed the man working his ticket. The man took it, then looked at Mike funny, because he saw Mike wasn't in there for five minutes. Before the man could say a word, Mike handed him five dollars, and said, "Keep the change."

As he drove and dug deeper into his dream-state, he decided to go see his son Tod. He figured since he lived over north, he could chill there until his class, which was being held at the YMCA, six or seven blocks from his house.

Halfway through his escape route, he put out the blunt. He was in a world of his very own. As he bobbed his head to the oldies radio station, "KMOG" was playing, he was enjoying the scene.

The north side, to Mike, was different. It was more laid back then over south, but he also knew it went down in these parts too. He saw the neighbor hood hustlers posted up on their corners, with smoke in the air. Crews of young sisters, pushing their strollers, side-by-side, like they planned to have babies at the same damn time.

Mike was moving through town without a worry in the world. No thoughts of his son, with the name of another man. No thought of them fools, popping up out of nowhere. He was high and feeling good.

For a minute or two, he sat in the car outside of his son's house. He felt the need to take in what was going around him. Across the street form his son's, he saw a family in their yard, having a barbecue. Due to the fact that there were a lot of people over there, he knew it had to be a family get together. As he got out of the car, he watched as two fools dressed in all red, came out of the house, the get-together was being held at. He didn't take his eyes off of them until he was sure they didn't see him. Satisfied that things were cool, he tapped his pocket, felt what he needed to feel, and he walked to the door.

All it took was two rings of the doorbell for Tammy to answer. There she stood, with Tod in her arms, and she too was dressed in all red, with a little black.

Mike took one look at her and thought, "What's up with this red and black shit?"

He didn't bother to investigate, he just took his son and walked into the house. He felt her staring a hole in the back of his head. Then he heard her close the door a little hard. He sat down in the rocking chair and looked at her one more time. To himself, he was like, "What the fuck is this bitch on? I got to see where her head is."

"Cuz, what's up with that shit you got on?" He asked.

"Dog, ain't shit wrong wit' what I got on," she fired back.

After cracking a smile, Mike thought, "Damn, how did they get to her, all the way across town? This shit don't make no sense."

It was only natural for him to laugh after such thoughts, which rubbed her the wrong way.

"What the fuck is so funny?"

Mike just looked at her, and said, "Everything's cool."

Not in the mood to go there with her, he turned his full focus onto his son. He bounced him on his knee, then pushed him around in his walker.

The sight of them playing so well consumed the bitterness that Pam tried to hold onto. Even though she spent many nights pissed off at him for not being there. Then telling herself over and over again, "Fuck him, Tod don't need no father!"

She needed a reason to justify such a change in how she felt, and she found it. She thought, "Five months is a long time to come up missing, but he was in jail."

More than willing to break the ice, she said, "Mike, have you talked to Lucky yet?"

"Not yet, but I need to. You go the number?"

Instead of a verbal reply, for a brief moment, as if lost in thought. She then picked up the phone and dialed the

61

number. Mike figured Lucky must have picked up, because she, " Hold on someone wants to talk to you."

Feeling proud that she did something good, because everyone knew how close he and Lucky were, she smiled as she handed him the phone.

"What's up fool?"

Was all Mike had to say, and Lucky was on it. " Aw, what's up cuz, when did you get out?" Lucky asked, excited to hear his homies voice.

"Yesterday, but it feels like I been out a month already."

"Your right around the comer at Tammy's right?"

"Yep," Mike replied, already knowing where this was headed.

"Don't move, I'm on my way."

When the line went dead, Mike just looked at the receiver, then hung it up. Tammy wanted to know what was up, so she asked, "What did he say?"

"He said he's on the way. How far do he live?"

The first part was all she wanted to hear. Without answering his question, she dashed upstairs.

Her quick departure confused Mike. But when she came back down with some different clothes on, that confused him even more. He would later find out that she was playing both sides of the fence, with the rest of her friends.

Mike picked up his son and rocked him to sleep, as he thought about Lucky. "I'm glad he's on his way over. I need to know what's really going on with him and the south side homies. I heard it's a lot of bullshit going on, but I want to hear it from him. I can't believe he set KeKe up for his car and rims. Shit, they use to be close as hell. KeKe was even fucking his little sister, Little Bit. If I'm not mistaken, they said he was over there seeing her, when the bullshit jumped off. Now there's a big war going on over this shit."

As Mike laid his son on the couch, there was a knock on

the door. Tammy got up from where she was sitting, and answered it. Mike watched, as Lucky and his little cousin, Brandon, walked in. He met Lucky halfway and gave him a big hug. The he said, "It's good to see you fool!"

"Yeah, it's good to see you too," Lucky replied, hype from seeing his main homie.

" I'm already knowin'," Mike fired back. " But fool what's really goin' on?"

" Man, I got so much shit I need to talk to you about... Cuz, so much shit went down since you been gone."

"Yeah, I heard."

Feeling it was his time to jump in, Brandon let it be known what was on his mind. "A Mike, smoke one Cuz?"

"You act like you know me."

"If it's one thing I've learned over the years of watching you two," Brandon stated. " Is if anyone got it, you do!"

Such a statement caused them all to laugh, even Tammy, because they know he was right. That's why Mike liked Brandon like he did, because he was dedicated to learn. Mike looked at his pager and saw it was 1:15 pm. That meant he had a little over an hour to make it to his class. So, not trying to let the little homie down, he told him go out to the car and grab the half in the ashtray.

Brandon frowned at him when he said half, like, "What's that gonna do for us?"

Mike understood such a look, and said, "Cuz, you know I don't fuck wit nothing but the best."

With those words, came a big smile on Brandon's face. Without another word said, he was out the door. Mike and Tammy watched, as Lucky looking down at Tod sleeping.

"Cuz!" Lucky stated, making sure he had everyone's attention.

"That don't make no sense. That boy looks just like you cuz!"

Mike cracked a smile, as he glanced at Tammy, and replied, "That's that potent shit I be squirtin' all up in 'em."

Tammy shook her head, and was like, "Boy, your sick."

"Only for you baby," was Mike's comeback, as he blew her a kiss, which tickled everyone's funny bone.

"Damn Tammy, can I get something to drink?" Mike asked between dry coughs.

Knowing the symptoms of cotton-mouth, Lucky said, "Damn Cuz, how many blunts you smoked today?"

"Shit, I lost count after five," Mike replied.

"Cuz, you need some help."

"Cuz chill out, you're killing me," Mike pleaded, between a lough and a few coughs. " Damn Tammy, can I get something to drink?" Mike then asked.

From the kitchen, she snapped, "You need to kick-back, nigga I'm coming."

By the time she made it back, Brandon was coming through the door with the blunt in his mouth. "Here Mike, take this Kool-Aid and y'all got to go out-back to smoke that."

They went where they were told, and Mike told Brandon to blaze it up. Before the last word was out of his mouth, Brandon had it smoking. Mike looked at Brandon, and said, "Damn Cuz, slow down!"

To Mike, that's what life was all about, seeing those around him enjoying themselves. The only way he knew how to do this, with his friends, was through drugs. When it came to the girls in his life, it was through sex.

Through a mighty storm of pain and many stressful years, Mike would pin-point such a reckless pattern.

He would realize how he was programmed by the actions of his family. In his world, when you're feeling down and out, you seek instant gratification, so partying was the answer. If you're not man or woman enough to truly look deep within yourself, you will never see it, so there's no way you can do what it takes to correct it.

Brandon handed the blunt to Mike, who passed it right to Lucky. Mike then asked Brandon if he was still hustling?

"Yeah, when I get someone to put me on, but fools be acting stuck."

They all know the last part had Lucky's name all over it. He passed Mike that blunt, and hit it twice before Brandon was smoking again. Mike then let Brandon know everything would be all right. "Don't trip lil' homie, I'm back now, and you know I got you. Y'all go on and finish that, I got to go and handle something."

Once in the house, Mike found Tammy in the bathroom, doing her hair. He let it be known what he was worried about. "Tammy, do my eyes look bad, cause they feel bad?"

"Hell yeah! You need to stop smoking so damn much. Look at yourself in the mirror."

Mike thought, "For what, when he already knew how he was looking." He knew he had to do something and quick, so he told Tammy to mover over let him get to the water. He cut the cold water on and started wetting his face, like that would wash out the redness in his eyes. When he looked up, Tammy, Lucky and Brandon were standing there, looking at him.

Fluffy let it be known what everyone else was thinking. "Cuz, you're tripping."

As they laughed, Mike let them know how serious the situation was. "While y'all sitting over there laughing, I got this after-care class I got to go to for my probation, in less than a hour."

"Boy, what the fuck is wrong with you?" Tammy asked.

"Look, I don't need that shit right now," mike fired back.

"Look, you got some shit for your eyes?" He then asked.

"All I got is some smell goods. Shit, you better going to the drug store and get something for your eyes real quick, and quit bullshitting."

"Yeah, that's what I'll do," Mike agreed. He then looked at Brandon and said, " A Cuz, I need you to hold somethin' till I make it that for me for a hour or two. Then I'll slide by the house and pick it up. What's the address?"

"1507 Queen, don't trip, I'll be out front.

Mike pulled out his bag of weed and work. He reached in his bag of work and gave Brandon five pills. After he told him to bring him back sixty dollars off that, he handed him both bags. The gun was the last thing he pulled out and handed to him. Then he looked at Brandon, and said, "Give me that back, I'd rather be caught with it, then without, and that's real."

Fluffy and Brandon both let Mike know how they agreed with the last statement. "That's right cuz, that's right."

Tammy had a few things on her mind that she needed to let Mike know, herself. "Mike, your son needs some shoes, and you really need to slow your ass down."

"Look Tammy, what size do he wear?' She said, "2T," and Mike walked out.

Before he pulled off, he rolled the window down. Then he told Fluffy and

GOING NO WHERE FAST
CHAPTER 7

Mike decided to go to the drugstore, which was no more then ten blocks from the YMCA. All the way there, he kept looking in the rearview at his blood shot eyes. "Damn, I don't know how I'm gonna pull this off," he thought. "I hope this shit works. Fuck!"

He rode past the YMCA, and he was glad he didn't see anyone out there. To him, that was good, because he didn't want the wrong person seeing him driving.

Once at the drugstore, he quickly parked and got out. Before he could walk in, he was stopped by an old black man, who had something to ask.

"A young Playa, you got a dollar to spare?"

Mike reached in his pocket and came out with a five. He gave it to the old man, and he said, "Thanks, now I can go get some milk for my kids."

After hearing such bullshit, Mike smirked a little, instead of flat out laughing. In a low tone, he let himself know he was far from a fool, as he walked in the store. "Man, I don't know why he's playin', he knows damn well he ain't about to buy no damn milk!"

Inside, he spotted a young lady that was on the job. Feeling desperate, he walked up to her, and asked, "Could you please help me?"

She took one look at Mike, and let it be know what she saw. "You need something for your eyes, right?"

"Damn! They look that bad?" Mike asked, surprised.

After she finished laughing, she simply said, "Come with me."

Hot on her trail, Mike looked at his pager to see the time. He saw he had 15 minutes to work a miracle. Now he just needed her to find the shit he needed. When she finally stopped, he was so grateful. He figured they made it to the right shelf, because she was picking up boxes and glancing at the backs. Not wanting to waste anymore time, he let her know what his situation was.

"I need the best stuff, and I don't care about the price."

She handed Mike a box and he opened it. After she looked at him somewhat crazy, he pulled out his bankroll to let her know his money was right. He pulled the little bottle out and looked at it.

"And is this gonna help me?" He asked. " It looks just like water."

"Trust me, it will."

After hearing all he needed to hear, Mike got down on one knee and held his head back. He then held the bottle out to her. She looked from side-to-side, then back down at him, and asked, "What do you want me to do now?"

"Look, will you please do it for me?"

She studied his face and saw how desperate he was. She knew he needed some help and she found herself feeling sorry for him. Knowing her boss would flip if he caught her, she still looked out for Mike. When she was done, she handed him the bottle, and said, "That's it."

Mike stood up and started blinking his eyes. To him, he was working the medicine into his eyeballs. Feeling a lot better mentally, he looked at the young lady and said, "Thank you forreal. Boy, you are truly a lifesaver."

With a new box of blunts and the medicine for his eyes, Mike made his way to the car. As he walked out, to his surprise, the old man was coming out of the liquor store, with a bag in his hand. The old man saw Mike and didn't say a word, he just kept walking. When Mike saw that, he couldn't help but laugh. Hoping the old man could hear him, he spoke his mind. "Ain't that a bitch! Boy, nigga's ain't shit. This fool act like I didn't just give him five dollars or something. I just hope you enjoy your sorry-ass-self, motha fucka."

Two blocks away, Mike stopped the car due to the light turning red. He looked in the rear view to take a look at his eyes. He couldn't tell if it was working or not, so he grabbed the bottle and went to work. Within moments his vision was a blur. He squirted so much in his eyes that he damn near couldn't see. There was medicine running down his face and everything. After some got in his mouth, he tried to spit it out of the window. It didn't make it that far, it landed on his arm. He said, "Damn!" and wiped it on the seat.

Once at the YMCA, he found a nice place to park, away from everything. With the car cut off, he sat there for a minute, getting his thoughts together. After he put the gun under the seat, and rolled up the windows. He got out and locked the doors. When he walked into the YMCA, he spotted a fool he was locked up with, named Rob. Mike just wanted to know one thing, "Where's the class?"

"Oh, what's up Mike, when did you get out?"

Not in a talking mood, Mike just replied, "Yesterday."

He figured Rob read his mind, because all he said to Mike after that was, "Follow me."

As they made there way to the door of the classroom, Mike saw some teenagers going in what seemed to be a game room, down the hall. He couldn't make out any faces, but he knew that someone he knew was most likely down there.

When they walked in the room, Mike was glad to see

everyone still mingling around, talking to one another. He hated coming in a classroom where everyone was already seated, because all eyes would end up on him. That's just how he usually showed up to a class, but today he was glad he broke that pattern. He wanted to fit in the best he could, on this stressful day.

Everyone sat down when the counselor finally came in. Mike made sure he sat in the mix of the crowd. He knew this was not the time for him to sit in the back, and bring attention to himself. He had so much going through his mind.

He didn't know if the smell-good he got from Tammy was working or not? His sense of smell was so fucked up, he didn't know what he was smelling. To remain calm, he decided to have a quick one-on-one with himself. He became his own inspirational speaker. "You got to keep it together for a hour, then you can let go. Man, you can do this."

From how everyone was sitting, he knew it could only mean one thing, "Open Floor," which meant, one-by-one, they would all say their name and what's been going on in there lives, good or bad. Realizing this, he knew he had some attention coming. For the first time, he sized up the class and saw there was only eight of them. If the order went like he thought it would, it would be on him, third or fourth. This meant, he had to get his shit together and quick.

It didn't take him long to zone out and drift off into his own world. When the fool next to him kicked his chair, to get his attention, he snapped out of it. Confused, Mike looked around the room, only to realize it was on him. He figured he was stuck for quite some time, because he didn't remember hearing the first fool say a word.

A hell of a story, which could explain his actions of being

so distant, was desperately needed, and he knew it.
The first thing that came to mind, was his son Putter. He
felt it was a part of the truth, so in a low tone, he said his
name, and told the group about his son, that was named
after another man. To take his performance a step further,
he put his head down, and said, "Right now, I just need to
get my thoughts together, so with that, I close."

The room went silent and no one bothered to give him any
feedback. Such a topic was left alone. Then after close to a
minute, the next fool started talking. There was no doubt in
Mike's mind, he knew he won their pity; so to them, his
actions all made sense.

With his head still down, out of the corner of his eye,
Mike saw a female walking by in the hallway. He lifted his
head up just in time to see her ponytail. He looked at the
door, and thought, "That couldn't of been Lonna."

Without a second thought, he got up and walked out. He
figured this move would also fit into his over all performance.
Out the door, up the hallway a bit, is where he saw her. As
she reached for the game room door handle, he called out to
her.

"Lonna!"

She turned around, and to her surprise, Mike was standing
right there.

Mike figured it was about a year since the last time they
saw each other. He like her a lot, but there was one
problem, she always ended up moving back to Chicago.
Back and fourth she went, but every time their paths
crossed, they were back together. Lonna was one of the
only girls he wasn't in a hurry to get into bed. To him, she
was special, and that's just how he treated her.

"What's up stranger," was the only thing Mike said, and he
gave her a hug.

"I see you're still smoking like always," Lonna replied.

"How you know that?"

"I seen it in your eyes, and I been around you long enough to know how you move when you're high."

"Been around me long enough, hell, you left me for a whole year, so what's that?"

"Shit, I'm back ain't I? Boy, you know I could never forget about you."

"Well look, don't you move. I'm gonna take you home. I got to go to this little class for 10 to 15 more minutes, so wait for me, like I been waiting for you."

"I'll be out front, but I'm not alone, my cousin Aleasha's with me."

"That's cool, look, I'll tell you what, to make sure you don't leave me, take my car keys. Y'all can wait in my car for me. It's the all-white one, off to the side, by itself."

Mike handed her the key, and she told him what he wanted to hear.

"I'll be out there."

Knowing she would, he looker her in eyes, and replied, "It's good to see you too!"

When he walked back in the class, he didn't care if they were watching him. He felt like a King; his Queen was back.

To Mike, it was torture sitting there, listening to them fools talking about nothing. He was ready to get back to Lonna. Past irritated, he was like, "Fuck it," and got up and left. To himself, he quickly justified his action. "Shit, they think I'm stressing anyway, and it was on the last fool, so shit should be cool."

As he walked up to the car, he was happy to see Lonna and her cousin, in the car waiting for him. With the windows rolled down and the radio playing, Lonna was behind the wheel, while her cousin was riding shot gun. Mike walked up to the back door and told Lonna to unlock it. As he climbed in the back, the two up front looked back at him, somewhat confused. He just stretched out, and said, "Baby, go on and drive. Shit you do know how to drive, don't you?"

"Boy don't play," Lonna replied. " Oh yeah, here take this. I see you still can't leave home without it."

"Damn, Baby, what was you doing under there?" Mike asked, as he took his gun from her.

"I wanted to see if you've changed any, which I see you haven't. Now where am I going?"

"Just drive, and Jet me get my thoughts together, Damn!"

Lonna didn't care to respond, she found herself feeling a little pissed. She had to take a look in the rear view, to make sure that was the Mike she knew. She thought, "Damn, he ain't never talked to me like that before."

After driving a few blocks in silence, Alesha said, "Mike, I thought you was in jail."

"Shit I was, I just got out yesterday."

"And you're already moving too fast," Lonna stated.

"How many times am I gonna have to hear that same shit?" Mike thought to himself.

" y'all hungry?" Mike then asked.

After they both said yeah, he replied,"Well, go to one of the spots around here, so we can grab something real quick."

"Well, what do you want?" Lonna asked

"I ain't trippin', you're driving, so drive," Mike replied as he laid back and closed his eye.

After a few moments he saw they were pulling up in Taco Bell. Realizing she was about to park, he said, "Baby go through the drive-thru."

At the ordering box, Lonna turned around to face Mike, and asked, "Mike, what do you want?"

"You know, just a large orange."

"I see you're still not eating shit."

73

"Just get what you and Alesha want, and keep in mind, I'll always be alright."

"Mike, you know what, I see something did change with you. You got a smart mouth, and I don't like it." Lonna stated firmly.

"Is that right?" Mike replied. " Well, I got a few things I don't like, but we'll talk about that a little later."

Once they made it to the pick up window, Mike was like, "Who's paying for this?" They both looked back at him, and he pulled out his bankroll. He peeled off a twenty, and handed it to Lonna.

She took it, and said, "I see you got jokes."

" Yeah, just like you know magic, with your disappearing act."

"I'm with you on this one Mike, she do know how to do that," Aleasha agreed.

"I see both of y'all got jokes."

"Baby, ain't no joking about this, it's the truth, and you know it."

After she paid for the food, Lonna handed the bag to Aleasha, and the pop to Mike. She then said, "Where to now Mike?"

Before he could answer, his pager went off, and it wasn't on vibrate. The two up front, both looked back at him.

Lonna said, "Damn, you sure work fast. You just got out yesterday and you already got bitches blowing you up?"

"Lonna, you need to cut the shit out."

"Mike, you always did put everything off on me. Tell me, why is that?"

Feeling things needed to be cooled off, in a joking way, Aleasha said, "Damn, when was the wedding, because y'all act like y'all are married already."

"Fuck all that," Lonna fired back. " Mike where do you need to go?"

"To the homie, Luckies, on 15th and Queen. But look, baby I didn't know you used such words."

"Well, I do, and can we smoke?"

"Shit, y'all smoke now?"

"Yep."

"That's real fucked up, y'all wouldn't smoke with me back in the day. But y'all let some other fool turn y'all out."

"Yep, he sure did. In more than one way too."

Sick of playing such a game, Mike decided to smooth things over. He knew she was tripping because hispager went off. So, in a low tone, he laid it on her. "Baby, if you want me to feel bad and cheated, well I do, but I forgive you, and I still love you."

Lonna hated being mad at him, because it would never last. There was something about him that always seemed to be smooth. She started laughing, and said, "Boy, you really got problems."

"You're right, I'm looking at her."

Aleasha felt it was only right for her to put her two-cents in, "Oh, y'all are so sweet together, that don't make no sense."

They made the turn unto 15th and Queen, and Lonna said, "Where to now?"

Mike spotted Lucky and Brandon sitting on their front stairs, so he replied, "Right there, where them two fools are."

As they pulled up, Lucky and Brandon were walking towards the car. Mike rolled down the back window, and said, " Brandon, roll up!"

Loving the sound of that, Brandon went right to work. Lucky saw who was driving, so he smiled, and said, "What's up Lonna? I see you're back. That's one thing about Mike, he's gonna track his baby Lonna down, if he don't do nothing else."

"And you know this man," Mike replied, which caused them all to laugh.

Lucky walked around to the passenger window, to get a better look. That's when he realized it was Aleasha. "What's up Aleasha? I ain't seen you in a minute. Where you been hiding at?"

"I ain't been hiding, I been around."

Brandon licked the blunt one last time, and climbed in the back with Mike. He handed Mike the weed and $250 dollars. Mike looked at the money and said, "What's this?"

"It's two-fifty cuz," Brandon replied. " I got all of that shit off and I need some more."

When Mike looked up, he saw Lonna watching him in the rear view. He knew what she was thinking, but he wasn't trying to go there. He looked at Brandon, and said, "Well look, later on I'll be back with a little something for you, but right now, let's smoke."

Halfway through the blunt, Mike said, "Brandon, I need you to do something for me."

"What's up cuz, you know I got you."

"Look, I need you to call this feen and let him know if he got the money, I'll be there in less than 30 minutes."

"Cool, I can do that."

Brandon took the pager, and he was on his way. From the look Mike gave him, he knew he had to call the bitch, and let her know he's on his way.

As Brandon walked away, Mike just looked at him. To himself, he thought, "I love that little nigga."

Mike liked him so much, because he could relate to Brandon's struggle. Brandon was the oldest out of five, and his mom was strung out on crack. So, he and his sisters and brothers lived with their grandma, along with Lucky and his sister. Brandon always come last, so he was worst off. So, ever since Mike knew him, he did what he could for him. It was like he was little brother.

Lucky put a stop to zone Mike was in, when he tried to hand him the blunt through the window.

Lonna said, "Boy, snap out of it. Damn!"

He took the blunt, hit it twice, and passed it to her.

"What's up Cuz, can I roll?" Lucky asked, then he looked at Aleasha.

Knowing what he was thinking, Mike was like, "Not right now homie, that's not what the situation is. I'm on one, I got to meet this fool over south, but I'll be back after I handle this biz."

"He's about to drop us off, and go pick up his bitch, that's what he's about to do." Lonna added.

By the time Lonna was done speaking her mind, Brandon was at the window, with the pager in hand. He handed it to Mike, and told him what was up. "That fool said he got the money, so he's waiting."

"Good looking out, lil' homie, I'll be back, don't trip."

Sick of hearing the bullshit, Lonna cut in and was like,

"Y'all's boy will be back with another bitch. I'm on her time right now, so we gotta get moving."

After she was sure Lucky and Brandon stepped away form the car, she pulled off. Mike didn't say a word, he wasn't about to blow his high. Not on the bullshit she was on, even though she was right.

They made it to Lonna's and they both got out. Aleasha said, "Bye Mike," while Lonna kept on walking. Mike climbed in the front and honked the horn. Lonna stopped and looked back. That's when Mike waved her back to the car.

She came back, and said, "What?"

"Can I come over tonight?"

"Yeah, if your bitch will let you," Lonna replied, then she walked off.

Mike just smiled, and put the car in motion.

GOING NO WHERE FAST
CHAPTER 8

On the drive back to the south side, Mike couldn't stop smiling. He replayed the events of the day, and he couldn't ask for a better start. He got his first bag of work off; now it was time to bust down this other ball of crack. He put his car in the shop, stayed high, made it through class, bumped into his old bitch, got some pussy, and saw all his kids, but one. Now he was on the way to pick up another bitch, fuck on her, get high, and make some more money.

When Mike thought about the last thing, he started shaking his head. Then he said to himself, "Shit, it can't get no better than this."

Laughter soon followed, as he reached in his pocket and pulled out his bag of weed. The sight of one last blunt worth of weed sent Mike into a panic. His smile turned into a frown, as he said, "Fuck! This ain't never good."

He put his bag up, and quickly sized up his options on fixing such an issue. He knew Blast wasn't coming off any more of what he had, so that was a no-go. Then it hit him. A smile washed over his face as he remembered where he was headed.

Kim's aunt, Ms. Willer was real cool, everybody that grew up in the hood knew her. When you wanted to get away from the streets and kick your feet up and chill, Ms. Willer's house was the spot. It had to be after five, because she ran a day care in the morning. When Mike remembered that, he looked at his pager and saw it was going on three.

"Fuck! I hope she ain't got no kid," Mike prayed.

When he got off the freeway, he pulled into S.A, to call Kim and let her know he was right around the coner. The phone rang twice, and just as he hoped, Ms. Willer answered.

"Hello, Ms. Willer?"

"Yes."

"This is Mike."

"What's up boy? When did you get out?"

"Yesterday."

"Well, when you coming to see me?"

"I'm on my way right now to pick up Kim."

"Oh, that's good, cause I'm sick of seeing her face."

After such a statement was made, they both couldn't help share a laugh.

"Well look Ms. Willer, I need some of that good stuff, I got one fifty. So can you make a call?"

"I'll see what I can do."

"I would appreciate it."

"I bet you would, well here's Kim."

"Alright."

"What!" Kim asked,n doing her best to have her panties in a bunch.

"Girl get off that stuck shit!"

"Whatever dude."

"Look, I'm down the street at S.A gettin' some gas, so quit actin' stuck. I should be there in like five minutes."

" Dude you be bluffin'... But We'll see."

"Look, I'm about to get off this phone, but tell Ms.Willer I'm on my way."

"Yeah, whatever," Kim replied, and she brought their call to an end."

Mike looked at the phone, and thought to himself,

"That bitch better be glad I need that bud, or I would leave her ass on stuck. Shiiit, I don't know why I'm even fuck wit' her bluffin' ass any way," Mike questioned?

Once he made it, he parked and got out. He walked up to the door and knocked. Then he turned around and looked kitty-corner, and saw his Aunt Rhonda was home, because her car was parked in front of her building.

As Kim opened the door, Mike made a mental note that he had to go over there and see how his Aunt Rhonda and cousin Joy were doing. His Aunt Rhonda was his favorite aunt. She was his dad's sister, and she did her best to pick up where his dad was slacking. Just about every weekend, when he was younger, he used to go spend the weekend with her. She used to spoil him, the best she could.

Before Mike went to jail, that's where he was staying most of the time. Such a living arrangement was the out come of he and his mother getting into it.

One night his mom came into his room tripping, because she was high. It just so happened, he had company, and she was embarrassing him by her actions. Before he knew it, she grabbed him and started shaking him, saying, "Go get your sister! She's in the alley screaming, don't you hear her?"

Mike was fully aware of the fact, that every since Tony got raped by their mom's ex-boyfriend, their mom would trip out about her.

Trapped in such a mood, She tightened her hold on Mike, and kept shaking him.

Un-able to take the humiliation any longer, foolishly he shoved her off of him, and she went flying. Boy was he grateful that she landed on his bed.

That's the night his mom said, "If you're grown enough to put your hands on me, you're grown enough to get the fuck out of my house, so you and your company got to go."

So, at the age of fifteen, Mike had to put together a quick plan and become a man. It wasn't like he was alone, he had Jackie with him. Her mom put her out a week earlier, so she was staying with him and his mom. Jackie's best friend, Nana, was also along for the ride.

Mike packed his shit, and he was thinking about what he was going to do. Then it hit him, he reached in his pocket, and pulled out a key. This was one time he knew his dad came through.

Just the day before, his dad gave him a key to an apartment downtown, that he had rented. What Mike liked about that, was the fact that his dad was never there.

Knowing things would work out, Mike started smiling. Jackie and Nana looked at him, and asked, "What's up?"

Mike just looked at them, and said, "We're gonna be alright."

They made the journey it to the apartment, only to find it completely empty. Right away Mike was glad that he told Jackie to grab the blankets on his bed, before they left.

The next day, Jackie and Nana set out to do a little shop lifting for household supplies. When it came to Mike, he stole a car, and did a bit of shopping. Then he went and picked up his house stereo.

While they stayed at the apartment, they lived off hot dogs, hamburgers, and $1.99 jugs of juice. The apartment quickly turned into the homie hang out, party spot. For that reason, their stay there was short-lived.

Due to the fact that Jackie was pregnant, her mom let her move back in. When it came to Mike, he was back and fourth, from his Aunt Rhonda's, over south, to Jackie's, over north. Within a month, Jackie and her mom moved back over south in the 30's. Even though Mike had clothes at both spots, he spent 90% of his time right there with Jackie. Back then Mike didn't have problems with the fools he had problems with now. Most of them were Jackie's cousins, so they use to come by the house, and Mike would smoke with them every now and then.

The only thing Mike was focused on was getting high and hustling. He had friends on both sides of the color code. He was what he was, but if it wasn't about progress, it didn't mean shit to him. He understood one couldn't gang-bang and get money. At this point in his life, he felt money was more important.

He found himself in the middle of a war. To add fuel to the fire, one day Mike came home, and Jackie's cousin and his crew was hanging out front. When Mike walked up, one of them said, "Man, we need to hit a stang!"

That's when another one said, "Shit, that's the man with the money right there," pointing at Mike.

"I see you got jokes," Mike replied, really not paying such an out burst no mind.

At that moment Jackie's cousin threw out the bait, "What up Mike, smoke one!"

Thinking nothing of it, Mike attempted too blaze up. When he looked up, he found that he had a pistol in his face.

Sadly, two days later, the one who pulled the gun on Mike, lost something, and he said Mike and his crew took it. Such heat forced Mike to move completely in with his aunty, as he laid low.

Mike walked in the house, and he asked Kim, "Where's Ms.Willer?"

"Damn, is that the only reason you came over here?"

"Oh come on baby, you know I'm here to see you, now give me a hug."

She tried to play hard, but she opened up and gave in. When their embrace came to an end, her hand shot down to his joystick. She then smiled, as she rubbed it. Knowing she had his full attention, she turned and walked into the living room. Mike stood there for a second, and thought, "Man, what's up with this freaky-ass bitch?"

He just shook his head and walked into the next room. Ms. Willer, her daughter Dee, and Kim were sitting on the couch. As soon as Ms. Willer saw him, she said, "That's on it's way."

"That's cool, but what's up Ms. Willer, how have you been? Dee what up?"

"I've been alright, just trying to keep the police away from here."

"What do you mean by that?"

It was Dee that felt she had to answer, "Tim and his friends came running over here and the police were right behind them. Shit, I told them they had to go because the police wont be kickin' my mommy's door in."

" Damn, thats crazy," Mike replied. He then looked at Ms.Willer and asked, "Can I roll up?"

" Dee grab him my tray," Ms.Willer instructed.

Mike watched as she reached under the couch for it. He really didn't need it, but he took it anyway. He busted the blunt down, and Dee handed him a little trash can.

Ms. Willer saw the blunt, and said, "Here we go with that blunt crap. Look at you, you're about to waste all of that good weed. Why don't you just roll me up a joint and y'all smoke the blunt.

"You don't got to say no more, Ms. Willer I got that for you," Mike replied, as he looked up and saw Kim just stearing at him. He didn't want her feeling like he was neglecting her, so he hit her with a dose of small talk.

"What's up Kim, how have you been?"

She saw right through his bullshit. She got up, and said, "I'll be upstairs when you're ready."

Mike didn't have to say anything, because Ms. Willer did, "Yeah, go upstairs with your flaky ass."

Mike just kept rolling the joint for Ms. Willer. He got done and handed it to her, she looked at it, and said, "It's a fat one too, thank you."

She blazed it up, as Mike finished rolling his blunt. He got done, and as soon as he was about to light, Kim was there, "Let me light that."

Mike looked at her and he knew a powerful struggle when he saw one. He figured this was one, he was willing to lose. He handed her the blunt and the lighter.

Ms. Willer just looked at her and started shaking her head. This time it was Dee that said something, "Girl, that don't make no sense."

Kim's comeback was quick and sharp, "Well, to me it do!"

Ms. Willer said, "Mike, I'm glad you're here to pick her ass up, because she needs some dick, so she can get her mind right."

Everyone started laughing so hard, Mike saw some tears. That's when Mike said, "Well, I got just what she need," and they laughed even harder. Their laughter was interrupted by a knock on the door.

Ms. Willer looked out the window and saw it was her friend with the weed. Before she walked to the door, she said, "Mike, give me the money."

He pulled his bankroll out and peeled off the $150 dollars, and gave it to her.

Everyone's eyes focused in on Mike's hand, and Dee said, "Mike, when did you say you got out?"

"Yesterday, why?"

Dee passed him the blunt, and said, "I see you don't waste no time getting back into the thick of things."

Mike just hit the blunt, as he looked at Kim. He thought to himself, "Let me get out of here and take this bitch to the spot so I can fuck the shit out of her."

It was Ms. Willer that made him snap out of his zone,

when she handed him his weed. Without a second thought, he grabbed her weed tray and put a nice amount of weed on it. "Good lookin' out Ms. Willer. Kim are you ready?"

Kim said, "Yeah whatever," and she got up and walked to the door.

Mike hit the blunt one last time, then handed it to Dee. Before he walked out of the room, he said, "Y'all take care and I'll see y'all later."

When he made it outside, he was somewhat glad to see that his auntie's car gone.

The trip to the building was made in silence. They both rocked their heads to the music the radio was playing. When Mike pulled up, he saw that all of block-players were out. He knew he had to get out there and get some of that good money. "That would come later, but right now, I got to knock a patch out of this bitch!" He thought.

After making plans with Tee to smoke one later, Mike and Kim walked in the building. His mom and Tony were sitting at the table playing tunk, when they walked in.

When his mom saw him, she asked, "How was your day?"

"Everything's been real smooth," Mike replied.

"And how are you doing, sweetie?" Mom then asked Kim.

"Fine," Kim replied some what nervous.

"Mom, has anyone been looking for me?"

"Yeah, your cousin Bee and T.Bone," she replied. "They said they'll be back. And that's about it, besides them fools outside."

Before Mike could ask any more questions, his sister Toney cut in, "What's up little brother, I been waiting for you."

"Yeah, I bet you have, but you got to wait some more, I got to take care of something first."

"Well shit, if you don't got it, I'm going upstairs."

"Girl, just sit yo ass down," mom ordered.

"He got it, he just got to bag it up."

"Oh, I didn't know that."

"Well, mom wasn't pose to know that either."

"Boy, I'm your mother, I pose to know everything."

Mike looked at Kim and saw how she was looking uncomfortable, so he said, "Look, I'll be out in a minute, I got to handle something real quick.."

"You're my son, so you know I know your minutes, and I bet ya'll do got something to do. Sweetie, just take it easy on my son, and Mike don't be to long."

They all started laughing, and Mike grabbed Kim's hand, as he lead the way to the room.

Kim sat on the edge of the bed, while Mike walked over to the radio and cut it on. With the volume at a five, he pulled his gun out and sat it on the floor next to the bed. Read for some action, he then laid back on the bed and told Kim to come lay next to him. She kicked her shoes off, and made her way on top of him.

They started kissing, and she was grinding on him at the same time. Mike rolled her on her back and gave her a soft wet kiss, then he went to work on her pants. He got the bottom open, zipper down, and the panties came off.

She looked down at Mike, as he looked at her pussy. It was hairy, just like he remembered it. He quickly climbed in between her awaiting, wide open legs. He worked his pants and pulled them down below his waist. He then grabbed his joystick, lubed up the head with a little spit, and drove it into her love-spot. Four strokes into it, he realized it was still bullshit, like he also remembered. It wasn't hot, it was luke-warm. It wasn't wet, it was damp. He made up his mind just to get one off, and be grateful for that. So, he just fucked her like a jack rabbit, no passion nor dedication. As he was working it, he couldn't believe she was trying to fuck him back. He knew she could be come a

86

good fuck, with some work, but he wasn't ready to
put the time into her. So, he just went with the flow and got
his off inside or her.

  With that out the way, Mike rolled over and pulled his
pants and boxers up. While he did that, Kim did the same.
Then she sat back on the edge of the bed. That's when Mike
told her to stand up. He reached under the mattress, and got
his last ball of crack. He then grabbed the plate and baggies
form behind the radio. With everything sitting next to him
on the bed, he pulled out his bankroll and started counting.

GOING NO WHERE FAST
CHAPTER 9

Mike looked down at his bankroll, and said, "I got to slow down."

Not realizing he said it out loud, Kim said, "You sure do." He didn't give in to her invitation to an argument, instead he said, "I need you to do something for me."

He then handed her the plate with the work on it.

She looked at it, and said, "What do you want me to do with this?"

"I need you t break half of that down for me. Do you think you can do that for me?"

" You act like I pose to just know how to do that shit," Kim replied.

"Don't trip, I'm gonna walk you through it."

Kim just sat there for a minute, as she got her thoughts together. She didn't want Mike to know how excited she really was about getting the chance to do this. She a few of her ex-boyfriends break down their dope, but non of them ever asked her to help. Even though she wanted to help and learn, she never asked. This time she didn't want to overdo her hard act, so she asked, "What do I got to do?"

"The first thing you got to do is take it out of the plastic, then I need you to take the razor and cut in in half. After you do that, put one half in a baggie, and hand it to me."

Still playing hard, Kim said, "Why can't you bag it up?"

"Because I got to take UA's, and when you touch it, it gets in your pores."

"So, what does that mean?"

"It means, it comes out in your U.A."

"Well, you smoke all the fuckin' time, what about that?"

"I got something for that, now is there anything else you need to know?"

"Don't get smart nigga, I wont do this shit for your ass."

"You know what, you're right. I'm sorry."

"I see you got jokes, Mike."

"Look, fuck all that. Let's just put this together," Mike replied; passed irritated.

" Well what do you want me to do?" Kim asked.

Wasting no more time, Mike gave out instructions, and Kim executed them gracefully. She did what he asked with the first half, and handed it to him. He took it and put it in his pocket. Then, using his pinky and thumb, he demonstrated the two sizes he needed her to cut the rest into.

She didn't miss a beat, her eyes were focused on Mike's every mover. Satisfied that she understood, she went right to work.

Pleased with Kim's work flow, Mike picked up the gun and laid it on the bed. His next move, he figured, would be getting his blunts out of the way. So, he went to work on rolling up his last four.

yearning to be stroked for the good work she was doing, Kim said, "Look Mike, am I doing this right?"

Mike quickly sized up her work, and said, "Yeah baby, you're doing your thang, with your fine-ass!"

Satisfied, they both went back to work on their projects. A minute later, Mike stopped in mid-motion, and gave Kim one last look. He like what he saw; she was truly dedicated to getting the job done. That's when he thought, "Man! I might be able to work with her after all. Shit, all it should take is a couple of days to invest in her, and she should be good to go." Mike then smiled, as he went to lick the last blunt closed.

With his kit rolled up and tucked away in his shirt pocket, he sat next to Kim. As she cut the last piece in half, there was a knock on the door. Startled Kim, jumped to her feet.. She would have dropped the plate, if Mike wasn't there to grab the it in time.

The sight of seeing Kim so scared, sent Mike into a frenzy of laughter. He said, "Shit's cool baby, calm down. It's only my sister."

"Shit ain't funny Mike," Kim fired back. " And I don't know why you're laughing."

"Because you act so hard, but you're scary as fuck," Mike explained. " Now take this plate and put it behind the radio, while I go get this door."

As he handed it to her, there was another knock at the door. Irritated, he said, "Kick the fuck back, here I come!"

At the door, he looked back at Kim and saw she did what he asked her to do. He then opened the door to see Bee and Tony standing there.

" Big sis what up?"

"I need something for thirty."

All Mike wanted to do was get Tony out of his face. So, he walked to where the plate was and picked up two pills with his bare hands. He walked back in the hall and gave her what she wanted.

Mike closed the door, and said, "Bee, I'm glad to see you."

"I'm glad to see you too fool. So what's up?"

Mike happened to look at Kim, and he saw how she was watching him. That's when he said, "What's up baby?"

"I thought you said you can't touch that shit!"

"Well, I can't, but I hope that little shit don't do nothing."

"Well, I hope so too," Kim agreed. " Shit Mike, you need to slow down, like you said yourself. "

" Yea, I know I do," Mike replied, giving it some honest thought. " But you know what baby?"

" What is it?" Kim asked, smiling a bit.

" I'll be al'ight!"

"If your hard head ass say so," Kim fired back. She found herself feeling stupid, because for some reason, she thought he would say something nice.

Mike had enough of that typed of talk, so he switched up, and said, "Bee, I need you to put this together for me."

Bee looked down at the plate, and quickly counted $1200 dollars worth of work on it. Loving the sight of that, he said, "Mike, it's on, ain't it?"

With a smile on his face from ear to ear, Mike replied, "This ain't shit, it's about to really be on!"

Mike was ready to get outside and make some more money. He knew he needed to get his hustle on, because his was bankroll was nice, but it could be a whole lot better. He had plans on seeing to it that it, and soon. He looked at Bee, and asked, "A Bee, when you came in was there a lot of fools out there?"

" Fool, you already knowing, so why did you ask?"

"Well hurry up, so we can get out there and get some of that money."

"Don't even trip cousin, I got you, but what's up with a blunt?"

"You know I got something for us, so hurry up, so we can smoke."

That's when Kim said, "Mike, you need to stop smoking so damn much!"

"I will, but not one day soon, you best believe that."

"I'm with you on that one cousin."

"Well, y'all both need some damn help."

"You're right baby, I do need some help. Some help gettin' rich. Now what part are you ready to play, to help me achieve such a goal?"

"You know what Mike? You really got me fucked up."

"Now do I really? Baby, you know you like what I bring into your life, so stop playing the role, and enjoy yourself. Because You know it's real over here."

" Is that right?" Kim asked.

"And you know this baby, now all you got to do is roll with your nigga, and everything will be alright."

Bee finished bagging up the last pill, and he put all of the work in one bag. After he counted it in his head one more time, he handed it to Mike.

" What's the count?" Mike asked, sizing up the bag.

"It was twelve on the nose when I started, but I had to fatten one or two up, so now it's eleven sixty."

"That's cool," Mike replied, as he slid the bag into his pocket. That's when he felt the other half that he put in there earlier. So, he pulled the half that wasn't broken down yet, out, and told Kim and Bee to stand up. He grabbed the gun and handed it to Kim. She looked at him crazy and took the gun. He then put the half, under the mattress.

When Mike looked at Kim, she was holding the gun with two fingers away form her, like it was going to bite her or something. Mike figured it was time for a little "Kim training," so he said, "Come on, let's go."

She responded just like he knew she would. "Here, take this," Kim demanded, trying to hand him the gun back.

"Baby, I need you to hold onto that, so find a place to put it. It's not gonna bite you, so quit trippin', and let's go."

She looked at Mike, and thought, "Damn, he ain't never acted like this before, but I like it."

Without another word, she stuck the gun in her waistband and pulled her shirt over it.

Once they made it to the dinning-room, Mike was glad to see his little sister was only one in sight. He walked over to the couch where she was sitting, and gave her a hug and kiss. "Mom's in the back right?" He asked.

"Yeah, Tony is too."

"Well, come lock this door."

"Ok."

When he turned around, Bee was already out the door, and Kim was holding it open. Kim didn't move until Mike was close enough to grab the door. She walked out and Mike was right behind her. He stopped outside of the door and listened, as his little sister put the lock in place.

Mike walked past Kim, and stepped outside to see Bee already sitting on the steps. Then he focused in on Tee and his boys, who happen to be leaning on the fence, with their backs to him. After he sat down next to Bee, Mike turned to see Kim still standing in the doorway. It was like she was scared to come out or something, he figured.

"Baby, come on out and have a seat, or you can go sit in the car and listen to the radio."

"Yeah, I want to sit in the car, so give me the keys."

"Look baby, take these keys, but you need to stay on point, for real."

Tee saw Kim walk by and he turned to see Mike and Bee sitting there. He said, "What's up Mike, can we smoke?"

Mike pulled out his box ofblunts, and said, "You ain't said shit, let's do this."

Mike stood up and started walking to the car. Bee and Tee were right behind him. Mike walked to the drivers door and got in. While Tee and Bee got in the back, Mike looked over to Kim and she was pointing in his drivers door window. He turned to see their new friend from across the street, standing there with a blunt in his mouth. Mike pointed to the back, and said, "Let him in."

He then handed a blunt to Kim, and told her to roll up her window. Before she could get it rolled all the way up, Mike

93

said, "Baby, go head and blaze it up."

She looked at Mike, and said, "I need a," before she could get the last word out, three lighters from the back, came flying up front. Everyone started laughing, and she said, "That don't make no sense."

That's when Mike pulled out his and handed it to her.

Mike liked what he was seeing; there were three blunts going at one time. The cars was filled with smoke and fools were coughing. He tried to pass Kim a blunt, and she said she didn't want anymore. Before he knew it, his eyes were burning from the smoke, and he loved every bit of it. He really liked how it seemed every time he passed a blunt, he was handed another one.

That was how he liked to kick it. It was always all the way, or no way, with Mike. He would deal with the consequences later; it was all about the here and now, fuck the later. He figured late might not make it, so why worry about it. If you were a true hustler, you would work it out, and find a way to make things right. This was his out look on life, so that's what he lived by.

The last blunt went out, and they all just sat there breathing in the smoky ass air.

"Fuck this, I got to roll down this window," Kim said.

Mike quickly said, "No you don't, once you're in, ain't no getting' out, so deal with it' by the way, hand me that."

Kim looked at him, and then said, "Oh yeah, here," and she then passed him the gun.

For the next five minutes or so, they sat there in silence. Everyone was in their own zone, off in their world. Kim broke it up, as she got out of the car because she couldn't take it anymore. She needed some fresh air and she got it. She also helped out the others because they all wanted to do the same thing. Their pride wouldn't let them give in, so they were all willing to suffer. One by one, everyone plied out of the car. As they did so, they all inhaled as much fresh air as they could. Mike leaned against the car, with Kim at his side. Tee's boys were laughing because it seemed no one could talk, due to the face, they were all so high. Mike found the words to ask Kim what time it was.

Kim said, "Look on your pager."

As he looked down at his pager, he said, "Oh yeah."

Kim looked and saw he didn't even look to see what time it was, so she said, "Let me see this," and she took his it.

He looked at her, and said, "Girl, you need to stop playin'."

"Boy, I ain't playin', all I'm trying to do is see what time it is for you."

She then looked, and said, "Boy, you shouldn't get high, if you're gonna be acting like that."

"Baby, I'm cool, I'm just getting my thoughts together."

"Shit, I bet you are."

Mike walked to the drivers door and got in. He told Kim to get in, and he pulled out his bag of work. When she closed the door, he handed her ten pills, and told her to put it up. Then he got out, and called Bee over to the car. Mike got back in and Bee got in the back.

"What's up?" Bee asked.

Mike handed him the bag of work, and said, "Look, I got to make a run real quick, so hang out and get some of that money for us."

"Don't even trip cousin, I'm posted, I'll be here."

"Alright Bee, I'll back in a minute."

With that said, Bee got out of the car. Mike looked at Kim, and said, "Did you put that up?"

"Yeah," she replied, and Mike cut the car on and pulled off.

GOING NOWHERE FAST
CHAPTER 10

Mike made it to the freeway, and rolled his window all the way down. As he was doing 70 mph, he kept his face as close to the open window as possible. He needed all the help he could get to stay up. All of his focus was on the road, as he passed cars up. He was shooting from lane to lane, as if he was in the Dayton 500. He knew he had to reach his destination quick, before his mind shut completely down, and the last bit of energy he had left evaporated.

With his eyelids feeling so heavy, and knowing how close they were to being shut all the way, he was surprised that he could still see. He looked at his companion, and the sight of Kim just sitting there with her arms crossed, just irritated him even more. "This bitch ain't no goddamn help! I know this bitch see me over here struggling. All she want to do is sit over there like a motha fuckin' manikin," was the only thing running through Mike's mind.

When Mike got too high, he needed to remain active or else he would pass out no matter where he was at. So, he knew he had to keep his mind working. He made it to his exit, and just his luck, the light turned red.

"Fuck!"

Kim looked at him, but she told herself it would be best not to say anything, so she just sat there. Mike sat there, and said, "Come on, come on, come on," like that chant would turn the light green, faster.

He didn't know if he fell asleep or what, but he knew the

manikin came alive, as she said, "Mike, the light is green."

He looked up to see the light green, and that's when he took his turn. Now that he was back on the street, he changed up his driving tactics. He knew he couldn't afford to get pulled over, so he took it slow. He passed up a mall of food spots, so he said out loud, "On the way back, we'll stop and get something to eat."

Again, Kim didn't say anything, she just looked at him. Then she went back to looking straight ahead.

They made it to Lucky's house and he parked, cut the car off, and said, "Let me get that." She opened up her hand, and there they were, sweaty as ever. Mike didn't say a word, he just took the ten pills, and thought, "That's why the bitch wouldn't say shit, because she was nervous as fuck."

Mike got out of the car, and told Kim, "I'll be right back." He then walked to the door and rang the bell.

Lucky's younger sister, little Bit, answered and said, "What's up Mike, when did you get out?

"Yesterday, but fuck that, let's talk about you."

"What about me?"

"Shit, I see you're still thick, with yo young ass."

"Yeah, but you want to fuck my young ass, don't you nigga."

"Baby, you're scared of me, I don't know why I don't want to hurt you."

"Yeah whatever nigga, are you corning in or what?"

"You know I am, I just wanted some one-on-one time with you, to see if we could come up with a understanding we both can be proud of."

"Mike boy, I seen you in action for years. I'll be damn if I become one or your little victims."

"Baby girl, I see you got your mind made up. But look, the door will always be open for you, so when you're ready, come on in and give yourself the chance to be happy with a real- one."

"Boy look, they're in the basement and they been waiting for you."

Mike walked in the house to find Lucky's Grandma Ann in her favorite spot on the couch, with her "Mickey" beer, at arms reach. "What's up Ann, how are you doing?" was all Mike had to say to get her started.

"All shit nigga, what do you want? Look, don't be having my grandson down there, smoking that crack shit."

"Ann, we don't be smoking no crack!"

"Yeah right, I ain't dumb, nigga."

"Alright Ann, I'm gonna leave it alone."

When Mike and Lucky used to live in the same building, Lucky would go down the hall to see what Mike was up to. Like always, Mike would end up getting Lucky high as fuck. They would then go back to Lucky apartment to use the phone or watch TV. Once they sat down, it wouldn't take Lucky no time to zone out and be come stuck. His grand dad would ask him something and he wouldn't respond. Mike would be right there laughing, and that's when Lucky's grand dad would say, "Ya'll been smoking that crack shit again? Mike, he left here just fine, now look at him. Every time he goes to your apartment, he comes back spaced out."

Mike would tell him over and over again, "It's only weed."

Lucky's grandpa would always say, "I'm not dumb, weed don't get you like that, look at him."

It would be an ugly sight.

Mike made his way down the steps of the basement, to find Lucky, Brandon, and the homie Lowdown, down there smoking a blunt. As soon as he made it into the room, Brandon handed Mike the blunt. Reluctantly, Mike hit it twice and passed it. That's when Lowdown said, "Mike, smoke one, you know I heard you got that sticky green shit."

"Cuz, I'm on one right now, so ain't shit crackin'. A Brandon, let me talk to you real quick."

They walked into the next room, and Mike handed Brandon the ten pills, and said, "I need one ten of that is that cool?"

Brandon reached in his pocket, and said, "Let me give you half right now."

"That's cool, hold your money and stack what you can. I'll be back sometime tomorrow, so do your thang."

"Bet, I got you Cuz, don't trip."

Mike walked back to the room, and told Lucky how he had to get in motion. Before Mike could turn around to leave, Lowdown said, "Cuz, can you give me a ride to the crib?"

"Come on, I got you," Mike replied as he lead the way.

When they got outside, Kim saw Mike wasn't alone, so before they made it to the car, she climbed in back. Once they made it to the car, Lowdown, looked in the back at Kim. Right away, Mike noticed a weary look on both of their faces. He brushed it off, and put the car in motion. As he drove, he realized there was a funny vibe in the car, and he couldn't figure out why. He knew he would find out in due time, so he went with the flow.

When they made it to Lowdown's spot, to Mikes surprise, Kim was the first one to get out. She said, "I'll be back," and she walked to the house next to Lowdown's.

Mike needed to get a better understanding on what was going on, so he asked Lowdown if he could use his phone. He needed to buy some time, to hopefully find out, what's the deal between them two. Mike knew it was deeper then what it seemed.

They walked in the house and Lowdown handed Mike the

phone. Mike decided to call Jackie to tell her that he would be over tonight. He knew that he didn't have to call and say that, but he wanted to make it look like he really needed to use the phone. Without Mike having to ask, Lowdown said, "Cuz, you know I be fuckin' wit' that bitch."

Mike smiled, and said, "Is that right? Well look cuz, take down my pager number, and get at me. I got to get up out of here."

"Bet, we can get together and smoke," Lowdown replied.

Mike made it to the car, and Kim was nowhere in sight. He got in and honked the horn once, and then he drove off. He forgot all about the food as he got on the freeway and headed back over south. He was wide awake now, and laughing to himself about what just happened. Then the thought of Lonna came back to his mind.

"I got to make my way back over there tonight. I will see if I can hook Bee's ass up with Aleasha."

He looked down at his pager and saw it was a little after seven. So, that's when he made up his mind that he and Bee would slide through to see Lonna and Aleasha, a little after elven. For the rest of the drive home, he drove with a smile on his face, as he bobbed his head to the sounds of the music "KMOJ" was playing.

When he pulled up to the building, he was happy to see that Bee was still out there. He was huddled up with a face that Mike knew was a friend. Mike got out of the car and walked up to Bee, and said, "What's up cousin?"

"Shit, it's on for real around here cousin. I'm glad you're back, where's baby at?"

"Fuck her, come on in and talk to me."

"Alright Mike, hold on, let me take care of this last fool real quick. Go on in, I'll be there."

"Don't be bullshitting, come on in and get at me."

Tee was still sitting on the steps in a zone, but Mike could tell his high was coming down. It was Mike that spoke first this time, "Tee, what's going on playboy, how you feelin'?"

" Come on now, you already know," Tee replied. "And I see you got your cousin out here, on one forreal."

"Yeah, you know we trying to do a little something around her."

"Well look Mike, I might need to holler at you a little later if shit don't come together like they should, feel me?"

"Don't trip, just get at me."

With that said, Mike just walked into building. He didn't knock, he just turned the door knob, and his house door came open. He stepped in to find everyone on the couch watching TV. When his mom looked up to see him, her only words were, "Your plate's in the oven and it should still be hot."

He went straight to the oven to find a plate of spaghetti and catfish. He looked in the small icebox and was happy to see a jug of grape Kool-Aid. He took it out and when he closed the icebox door, Tony was standing right there, "What's up Tony, what do you want now?"

"Is that your shit, Bee got?"

"Yeah, why?"

"Because, I don't think you should be letting him hold your shit like that."

"Everything's cool, don't eve trip, I got this."

"Well, if you say so, but look, let me get one for this ten dollars, and on everything, I'm done fuckin' with you."

"Damn girl, give me the ten, and go tell Bee I said give you one."

Before the last word was out of his mouth, Tony was in motion to find Bee. Mike found him a glass and got himself some Kool-Aid, and put it back in the icebox, he got his plate and Kool-Aid, and made his way to the dinning-room table. He was glad to see a fork on his plate, because he sure did forgot to grab one. Just when he was going in for his first bite he heard the door opening. He looked up to see Bee and Toney coming in. Right away, Bee focused in on Mike's plate, and went straight for it.

"Man cousin, let me get some of that," was the only thing Bee said, as he took the fork out of Mike's hand, and went to work.

Mike's mom put a stop to that, as she said, "Boy get your own, it's in the kitchen, and let him eat."

Mike took his fork back, and asked Bee, "Did you give that to Tony?"

"Yeah, I gave her one like you said, right?"

"Yeah, it's all good."

Mike got up with his plate and Kool-Aid in his hand, and headed to his room. He made it to the door, then stepped aside to let Bee open it. He followed Bee in, then he kicked the door closed.

Bee pulled out the bag of work and the money. He counted out five hundred and thirty five dollars, and slid it between him and Mike.

Mike put down his plate, picked up the money, and put it with the rest that he had. That's when Bee said, "Cousin, how are we gonna do this?"

"Look, we got to get this money right, so I can get somethin' real nice from my Big homie. So be cool, just help me get this little shit off, then on the next run, I will slide you something."

"I feel you, well look, I'm going back outside. When you're done eating, come out there."

"Bet," Mike replied, as he got back to his meal.

Bee walked out and closed the door behind him. Mike sat there and ate a fast pace, because he was ready to get out there and get his money on. He got done eating, and took his plate and glass into the kitchen. As he was walking out, his mom was coming out of her room. "Mike, come here and let me talk to you."

"Yeah mom, what's up?"

"Look baby, don't be having your cousin all in your business, do you hear me? Don't be stupid, you better listen to what I'm telling you!"

"I got you mom, don't trip."

"There you go being hard-headed. You're gonna regret not listening to me, like you always do."

Mike heard all that he cared to hear. He said, "Mom, I hear you," and headed out the door.

Before he made it, his mom said, "And you better watch your back out there."

Mike didn't respond, he just walked out. Once in the hallway of the building, he thought, "Man I hate when she be trippin'."

Mike made it outside to see Bee huddled up with another fool. "Damn, Bee's doing his thing out here," Mike thought, as he watched him in action. Mike looked down and saw Tee's boys must have left, because it was only him and Bee out there.

To liven up the party, Mike sat down next to Tee, and pulled out a blunt. Tee looked at Mike, and said, "What's up Mike, I see it's time for another session."

"And you know this, man," Mike replied, as he blazed up the blunt.

Bee walked up, and said, "I see it's on once again."   ..

"You already know, it was only a matter of time before I put something else in the air."

Out of the corner of his eye, Bee saw a police car riding by slow. He said, "Mike, cuff that, one time."

Hearing those words made Mike's heart skip a beat. He cuffed the blunt in one hand, and jumped up and slid into the building. He didn't care if he looked spooked, all he wanted to do was get as far away as he could. He went straight in the house and locked the door behind him. Everyone looked up at him, as they sat on the couch. The fear must have still been on his face, because his mom said, "Boy, are you alright?"

"I'm cool. I just had to come in for a minute."

Tony said, "Yeah whatever, I bet the police rolled by, didn't they?"

Mike didn't say anything, he just went to the table and sat down. He then looked at his blunt and saw how it went out. Once his heart stopped beating so fast, he walked to the window and looked out. He had to make sure the coast was clear. He saw his awaiting party got bigger. Joker and is crew were also out there. He was glad to see them. The more bodies, the tougher it would be for the police to get to him, he figured.

He made his way back outside, but before he closed his apartment door, he said, "Don't lock this door."

As soon as Bee saw Mike, he said, "Damn cousin! You got in the wind quick as fuck! I never seen you move that fast."

"Shit, I ain't got no time to be playing with them bitches, and you know this. What up Joker, how you feeling Cuz?"

"I'm cool you know, just ready to get into something, so what's up?"

Mike pulled out his blunt, and said, "You know we can smoke."

Joker looked at Mike, and said, "Cuz, you know we need more then that."

Mike looked down at his pager and saw it was 7:45. That's when he said, "Cuz, we got 15 minutes to get to the LQ, so what's up?"

Joker said, "That's what I'm talking about, I got whatever, on it."

Mike looked at Tee, and said, "What's up, you in?"

"Come on, you know I am."

"Well look, me and my cousin gonna make the run to the liq. We will deal with money when we get back. Joker Cuz, go to SA, and get some orange-juice, cups and some ice, and we will be right back."

Bee was already in his car with it started up; Mike got in and thy were in motion. Due to the fact that they were cutting it close, the ride to the liquor store was made in silence. They pulled right in front of the liquor store door, and parked. Then they ran in as fast as they could. Mike knew they just made it, because the man working there was on his way to lock the door. Before the man could say a word, Mike said, "We want a liter of Gin, and two cases of Old English, and we are out of here."

The man looked at them and saw they were not willing to hear no, so he said, "Com on, let's make it quick."

GOING NOWHERE FAST
CHAPTER ll

They made it back to the car and Bee put the drink in the back, started up the car. He said, "Mike, what's up with some Burger-King?"

"It's all good, cousin I got you. Just go through the drive-thru."

Bee didn't really want BK, but since it was right in the same little mall, he knew Mike wouldn't trip.

As they pulled up to the order box, Mike saw Blast two cars ahead. He said, "Look cousin, order what you want, I got to do something."

Mike got out of the car and crouched down as he made his way in front of Bee's car. Then he worked his way to Blast's drivers-side window. When he saw it was down, like he hoped it would be, he popped up, and said, "What's up fool!"

Blast shot toward the passenger-side so fast he was in Big Cie's lap.

Mike saw that while Blast was leaning, he was also reaching for what Mike knew was his Chrome 44. "Ce cool Cuz, it's only me," Mike joked.

When Big Cie and Blast realized it was Mike, they all started laughing.

Big Cie was the first to speak, "Cuz you need to kick back."

Mike said, "Cuz, it ain't my fault y'all was slippin'."

That's when blast said, "Cuz, I knew that was you."

After hearing such bull shit, they couldn't help but to laugh.

The people in the car behind Blast honked their horn. Not really playing the honking party any mind, Mike said, "Look Cuz, when y'all get y'all's food, slow up."

Mike turned to walk back to Bee's car.

Blast looked in the rear view and said, " Cuz, fuck that, what's up?"

Blast wanted to get some cool points back, due to the fact he lost some, when Mike crept up on him.

Mike stooped down at Blast's window, and said, "Look, we got some drink and some of the homies are at my building. We're about to just kick it, so why don't y'all slide through."

Blast said, "Cuz, I got some drink in the trunk too. And I know you got good trees?"

"I got a little something, but shit, I know y'all got it for real."

Big Cie said, " Cuz, don't trip, we'll be through there."

After hearing what he wanted to hear, Mike headed back to the car. When he made it to bumper of the honker, he heard doors being locked. He looked a the driver to see a red face white man. He started laughing, as he looked back to see Blast still sitting there.

Mike made it to the car, and as he closed the door, he saw Blast was just pulling up to the pick up window. Bee said, "Damn cousin, y'all be trippin'."

"Man shut that shit up and kick back. It's on for real now! Blast and Cie said they're gonna meet us at the building, they got drink and trees too. So you know it's gonna be a long night."

Bee didn't care to respond to Mike's shit talking. Even though he was older, he didn't feed into Mike's shit. There were many times he didn't like how Mike talked to him, but he always kept it you himself. He knew how Mike could quickly take it somewhere he wasn't trying to go. Everyone that was real close to Mike knew he was a "to the extreme" type of person. It was all the way, or no-way with Mike. Knowing this, Bee didn't want to be on the wrong side of Mike's anger, so he just let the shit slide.

They made it to the pick up window; Mike handed Bee a five; Bee paid for his food. As they pulled out of the parking lot, Blast pulled up behind them and followed them back to the apartment. On the drive back, Mike was in a world of his own, thinking about Lonna. He knew there was no way he was about to make that trip to see her, and that bothered him. He figured that would be his mission for the morning.

Bee pulled up in front of the apartment and parked. Before he cut the car off, he dug in the bag and gathered up the change. He then interrupted Mike train of thought by handing it to him. Mike looked down at the change, put it in his pocket, and got out of the car.

When Mike finally looked towards his front yard, what he saw took him aback. It had to be as least fifteen of his homies out there. It was Joker and his crew, Face and his crew, and C-Rider and his crew.

Mike stood there shaking his head when he heard Blast call Face. "Face, Cuz y'all come get some of this liq."

That's when it hit Mike, all of this was already planned.

That's when Cie walked up to him and handed him a blunt, and said, "Welcome home Cuz!"

Mike stood there smiling, proud as ever. Right as he took his first step to cross the street, he heard nothing but bass coming his way. As he turned to look, C-shot pulled up and stopped right in front of him.

C-shot cut his music down and stuck his head out of the window, and said, "What's up Cuz, where can we park?"

Mike looked behind him and saw a car full of the home girls behind him.

Mike then looked up and down street, only to realize it was packed with cars. Seeing this, he told them to park on the side street.

C-shot turned his music back up, as he pulled off, and hit the corner.

Mike stood there in the middle of the street taking everything in. Blast had his trunk open, and the homies were coming out of his trunk with 40's of Olde E. C-shot and his crew had bags in their hands and Mike knew it wasn't food. Bee already had a blunt in his mouth, and Tee was rolling one up.

Mike's new friend from next door, was sitting on his steps with two of his friends. While Mike's friend from across the street, was hanging in his yard with his boys, getting their hustle on. Everyone was getting a look at the new king on the block, and Mike loved it.

He wasn't surprised to see Tony hanging out, acting like she was looking for him. Tony saw Mike walking up, she said, "Mike, mom wants you."

"Yeah right, I bet she do, Tony don't be playing."

"Boy, I'm not playing. Will you go see what she wants?"

As soon as Mike walked into the yard, the love was apparent, as everyone came up to him to show him love with a hand shake or a pound. Mike made his way to the door, and Cie was right behind him.

Cie said, "Mike, I got to put something in your ear, so can I come in to talk to you?"

"Come on Cuz, don 't disrespect me like that, you know it's all good Cuz, come on."

Mike looked up to Cie and he had mad-love for him, not just because he was the "Big Homie." Mike always looked at him as a big brother. Cie knew Mike's family, so to Cie.

Mike was family, and Mike felt the love.

Mike and Cie walked in the house to find Mike's mom standing right there. "Mike, is everything alright?"

" Ma' everything's cool," Cie re-assured. "Some of the homies wanted to slide by to see Mike, now that he's home."

Mike was stuck trying to figure out, was his mom tripping because she was high, or was she really worried?

"Ok, you know I got to make sure my baby's alright."

"Yeah, I know ma', he's a'ight. I got him."

Mike was satisfied with Cie's comebacks to his mom, so he made his way to his room without saying a word. He reached for the door knob, he turned to see Cie standing there right behind him. He opened the door, walked in, and went straight for the radio. Cie came in and closed the door behind him.

Mike turned around, and said, "What's up Cuz?"

"Cuz, I got a half zip left and I want to slide it to you, if shit's looking good on your end. You know I'm making that run back to the city real soon, so I got to get together all of the chips that I can."

Mike pulled out his bankroll and counted out thirteen hundred, and handed it to Cie.

"Here Cuz, that should handle the two, if you need a little more, let me know and I'll put something together, hopefully by tomorrow."

"Cuz, don't trip, it's on and cracking."

Mike picked up his mattress and put it next to the other half zip he had left, then he put the mattress back down.

Cie looked at Mike, and said, "Cuz, what are you doing tomorrow?"

"Shit Cuz, why what's up?"

"Well, I'm gonna come get you tomorrow, so we can kick it."

"Cuz, I got you, just let me know," Mike replied.

"Well, let's get back outside and fuck with the homies," Cie shot back, as he opened the door and walked out.

Mike stood there and gathered his thoughts. To him, everything seemed to be getting better and better. Mike cracked a smile and walked out of the room and closed the door behind him. He didn't feel like being bothered, so he walked right out of the front door and before it closed it behind him, he said, "Lock this door."

As soon as he stepped outside, he saw Bee in the middle of two men and one lady, making a transaction. He was really glad to see that because he knew his bankroll was down to less than $400 dollars, and he needed to get as much money as he could, and as fast as he could.

He looked at everyone else drinking, smoking, laughing and just fucking around. There seemed to be more homies out there now, then when he first went in. The sight of everyone moving around, having a good time, made Mike a bit nervous. He hated being in crowds. He did not feel safe around a lot of people, due to the fact that he was always on guard. It was hard for him to watch twenty or more people at once. He didn't care who they were. Ever since those fools tried to kill him at school, he was very cautious of everything around him.

The day after that fool lost an arm, Mike went to school anyway, because he thought he was on some hot-shit. He knew they thought that he had something to do with the shooting, because after it happened, he got a page from Jackie. When he returned her call, she asked him if he was involved.

Mike said, "No, why would you ask me something like that?"

"Because, my cousin said it was you and those two fools that you be with all the time."

Mike started to laugh, and said, "Baby, I did not have shit

to do with that one."

So, the next day, even though he knew it was known what school he went to, he went anyway. He showed up for the last two hours, like he always did. He would show up at lunch, with his fresh finger-waves, a fresh outfit, weed, and a trunk full of liquor. All for a young lady or two that wanted to kick it.

On that day, he showed up in a cab because his car was to hot to drive. He timed it just right; lunch was just starting. Focused on getting some hot chocolate chip cookies and a milk, he headed to the lunch-room. As soon as he stepped into school, the crew of females he always kicked it with, were walking his way. Keita and everyone else, was there. The only one missing was Pam.

When they saw Mike, they knew what time it was. They all looked at each other and started smiling. Mike walked up, and Keita said, "Mike, where are you parked? I know we about to kick it."

"You're right about one thing, we're gonna kick it, but we got to walk around to the park. The funk is on, so fool's are lookin' for my car. So right now I'm cabbing it."

Keita said, "Yeah, I heard about that one fool gettin' shot last night. So Mike yea, you better be careful, and watch your back shiiit!"

"Look, fuck all that, are y'all kickin' it or not?"

Keita looked at her girls, and said, "Are y'all wit it or what?"

Like always, They all said, "Yeah, it's on."

"I got to get my cookies, be we do anything," Mike corrected, leading the way.

Mike stepped in the lunch room, and right away he heard someone talking about the fool that got shot. He brushed it off, and made his way to the front of the line. He got his snack, and walked back to where the girls were waiting.

They made it to the park, and Mike blew their brain's back. Twenty minutes later, he had them so high they were all scared to go back to school. He wasn't complaining, he was loving their company.

Five minutes before school let out, they pulled themselves together and walked back. In the school parking lot, Mike saw one of his homies picking up his little sister, and he had another homie in the car with him. Right away he figured, that could be his ride up out of there.

Mike looked at the girls, and said, "I'll get up with y'all later."

"Alright Mike, take care and be safe," Keita repied for the group.

Mike then walked up to the driver's side window of his homies car, which was rolled down, and said, "What's up cuz, can we smoke?"

"Cuz you're already knowin'," they both replied in agreement.

"Cool, let me take care of something real quick," Mike fired back, and he was off.

He ran to where the school buses were lined up at, and found the bus he was looking for. While he was trying to talk a young lady off, two reddish cars roll by. Even though he saw them, he paid it no mind. The only thing he was focused on was talking baby off that bus.

Out of nowhere, a fool ran up to Mike and sucker punched him from behind. Mike didn't fall, he took a step back to set up a defense against his attacker. That's when the school police came up and grabbed the fool that struck him. Out of the corner of his eye, Mike noticed another fool headed his way.

As he turned to face his next would-be attacker, Mike zoomed in on the gun in his hand. At the same moment, he saw the fool finally noticed the school police had his partner. That's when he changed directions, and ran off without doing what he came to do to Mike.

There was no question about it, Mike knew just that. Mike's homies at the car, were calling him. When he looked over to them, they were waving for him to come on. Mike ran to the car and got in the back with his homie's sister. The homie driving, put the car in motion, and said, "Cuz, them fool's are three cars deep."

Mike didn't say anything, he was trying to gather his thoughts. His train of thought was broken, when he noticed the car stopped. He looked up to see both of his homies hanging out of the window, throwing up gang signs. He then looked across the street, to see who they were disrespecting. When he saw the fool that ran off when he saw the police, his only words were, "Y'all got heat?"

After they both said no, Mike just shook his head, and said, "Cuz, you need to drive!"

Mike didn't like how he was feeling. To him, feeling vulnerable was the worst of all. At that very moment, such a state consumed him. He was about to grab his gun, before he left the house, but he told himself he wouldn't need it. Now he was mad at himself for not having it.

The homie put the car back in motion, and Mike kept looking back to see if them fools are following them. He knew they would be, and he soon realized he was right. They weren't behind them, they were on the next block over. They would speed down the block and stop at the intersection, and wait. Once they saw Mike and his homies drive by on the block over, they would speed off to the next intersection.

Thinking he lost them, the homie driving pulled up in the alley behind his sister's house and let her out. When they made it to the comer and tried to make a right, the car full of fools rammed them, head on. The same fool from the school jumped out and started firing rounds into the car Mike was in. He was trying to finish what he came up to school to do to Mike.

Mike was stretched out in the back on the floor. Every time he looked up, all he saw were flashes and sparks. He told the homie driving to put the car in reverse. Out of fear, he put it in neutral and all it did was rev up.

The homie in the passenger seat said, "Move Cuz!" and he put the car in reverse. Mike looked up to see those fools were still following them, as they drove backwards.

Mike knew they were reloading their gun, and he kept thinking, "Should I get out and get away on foot, or keep trusting Cuz, and his driving?"

The homie made a drastic move and drove on the sidewalk, as he put the car back in drive and floored it. They got away and made it to another homies house, that stayed close by.

Thay all got out to look at the damage, and the homie driving just dropped to his knees. The sight of the shattered windshield, bullet holes in the hood, which anti freeze and smoke was escaping from, was all to much for him.

" My mom's gonna kill me," he cried out. "What the fuck did you do to them niggas cuz? Damn!"

Speechless, Mike walked in the house and called a cab. That night he went out, and when he finally made it back in, he felt pleased with himself. His gun was put up, never to be seen or used again.

"Boy it feels good to be home," Mike thought, as he walked up to Blast, and said, "Let me hit that!"

Everyone sat around getting high and drinking. C-shot and his crew were the first to leave. Then Blast and Big Cie got in motion. As they were pulling off, Big Cie said, "Mike don't forget 11:30 to 12:30 tomorrow."

"Cuz I'll be waiting," Mike replied.

Within a half hour, Mike, Bee, and Tee were the only ones left. Bee was still hustling, and Mike and Tee just watched him in action. The two of them sat there sipping on gin and juice, and smoking a blunt. Tee looked at Mike and said, "Mike, bless me for this buck-fifty."

Mike said, "Don't trip, I'll be right back. A Bee!"

"What's up cousin?" Bee asked, talking louder than ever, with his blood shot eyes

"Come on, we got to go in and take care of something, so come on."

They went straight to the room and Mike closed the door behind them. He grabbed one of the halfs and handed it to Bee. Then he said, "I need a ball."

"Where's the plate?"

"Behind the radio."

Bee reached into his pocket and counted out $230 dollars and handed it to Mike.

Mike put the money up, then said, "Bee, how much work you got left?"

"Just six pills," Bee replied, as he sized up the bag. "You want me to bust all down that?"

"Yeah, you can do that," Mike confirmed; all the while taking a mental note of just how tired he was. "But first let me get that ball."

GOING NOWHERE FAST
CHAPTER 12

Mike jumped up and looked around the room. He tapped his right pocket and felt his gun. He tapped his left pocket and his mind was put to ease, as he felt his bankroll. Then another worry erupted in his mind; Bee was nowhere in sight.

From the sight of the sun, and hearing the birds singing, Mike knew he passed out last night. Mad at himself for doing it, he stormed out of the room. The only thing on his mind was finding Bee. When he made it to the front room, his frown quickly turned into a smile. He saw Be was sound asleep on the couch.

With his mind at ease once, he made the trip back to his room to find something to put on. He dug in his bag and pulled out a pair of fairly new tan Dickies, boxers, a new T-shirt, and some socks. He gave the Dickies a once over, and figured he could get away with not putting any heat to them. He then laid his outfit for the day on the bed, as he headed for the shower.

With his towel wrapped around him, and his dirty clothes in hand, Mike tiptoed back to his room. He closed the door, and removed the contents of his pockets, and laid them on the bed. When he got to his pager, he looked to see it was a little after six. At that moment, he quickly mapped out his morning. "I need to see about my car. Shiiit, I hope it's done, then I can take it to get painted. I also got to slide through Jackie's, then make it back here to meet Cuz."

He got dressed, and put his dirty clothes in the closet. Just as he was walking out of the room, he remembered about his box of blunts that were still in his Dickie shirt. He ran back to the closet and found what he was looking for. Now he had his daily paraphernalia intact: money, gun, and box of blunts, he felt complete.

As Mike made his way through the house, he was glad everyone was still asleep. Due to the fact that he wasn't high yet, he didn't feel like being bothered. With one shake of Bee's shoulder, Bee rolled over and looked up at Mike. Still half asleep, he mumbled a few words Mike was in the mood to hear, "Cousin, it was on last night."

"Yeah, is that right? Well look, get up, we got to get in motion."

Bee laid there for close to a minute longer, trying to clear his head. Once he was satisfied, he stood up and stretched. As he slowly let his arms drop, he glanced at his watch. The sight of the time really got his blood pumping. "Damn cousin, it's only 6:36."

"I know, but you know how I get down, the earlier the better, so let's go."

"Yeah, whatever nigga, shit, I just went to sleep around four. Them feens kept throwing rocks at the window."

"Fool-ass nigga, you got feens throwing rocks at mom's window! Nigga, what's wrong with you?"

"Shit, I was chillin' in the window and they would walk up, and I would tell them I'll be right out. When I tried going to sleep, they kept coming back. When I wasn't in the window, they started throwing the rocks. I told them to stop, but they did it anyway. You know how they get about this shit."

"All that shit sounds good, let's just get the fuck out of here."

For the first time since Mike had been home, when he got

outside, he seen that nobody was out. He just stood there on the top of the steps, taking in how calm things seemed. With peace on his mind, he pulled out his box of pre-rolled blunts, and put one in his month. With a little smile on his face, and a great sense of pride, he walked to Bee's car. As soon as he got in, Bee handed him a roll of money. He started counting it, and Bee said, "It should be $800 and I got two fitty left on the work side."

Mike stopped counting it and put it in his pocket with the rest of his money. He sat there, and thought, "Damn, it was on for real last night. Bee did his damn thing. I wonder how much he stashed for himself? Fuck it, he deserved it."

Bee put a stop to Mike's self-time, when he said, "Mike, where we going?"

"Let's go get some breakfast."

"Where at?"

"Shiiit, you're driving, I don't care," was Mike's response, as he blazed up his blunt.

When they made it to Perkins, they sat in the car and finished the blunt. Once the blunt went out, they floated in and found a table. They both ordered hotcakes, cheese eggs, turkey bacon, milk, and orange juice. As soon as the food showed up, it was all eating and no talking.

When they got done eating, Mike looked around and saw that there was no one that worked there in sight. Bee watched as he was surveying the scene, and he already knew what Mike was on. So, without a word said, he got up and walked out. By the time the door closed behind Bee, Mike was in motion. When he made it to the car, Bee had it in drive, ready to move. As they drove off, Mike looked at Bee, and said, "I'll pay them on the next round."

They both started laughing, and Mike reached for another blunt.

As Bee took the blunt Mike was handing him, he said,

"Mike, where to now?"

"We got to stop by the car shop, so I can see what's up with my car."

"Is it already done?"

"Shiiit, I hope it so. But look, if this shit come together like it should, it's about to really be on."

Out of the little crew Mike hung with everyday, he was the main play maker. He loved that position. It gave him a sense of power and worth. When everyone would look to him for an answer, or a way out of their of struggles, he would love to help.

To be such a little guy, he played his position to the fullest. Weighing 125, standing at 5'4", light-skin baby face, with long black permed hair, one couldn't tell he could really flip out. Mike was the shy, passive type, that just liked to have a good time, until someone pushed him to far. He hated when that happened, because it was hard for him to turn off his aggression. So, he did his best to also play the position of a peacekeeper.

Happy to hear he was missed, Mike looked straight ahead, and said, "Don't even trip cousin, I'm back home, and I'm ready to really turn up this time for real."

"Mike, you ain't got to tell me, I'm already knowing. But look, can I hit that?"

Before Mike passed the blunt to Bee, he took a real long hit off it. Then he laid back as far as he could in the leather Cadillac seats. He closed his eyes, and let the smoke escape from his nose. After he let the smoke out, he sat there for a second or two, then he said, "Here Bee."

Without opening his eyes, he passed it to him.

When Bee said, "Here," Mike would open his eyes to get the blunt, then he would close them again. He did this all the way to the shop. To Mike, that was how you rested your mind.

They made it to the shop, and Mike told Bee he'd be right back. He got out and walked in, as soon as he did, he saw his car was still in the air. The clerk that he dealt with the day before must have saw the disappointment on Mike's face, because he said, "Your car is ready, I was just checking the muffler, and it looks good."

"I'm really glad to hear that, how does everything else look?"

"You're ready to roll, you got an oil change, new spark plugs, new plugs, water pump and all. You shouldn't have any problems for a while. All I need is $36 dollars, which is the difference."

Mike pulled out his bankroll and found the few bucks and handed it to him. The shop clerk took the cash, and yelled, "Tim, let his car down."

"Thanks my man. A, do he got the keys?" Mike asked.

"Their in your car already."

Mike walked over to his car and jumped in. The mechanic named Tim, closed the hood. That's when Mike turned the key one time and the car came to life. Mike smiled at Tim, and Tim gave him the thumbs up. Then he hit the button that sent the garage door up. When the coast was clear, Mike was in motion. When he made it to the parking lot, he did a brake stand, to test the cars tightness. Boy was he was proud of the results. He filled the parking lot up with smoke, as he put on a show.

Mike stopped in front of Bee's car, rolle his window down and said, "Follow me! I got to drop my car off at this other shop across the street from BK, on Lake."

With the last word said, Mike pulled into traffic, and Bee was right behind him.

On the way to the next shop, Mike found himself sizing

up his plans for his car. He got the tune-up out of the way, now he was taking it to get painted. Then he figured the next move should be getting the windows tinted. He looked at the old ass tape deck, and thought, "Tonight, I'm going out to hit a lick on some real beats. I'm gonna make sure this motha fucka is bangin'!!"

He knew coming up on some nice rims shouldn't be hard. Some of his childhood friends were into car jacking, but if push come to shove, he too would get his hands dirty.

Mike made it to the shop, and got the feeling that it was still closed. He got out and walked to the door, and just like he thought, it was. He saw the sign said: Open at 8:00, then he looked at his pager and saw that it was only 7:45. To Mike, time meant everything, so he was not up to sitting around for a half-hour, doing nothing.

Within no time, he had a plan. Wasting no time, Mike walked over to Bee's car and got in.

" What up, whats the move?" Bee asked.

"It don't open until eight," Mike replied. "So this is what we are going to do. I want you to go back to the building, and hold the spot down. I have to make a run, then I will meet you there."

"That sounds like a plan," Bee agreed.

Ready to get at it, Mike got out, and Bee pulled off. As soon as Mike made it back to his car, he said,"Fuck! I should have got a few pills from that nigga before he left."

There was no doubt in his mind, he knew Jackie's mom would want something, once he got there. As Mike cut the car on and got in motion, he made up his mind that he would slide by the building first, to see Bee. He knew he couldn't miss no money.

Just his luck, when he pulled up, Bee was getting out of his car. Bee looked and saw him. Bee turned around and walked up to Mike's window, which was already rolled down. "What's up cousin? I thought you had to make a run?"

"I'm still on it," Mike replied. " I just need two pills."

Without another word said, Bee came out of his pocket with two pills, and handed them to Mike.

Mike took them, and they found their way under his tongue. "Look cousin, I will see you in a minute. I have to roll."

"Cool," was all that Bee said, as he backed away from the car, and Mike pulled off.

Once at Jackie's, Mike cut the car off and sat there for a few minutes getting his thoughts together. "Man, I hope this bitch ain't on no bullshit, because I am not in the mood."

After looking at himself once in the rear-view, he got out and walked to the door. All it took was two knocks, and the door opened. Jackie was standing there with her daughter in her arms.

Mike quickly noticed she was wearing the same big T-shirt that she had on the day prior. Before any words were said, she handed Mike the baby and walked back into the house. Mike looked at his little girl and smiled, as he stepped in, and closed the door. He walked in only to find Jackie laying on the couch in the same position that she was in the day before. He didn't like the thoughts he was having about Jackie, but her actions were turning him off.

To him, it was like she was giving up on herself, and he needed more out of her than that. He sat down beside her and in joking way, he said, "Damn Jackie, your feet stink."

"You are a lie, I got in shower last night before I went to bed. You would have knew that if you were here."

From her comeback, Mike got what he was looking for. Hearing the shower part made him feel a little better, but he still didn't like what he was seeing. He could not believe how he was feeling. For the first time, he was not interested in fucking to her.

Mike almost lost track of time, as he played with his daughter. If it wasn't for his pager falling on the floor, he would not have looked to see that it was after eight. He handed Shonna back to Jackie, and said, "I'll be back, I got make a run."

"Yeah, I bet you do, just like I know you 'll be back."

"Look, take down my pager number, and if you or anyone else needs anything, page me, I will be right over."

"Shit, what do I have to write it down for if you're already coming back? I'll get it then."

Mike looked at Jackie and realized it was a no win situation. So, he bent down and kissed her and his little girl on the forehead. Then he made his way to the door.

When Bee saw Mike pull up, he damn near ran to the car. "Damn cousin, we got to get back on," Bee explained. "All I got three pills left, so what's the move?"

"Don't trip, we already got a little something put up," Mike explained. "But right now we need to make that trip."

Mike pulled up into the shop parking lot and got out. This time he decided to leave his car on. He walked in and a man waved him over to the desk where he was sitting.

"How you doing today?" Mike asked, trying to be cool.

"Just fine, how can I help you?"

"Well, I just wanted a basic black paint job on my car outside."

"Well lets go take a look,"

When Mike got outside Bee was sitting on the hood. Bee said, "What's up cousin, are you about to get it painted?"

"Yeah, that's the mission."

The man did a once over, and said, "I can do a good black for you Three- ninety-five."

"That's cool, when do you think it can be done?"

"Well, we can get right to it for you, and I believe by tomorrow, it should be done."

"That's cool, I couldn't ask for anything more."

"O.K then, well let's go inside and get the paperwork together so we can get things moving."

Mike said, "Cool", then he got in the car and cut it off.

Once inside, the man didn't waste no time on putting the paperwork together. Sure that every thing was in line, he handed them to Mike to sign. With a smile on his face Mike did his best at writing his name. He then pulled out his bankroll, and gave the man $300 dollars." I'll have the other when I pick my car up."

"Well, let me give you a receipt for that."

"Cool but look, I put my pager number on that paperwork so page me as soon as it's ready."

"I sure will."

Focused on getting back to the building, Mike was like, "Alright then, I'll see you tomorrow."

Smiling form ear to ear, the man said, "I'll be sure to page you right away."

"Cool," was Mike's only reply, and he was on the move.

As Mike got in the car, and closed the door Bee put the car in gear. Bee then asked one thing, "where to now?"

Looking straight ahead, as if success was in clear view, Mike simply replied, "back to the building to see what's really good."

"Shit, that's what I'm talking about. Let's get this money."

"Don't eve trip, you know we got to do that."

"Man, I'm glad you're home."

"Me too... Me too...." Mike replied, feeling real good about things.

GOING NOWHERE FAST
CHPATER13

Mike walked in the house and found his little sister and brother at the table. They were eating eggs and toast. He walked up to Tasha and gave her a kiss on the head. Then he walked over to Sam and gave him a few punches to the ribs.

"Quit playin' Mike, why don't you leave me alone?" Sam cried out, as he tried to block his brothers blows.

Tasha like what she was seeing, and she said, "Mike don't stop, he was just hitting me before you came."

"What, you was just hitting her?" Mike asked, really going in on him now.

"Man stop playin'," Sam begged. " I didn't do nothing' to her."

From the kitchen, his mom heard what was going on, so she walked in the room. She took one looked at Mike, and said, "Yes he was."

" Oh yea," Mike asked, and he really went in on his little brother.

As Sam cried out, Bee walked in, and said," Damn, what's goin' on!"

"You better be glad I got something to do," Mike told Sam, as he punched him once more.

" Man you play too much," Sam cried out as he watched Mike and Bee walk off.

Once they made it to the room Mike went straight for the stash. He grabbed the half zip and just sized it up.

Bee closed the door behind him, and said, "You forgot you even had that, didn't you?"

"Come on cousin, you know I don't never forgot about shit."

"Yeah right, I just bet."

"Come one, you know me."

"Yeah, that's the point."

With that said, they both started laughing because they both knew he forgot. Mike handed Bee the half zip, and said, "Here you go, do what you do, I got to make a run real quick. Do you got something on a sack of trees?"

"Yeah, I got a dub on it. Just get it, and I'll hit you when I get back."

"Cuz, don't be on no bullshit."

"Man I got you, stop trippin'."

"A'ight, I'll be right back," Mike replied.

As he walk past his mom's room, Mike thought he heard her and her boyfriend arguing. In the mood to bust a nigga's shit wide open, he doubled back and walked in.

" I'm really not in the mood for all that!" Mike snapped.

He knew his message was apparent, because the room went quiet. Sure that he was understood, he closed the door and got on his way. When he made it to the door, he looked at his brother, who was in the living room, and said, "Come lock this door. And let me know if they start arguing again."

As soon as he got outside, a lady was walking up. Mike waited for her at the top of the stairs.

" What up now?" Mike asked.

"You know where I can get two for $30 at?"

"Yeah," Mike confirmed, ready to go get Bee.

Right then, he remembered about the two pills in his mouth. He turned around, and said, "Come on in, I got you."

She stepped in the hallway, and Mike spit out the two pills

and handed them to her.

She handed him the money, and said, "If this is any good, I'll be back to deal with you some more."

Mike looked at the lady, and said, "Well, you'll be back then.?"

She looked at Mike, smiled, and said, "We'll see," then she walked out of the door.

Mike gave her a minute, then he made his way to his car. He drove around the comer to S.A. He figured he would get some gas and some blunts, while he was there. He walked in the store and heade straight to the counter. He had to wait because a native fool was in front of him getting a box of blunts.

When Mike saw that, he cracked a smile, and said, "A my man, let me talk to you for a minute."

The native fool looked at Mike, and he already knew what Mike was on. He simply said, "I'll be outside."

Mike paid for his items, then walked outside. The native fool was posted up on the wall, and Mike walked over to him.

"What's up my man, who got the trees around here?" Mike asked.

"I got some nice dimes of some good green buds."

"Cool! Let me see a couple bags and if they're fat, then I need three of them."

"Well, I got to walk to the house down the street to get them for you."

"Look, let me pump my gas, then I'll give you a ride, so I can know where you're at."

"That's cool, we can do that," the native fool agreed.

Once at his house, he told Mike to park in the back. They went in the side door, that led into the kitchen. That's where he told Mike to wait.

Mike watched the fool go into a side room, and he came

back in the kitchen with a bag full of dimes. He dug in the bag, and handed Mike three.

Mike looked at the bags over and saw they were nice size.

"Let me get a nice deal on a half?"

"I can't do it. I need dime for dime, that's all I can do."

Mike didn't like what he was hearing, so he made a mental note of how the fool was acting over his shit. Mike was a weed head, but he was far from a "vic". Instead of the half, he figured if he got two, he wouldn't feel so bad.

So, he said, "Look my man, let me just get two."

"That's cool, here you go," the native fool replied, and handed Mike two of his fattest dimes.

Mike took them, and handed him the first three back. He then dug in this pocket and felt the butt of the gun. Right then he entertained the thought of taking all of the fool's shit. He talked himself into giving the him a pass, but he told himself, "This fool got one strike against him."

Mike found his bankroll and gave the fool a dub, and said, "I'll be back to spend."

"That's cool, someone's always here. Just come to the side door."

"Bet," Mike replied, on his way to the door.

Mike didn't go home the same way he came. He wanted to ride past his cousin, La'Don's old bitch's house. Every since La'Don went to the joint, the bitch been acting real stuck, and Mike didn't like that shit. He rolled by her house real slow. When he saw the Big-boy Bronco parked in front of her house, he smiled. Right away, he knew two things, "That's why the bitch been acting stuck, she got a nigga up in my cousin's shit. I bet that Big-boy got good beats in it. I'll be to see you tonight!" Mike told himself.

He made it back to the building, and saw that is mom's boyfriend's car was gone. He was glad to see that, because that meant he was gone too. Mike got out of the car, and what he saw was what he was used to seeing, things were speeding up. The two houses across the street were open for business, and the boys next door were out. He saw groups of people moving up and down the block, and he knew they were trying to get their high on.

As Mike walked up to the building, he said, "Can I hold something," to his friend next door?

"Shit, I should be asking you. Everybody knows you're the man."

"Yeah, it sounds good."

"Come on Mike, you it's the truth."

"It sounds good," was the last thing Mike said, as he walked in the building.

He tried to open his door and it was locked. After he knocked around six times, his mom opened the door, and said, "Boy, why don't you use your key?"

He looked down at his keys in his hand, and just shook his head.

"You forgot you had your own key, didn't you?"

"Come on mom, how could I forget about that?"

"Boy! Just get in this house."

"Man, I thought you wasn't gonna let me in or something. You know the way you was standing in the doorway."

Mike pushed his way past his mom, and she popped him upside the head.

She then said, "Boy, you need help," and they both started laughing.

When Mike walked in the room and closed the door, Bee looked up to see it was him, and he went back to work.

"What's up cousin, how's things looking over there?" Mike asked.

"Shit's all good, the count right now is twelve hundred. So what's up, did you get some trees?"

"Yeah, but it ain't right. I just got something to hold us for a hot second. Are you almost done?"

"Yeah, just give me five minutes, and we can roll."

"That's cool, that gives me five minutes to roll up this blunt."

"Yeah Mike, do what you're best at, so we can smoke."

"Bee, you need to respect my mind, and just finish doing what you're doing, for real."

When Bee failed to respond, they both went on doing what they were doing, in silence. Bee was done first; he put all of the bagged up work in one bag. Then, he laid the bag by Mike, and put the plate behind the radio. Mike finished rolling up and he put it in his mouth. He picked up the bag of crack, and said, "Bee, hand me another bag."

After Bee handed him the bag, he put half of the work in it, and put it under the mattress. He then looked at Bee, and said, "Come on cousin, let's go outside and get this money."

They made it outside and found their spots on the steps. Mike blazed up, and they sat out there hustling. Mike liked how things were moving fast. He figured if things kept moving like they were, he could call it a night early. It was like ever since they stepped out, they became the peoples choice. The fiends kept coming and Mike loved it.

Mike noticed how the crew from next door kept looking over at him and Bee. To himself, all he kept saying was, "I hope I don't have to burn nobody, I hope they stay in their place, because I don't mind letting them have it."

His self time was interrupted by Bee tapping him. He looked at Bee, and said, "What's up?"

Bee just pointed to the street, and Mike saw Cie in a renter car, waiting for him.

Mike said, "Damn! Look cousin, take the bag, I got to roll with Cuz. I'll be back, so do what you can."

"That's cool cousin, I got you. If I leave, I'll be right back because I got to run home and change."

Mike said, "Alright cousin, just do the right thing, and you know where the other shit it, if you need it. I'm gone."

With that said, Mike ran to the car. He was surprised that Cie was by himself.

"What's up Cuz, how are you feeling?" Cie asked,

"Shit Cuz, everything's everything, you know."

"Yeah Cuz, I feel you," was Cie's reply, as he put that car in motion.

Mike pulled out his bankroll and counted out $650 he owed Cie, he then handed it to him. Not one time did Cie take his eyes off the road. He didn't even bother to count the money, he just put it in his pocket. Then he said, "Cuz, I see you did your thing last night after we left."

"Yeah Cuz, you can say something' like that."

"That's cool Cuz, just keep doing your thing, because shit's really about to be on around here, like the old days. See, I'm about to make that trip back to the city, so get your money right."

"Cuz, I'm already knowing, so you best believe, I'm gonna be ready."

"Cuz, I'm gonna give you the number down there, so when you're ready, you can give me a call. Then we can put things in motion."

"Bet that Cuz, when are you leaving?"

"Real soon Cuz, but right now, I got to make some stops to pick up this paper."

For the next three hours, they made a handful of stops, as Cie picked up his money. Mike lost count on how many blunts they smoked. It seemed every stop they made, blunts were getting passed to him. Mike knew they made their last stop, when Cie said, "Cuz, do you need to make any stops?"

Mike just sat there for a minute, as he tried to get his thoughts together. Cie started laughing, then he said,

"Cuz, are you alright?"

"Yeah Cuz, I'm cool, but now that I think of it, I do need to go to Kid's Footlocker, to get my son some shoes."

"Cuz, don't even trip, we're there."

They made their way downtown, and Mike got his son some blue and gray Nike's. They then went to Dairy Queen, Mike had to get something real cold to drink on, because his mouth was dry as fuck. After they got their DQ, Cie said, "What's up Cuz, you wonna drop those shoes off to your shorty?"

"Yeah Cuz, we can do that."

To Mike, the more he hung out with the Big homie, the more influence in the hood, he would have. He also had mad love and respect for Cie, and when it came to his loyalty to him, there was no limit. He knew Cie knew this, because Mike made sure his honor to Cie was apparent, at all times.

They made it back to the car, and Cie said , "Cuz, where does shorty live?"

"Over north, down the street from the YMCA, on Broadway."

Cie started up the car, and said, "After that, do you got anywhere else you need to make a stop at?"

"That's it Cuz, after that, it's all you."

After that was said, Cie put the car in motion. He jumped on the freeway, and as soon as they got in traffic, he looked over to the car next to them. All Cie said was, "Cuz, there go them fools, right there!"

Mike's hand went straight in his right pocket, where his gun was. He then looked over to see the two fools. The fool driving, must have read Mike's mind, because he shot to the shoulder, to pass the car in front of him. Then he punched it. Cie made a move of his own, and they ended up right behind the car the fools were in.

At that moment, Mike rolled his window down.
The chase was on. They shot from lane to lane, as they
pushed their cars to the limit. Just missing cars by inches,
as they made their moves. To Cie, it was a game, and to the
fools, they felt their lives were in danger. The fools sped
past Mike and Cie's exit, but Cie slowed down. When he
took their exit, they both looked at each other and started
laughing. Cie was the first to speak, "Cuz, did you see how
spooked them fools were? They thought we was on one for
real! You know what I'm saying Cuz, and why did you roll
down your window?"

Mike looked at Cie, and thought to himself, "This nigga
was just playin'! Shit, he don't even know how close I was
to letting them fools have it. I'm glad he didn't pull up on
the side of them, because I would have aired their ass the
fuck out."

Cie looked at Mike after he didn 't say anything, and said,
"What's up Cuz, what's on your mind?"

"I'm cool, homie. I'm just getting' my thoughts together,"
Mike replied.

GOING NOWHERE FAST
CHAPTER 14

They made it to their destination, and Mike and Cie walked up to the door. Mike rang the doorbell, and his baby's mom's friend Shell, answered. Mike couldn't believe what he saw; she was draped in red and black, from head to toed. She had on some black Nike's, with some red fat laces, and some bright red pants, with a Chicago Bulls black and red T-shirt on. To top it off, she had the nerve to have a red bandana tied around her head.

Mike saw her and just shook his head. In his mind, he was screaming, " What the fuck is going on!"

He stood there stuck and Shell brought him back. She said, "Damn nigga, are you coming in or what?"

Trying to keep his pride and anger in tact, he just walked in. He looked back at Cie, and said, "Come on Cuz."

When they made it to the front room, Mike saw his son in his walker. He put the bag with the shoes in it down. Then he walked over to pick up his son, and Cie found a spot on the couch to sit down. Shell just stood there with her arms crossed, like she was overseeing things. At that moment, Mike's nightmare went from bad to worse. His baby's mom came downstairs, and she too was in black and red, from head to toe. It seemed that she and her friend took it a step further in coordinating their outfits. When it came to her shoes, instead of black and red laces, she had red shoes, with black laces. Black pants, instead of red, red T-shirt not black, and black bandana, while her friend had a red one on.

Mike couldn't believe his eyes. "Never have I ever felt
this embarrassed," he thought. He hated that he was
subjecting his Big homie to such bullshit. The room was
silent; Mike figured everyone was trying to guess what the
next was thinking.

Mike felt this would be a good time to turn things around,
and make a statement. He handed his son to Cie, and said,
"Cuz hold him why I get his shoes."

Mike took the shoes out of the box, and started putting
them on his son. Everyone in the room watched his every
move. His message was oh so clear, as he tied up his son's
blue and gray Nikes.

Mike was far from prepared for his babe's mom's
comeback to his move. She looked at her friend and said,
"Girl you know Blood balled and he said he will be over by
bix!"

Shell got it clearly. Wasting no time, she fed in as she
said, "Blood is bool as hell. I'm a bick back till he bomes
over! I hope Dog is wit him, blood is brazy as fuck!"

Mike couldn't it no more, so he his son and placed him
back in his walker. He then looked at Cie, and said,
" Come on cuz lets roll."

It was one thing to dress like she did, but when she started
changing every C-Word into a B-Word, it was too much for
him to take.

They made the trip back over south in silence. Mike was
mad as hell and Cie could tell. He handed Mike a blunt, and
said, "Here, put this in the air!"

Mike watched as Cie took the exit on the wrong side of
Lake Street. At this point he didn't care where they was
headed because he was ready to release some anger. He
passed Cie the blunt at the same times as he was pulling
over to park.

Mike looked around, and Cie said, " Come on cuz."

Cie then cut the car off and got out. They then stood outside of the car and finished the blunt.

Mike followed Cie as he walked up to a house that he never been at before. "Damn, who lives here?" He thought.

Cie rang the bell, and Mike was surprised to see Cie's son answer.

Before Cie said a word, his son said, "What's up cuz!"

Cie gave him a pound of the fist, and said, "Everything's cool Cuz." Then Cie walked in the house.

Mike followed Cie into the house, and Cie's son greeted him the same way, and he closed the door.

Cie looked at Mike, and said, "Cuz, you can have a seat." He then pointed to the couch. Mike was glad to see the couch, because he was high as fuck. He made it to the couch and he didn't waste no time getting comfortable, as he laid back.

Cie went into a back room, and Mike heard him talking to who he figured was his baby's mom. Mike put both of his hands in his pockets. He had one on his money, and the other on his gun. Feeling safe, he closed his eyes and let his mind rest. He then reflected on everything that he's been through for the day.

He didn't know how long he had his eyes closed, but when he heard the front door open, his eyes shot open. The first figure took Mike aback, as he walked through the door. When the second one came in, Mike's heart stopped. He pulled his gun out real smooth, and tucked his hand under his T-shirt. He didn't sit up, he remained laid back. He couldn't believe it, here he was in the same house with two of the fools. It was their Big Homie, and he had one of their known shooters with him. Just like Mike's baby's mom, they were dressed in all red and black.

Confused, Mike tired to keep his cool while he kept his finger hugging the trigger. They looked at Mike, and he made sure they understood where he was willing to take it. He put his left hand back in his pocket, and he kept the other one under his T-shirt. He made sure the form of his gun could be seen.

The older of the two called out, "Sal."

That's when Cie came out, and said, "Come on Cuz, let's roll."

Mike stood up and tucked his gun in his waistband, and made his way to the door.

Cie's son came running out of the back room, and said, "I'll see you later Cuz."

Mike cracked a smile and gave him a pound. Then he walked out to the car, and Cie was right behind him. They made it to the car and got in traffic. Mike couldn't keep it to himself. He needed to get an understanding on what just took place, so he said, "Cuz, what's up with that shit back there?"

Cie looked straight ahead, and said, "Cuz, them fools are my baby's mom Sal's brothers. Yeah Cuz, I know shit's real crazy, but fuck em! They can still come up missing, and that's real."

Mike pulled out his gun and laid it on his lap. Then said, "Cuz, this shit's crazy as fuck."

With that said, they both started laughing. Mike had enough of having close calls. He figured it was time to get into something that would put his nerves at ease. So he said, "Cuz, I need to get back to the building."

Mike looked up and saw the building. He sat there, for close to a minute, as he got himself together. When he was about to get out of the car, Cie handed him a number, and said, "Cuz, here take this number and call me when you're ready."

Mike took the number, and said, "Good looking out Cuz, I'll be calling soon."

Cie then said, "Cuz, put $4,500 hundred together, and I got a nine piece for you."

"Cuz, you don't got to say shit else, I'll be calling real soon," and with that said, Mike got out of the car.

Mike saw that his mom's car was there, but Bee wasn't. Now he had to track him down, and he didn't like the thought of that. He looked around and saw the faces of the same old playa's, out doing their thing. He walked in the building, and this time, he remembered to use his key. When he walked in, he was surprised that nobody was home. He walked to his room and checked under the mattress. He was glad to see his bag of crack was still there. He made up his mind that he was going to sit outside and get his hustle on for a minute.

He sat and did his thing for less than a hour. Then he started thinking about Lonna. Just the thought was all it took, he jumped in the car and hit the freeway.

It didn't take any time to make it to her house. He pulled up into her parking lot, and saw her little cousin, Tooty. He hit his horn a few times and she looked. When she saw it was him, she ran up to the car, and Mike rolled the window down.

"What's up Mike, are you looking for Lonna?"

"Come on now, you know I am. So where's she at?"

"She's at the park, I could take you over."

"Well, why are you still standing out there, get in."

She got in and Mike turned around and drove out the same way he came in. As he looked straight ahead, he said, "So what park is she at?"

She said, "The one right behind the building, right there," and she pointed her little finger.

Mike thought, "Damn, we could of walked."

They pulled up to the park, and Tooty said, "There she go, right there."

Mike spotted her and he kept on driving. He drove over the sidewalk and into the park. Halfway to Lonna, Tooty said, "Boy you crazy, I can't believe you're driving in the park."

When he saw he had Lonna's attention, he stopped the car and got out. While he walked the rest of the way to Lonna, Tooty ran. Lonna just stood there with her hands on her hips.

When Mike was close enough to hear, she said, "You need to get that car out of the park before the police come."

Mike walked up to Lonna, gave her a hug, and whispered in her ear, "I'm glad to see you too."

He then strolled over to the table where Aleasha and her mom were sitting, and said, "Hi."

Lonna saw that he left the car on, so she decided to park it herself. " He get on my damn nerve," she thought as she handed Mike his keys.

Mike liked what he just saw, so he smiled, and said, "I see momma's gonna make sure her baby's always safe."

Aleasha's mom started laughing, and Aleasha said, "Boy, you're a fool."

"Yeah, only for Lonna's love, and y'all know that."

Aleasha's mom said, "We sure do, don't we Lonna?"

"I don't know nothing," Lonna fired back firmly.

Mike hated when she was on that mad shit. It took away from her inner peace, and thats what he found so beautiful. He would do his best to over look it, but at times, it was hard.

"Mike, do you want a burger or hot dog?" Tooty asked.

For the first time, Mike realized it was a barbecue. Then it hit him, he'd been doing all of that smoking, and the only thing he ate was breakfast.

He looked at Tooty, and said, "Yeah, I'll have a hot dog."

Tooty put it together for him, then handed it to him.

She then said, "That's a shame I had to ask you."

Knowing Tooty's words were for her to hear, Lonna shot back, "Ain't nobody asked you to do nothing!"

It was the sound of Mike's pager going off, that interrupted such a heated moment. All eyes were on him and knew it. Without even looking around to see, he put his hot dog down on a plate on the table. Then he lifted his T-shirt, to get his pager. He glanced at Lonna and her eyes got real big, like she was surprised or something. Then, she looked from side-to-side, then behind her. Mike looked down and saw he had his pager in one hand, his shirt in the other, and his gun was showing. He forgot he even had the it.

He put his shirt down and dusted it off, like he had something on it. He then saw everyone was watching him, so he looked down at the number. He hoped it wasn't that punk ass bitch Kim, but he saw it was Bee. He was glad it was him, and it must have shown on his face.

Lonna said, "Damn! What bitch got you in a good mood, all of a sudden?"

Mike smiled, and said, "Baby look, I need to use the phone, it's about some money, on everything."

She looked at him, and said, "It better be about some money, now come on."

Mike picked up his hot dog, and said, "Lonna, I love you too."

He knew that would get everyone laughing, and it did.

Lonna walked off, and said, "Come on, if you're coming."

Mike was walking behind her, looking at her ass. He was thinking about how good he knew her loving was. Aleasha's mom must have read his mind, because she yelled, "Don't y'all be up there doing nothing y'all shouldn't be doing."

Mike looked back and smiled, as he said, "Y'all know I'm

always on my best behavior."

Mike had to break into a nice run to catch up with Lonna. He said, "Damn baby, why are you moving so fast? If you don't want me to walk with you, just say so."

"Mike, I see you're really pushing it today, ain't you?"

"Shit, I thought I was being good."

Lonna just shook her head, and said, "Boy, come on, you're too much for me."

They made it in the building with no problem. Mike did get his hands slapped a few times, when he tried to get a quick feel of her ass. Once in the apartment, Lonna handed him the phone. She stood right in front of him while he called Bee. Bee answered, and Mike said, "What's up cousin?"

"Shit, where are you at, the building?"

"I'm over north at Lonna's, but what's up, you wonna take a trip to the spot on Rice? We can spend a dub or two."

"Shit, y'all two go, I don't got no bitch that I feel like being bothered with."

"Cuz, her cousin is here too, so I'll bring her."

"Man cousin, is she cool or what?"

"Nigga, just meet us out that way in a hour, and get some trees."

Before Bee could respond, Mike hung up the phone. Lonna took a step closer to Mike, and said, "That didn't sound like it was about money to me, and what's on Rice?"

"A cool-ass Go-cart spot, me and the homies be going to."

For some reason she had a frown on her face. Mike didn't like it, so he said, "Quit acting like that, Damn!"

Before Lonna could respond, Aleasha walked in. Mike said, "Aleasha, I'm glad to see you. Look, do you wonna go Go cart racing with me, Lonna and my cousin?"

He saw how she looked when he mentioned his cousin, so he said, "Girl, he's cool, you know I wouldn't hook you up with no bullshit-ass fool."

A smile appeared on Aleasha's face, and she said, "Since you said that, I'm with it."

Mike sat down, and pulled out his bankroll, and a dime bag fell on the floor. He looked down at it, and said, "Damn, I forgot all about you." He put his bankroll up, then he picked up the dime and kissed it.

After Lonna saw what he just did, she couldn't help but say, "That don't make no sense."

Mike came right back with, "Yeah, the way I love you."

Seeing where this was headed, Aleasha said, "Come on y'all if we're going. Mike, you got me all geeked to go, now y'all want to sit around and bullshit."

Mike said, "She's right Lonna, let's get out of here."

He then stood up and walked to the door. When they made it to the car, Mike handed Aleasha the dime and blunt. He didn't have to tell her to roll it, she already knew. By the time they made it to the freeway, she had it rolled up. She tried to hand it to Mike, and he told her to light it.

They made it to the Go-cart place, and Bee was there waiting for them. Mike introduced Bee and Aleasha, and they hit it off right away. They rode the Go-carts three or four times, before Lonna said, "I'm ready to go home."

Mike wasn't surprised when Alesaha said, "Y'all go ahead, I'm riding with Bee."

He and Lonna just got in the car and pulled off. Bee was following Mike at first, but when he made it to the exit that lead over south, that changed. When Mike saw the south side exit, he looked in the rear view, and just like he thought, Bee took it.

Mike made it to Lonna's, and before she got out, he said, "I'm gonna slide through here tomorrow, alright?"

"If you say so," was all she said, as she got out.

Mike sat there and watched her walk off. Once she made it in the building, he pulled off, not knowing where he was headed.

GOING NOWHERE FAST
CHAPTER 15

Mike made it to the stop sign at the end of Lonna's block, and he sat there longer than the law required. As he calculated his next move, he looked down at his pager and saw it was to early to go on the mission to get the beats for his car. He was in the mood for company, so he really didn't feel like going back to the house and hustle by himself. He figured his best move would be to go over Lucky's and hang out, since he was already over north.

As he got halfway to Lucky's house, it hit him, "Damn, I didn't even get no bud from Bee, and I don't got shit left. Well, Lucky's gonna have to take me to get some," he told himself.

He didn't like the feeling of being without his bud, because to him, that meant he was slacking. For him not to have any, was like the President walking around alone, without the Secret Service; it just isn't suppose to happen.

The fact that he didn't have any, to him, would take away from his character, when it came to certain people. He did his best to seem like he had it all together, at all times. That was on the outside; while on the inside, to him, everything was missing.

In the eyes of so many, he seem to be one of the happiest young playa's. Only if they knew under all of the deception, he was truly unhappy. For so many years, that was the problem Mike would be stuck trying to figure out. Why he felt the way he did? He had the life any young playa in the hood, would want to have, but still he felt how he did. It

145

would take the many years to figure out, True Love played a big part.

He made it to Lucky's, to find him and Brandon sitting on the front steps. As soon as they saw Mike pull up, they got up and walked up to the car. Before anyone could speak, Mike said, "Come on y'all and take me to get some more bud. I only got a little left."

His pride wouldn't allow him to tell them the truth, that he didn't have any at all.

With no questions asked, Brandon got in the back, and Lucky got in the front. Lucky was the first one to speak, as he told Mike, "Bust a U, and turn around."

Still mad at himself, Mike didn't say a word, he just did what he was told. Then without a word said, Brandon tapped Mike on his shoulder, and when Mike looked back, Brandon handed him a little stack of bills.

Without counting it, Mike put it in his pocket, and said, "Good looking out cuz."

Mike didn 't want to get in a real conversation until he got his weed, and felt better about himself. He figured they both realized he wasn't in the talking mood, because they rolled in silence.

The only words said, was when Lucky gave him the directions to where they were headed. He told Mike to take a right, then he pointed, and said, "Park right there, it's the fourth house."

Mike pulled up and parked behind a van, a house from where Lucky pointed to. He put the car in park, then looked at Lucky and asked, "Cuz, what do they got?"

"Shit, some cool-ass green buds."

"I can dig that, but what about the bags?"

"Oh right, shit Cuz, whatever you want, they got it and the prices are cool as fuck."

Mike reached in his pocket and found the bills Brandon gave him, and counted out $80 dollars, then handed it to Lucky. "Here Cuz, see if you can get a zip for this."

Without a word said, Lucky got out of the car and walked to the side-door of the house. Mike watched, as his homie knocked on the door. Three times was Mike's count, and someone answered. The only reason he could tell, was because a fat head of a Brindle Pitbull, poked his head out of the door, causing Lucky to take a quick step back. The sight caused Mike to let out a little laugh, as he thought, "A Pitbull, that's what I call security."

Brandon must have saw what took place too, because he said, "Yeah Cuz, that fool got a big ass Pit!"

"Yeah, I seen that. And you can tell it means business by the size of it's head. You know!"

"Hell yeah!" Brandon replied, which caused them both to laugh.

As Mike sat, he found himself thinking about Lonna. He replayed the time they spent together earlier, and the vibe he was getting from her. He then decided to end things with her, because he felt there was no room for progress.

Right then, the sudden sound of the car door slamming, startled Mike, as his trance was broken. His instincts sent him leaning as close as he could to the drivers door. At the same time, he looked over to see a worried look on Lucky's face.

"Damn Cuz, it's only me!"

"Shit Cuz, you better slow down! Boy it was about to be on, in this bitch."

"Here Cuz, take this bud! Nigga, you need to smoke and calm down."

"Yeah fool, you're right about one thing, I do need to smoke, but calm down? Hell naw, I got to stay on my toes at all times around this bitch!"

" Cuz you was nowhere near on you're toes my nigga," Lucky replied. " I don't know where you was at but you wasn't here!"

"Yeah Cuz, I did zone out, didn't I?" Mike agreed, smiling. He then looked back at Brandon to see him shaking his head.

Brandon said, "Yeah Cuz, you was gone."

Then they all started laughing. Mike put the weed in his pocket, as he put the car in drive and pulled off. They were all still laughing, when Mike said, "You know what? Fuck both of y'all!"

That last outburst from Mike sent Lucky and Brandon into tears, as they laughed even harder. The sight of seeing Mike off his square was pure joy to their eyes and ears. For once, Mike was on the receiving end of the jokes, and they loved it.

Out of desperation, Mike said, "Y'all go head and enjoy y'all self right now, but you best believe I will get the last laugh."

He hoped the threat of revenge would shut them up, and to his liking, it worked.

After the little left over snickering came to an end, the car went silent. To polish up his tarnished pride, he said, "Don't stop laughing now, go ahead and enjoy y'all selves, I ain't trippin'."

This was one of his favorite tactics to make it seem like he wasn't bothered by their actions, and he was still in control. He knew they wouldn't start laughing again, but he wanted the message to be clear, that laughing wasn't getting to him, when it was.

Once again proud of himself for regaining control of the situation around him he turned the radio on for the first time. After hearing the smooth voice of Marvin Gaye,Mike realized it was the dusty hour, and that changed his whole demeanor. His foot got lighter on the gas, as he slowed down their motion. He found himself in a deep gangster lean, as he bobbed his head to the rhythm. In the zone he was in, no one could tell him he wasn't a playa. Instead of his usual, "A Cuz, do one of y'all got some blunts," it was, "Do one of y'all playa's got some blunts?"

Lucky and Brandon both said, "No," at the same time. co

"I can dig it baby, well I got to slide by the store and pick up a box."

As he drove down Penn Avenue, he was enjoying the sight of so many families standing outside of their homes, enjoying each-others company. Mike loved to see strong families together he admired the love they had for one another, which was so apparent. Mike's slow pace was brought to a complete stop when the traffic light turned red. Right then, the sound of Al Greens, "Let's Stay Together," sent Mike into a world wind of memories. He closed his eyes, as he replayed how strong his family used to be. All of the Sunday dinners, the big Family gatherings, and the best of all, the support everyone had for one another.

He was brought back to the present, when Lucky said, "Cuz, the store is right there, don't you got to get some blunts?"

He opened his eyes, looked to his right, and pulled over and parked. Then he sat there for close to a minute, thinking about how his family was now. Everyone seemed to be out for self; there was no support, no gatherings, no dinners, no nothing. From the thought of that he just shook his head and walked into the store.

Mike got his box of blunts and walked back to the car. As soon as he got in he turned off the radio. He looked at Lucky, as if he was about to say something. When he was satisfied that Lucky didn't have anything to say about the radio, he handed Brandon the box of blunts and the weed, and told him to roll up. He put the car in drive, and made his way back to Lucky's house. As soon as they pulled up and Mike parked, Brandon said, "Here Cuz, I rolled up a fat one!"

"Nigga, I bet you did roll a fat one," Mike fired back, which had everyone was in tears.

"Cuz, go head and blaze it up and hand Lucky the kit, so he can roll one up another one."

They sat in the car and smoked the two blunts, then sat in silence, while each one was in his own zone. Somewhere between the first and second blunt, Mike turned the radio back on. He was the first one to come out of his zone. He figured the others were willing to sit there, stuck, until the sun came up. He turned off the radio and reach and grabbed the weed and blunts off of Lucky's lap, as he said, "Cuz, I got to roll, but I'm gonna get with y'all tomorrow."

They both said, "Alright Cuz," in slow fashion, as they fell out of the car and slammed the door.

Seeing his homies so high gave Mike feel good, because he knew his job was done. He showed them a good time.

Mike knew it was time to make the trip back home before he passed out, and would have to spend the night. He put the car in motion and rolled down his window to get some fresh air. He needed all the help he could get to stay up, so he knew he had to make it to the freeway quick. Just like he'd planned, the wind coming through the window kept him awake. The trip back home didn't take anytime. As he pulled in front of his house, Mike was surprised to see Bee and Aleasha sitting on the steps.

He cut the car off and sat there for a minute, getting his thoughts together. He then got out and closed the door, but before he could make the trip to the stairs, he had to catch his breath. The tasks of standing up took a lot out of him, "Damn, I didn't realize I was so high," was all he could think of. After he got closer, his vision became clearer, and the sight of Bee and Aleasha, all hugged up, sent Mike into a state of disbelief.

He walked up to them, and all he could do is put his head down and shake his head from side to side. Aleasha was the first to speak, "Mike, what you shaking your head for?"

As if Bee already knew what Mike was thinking, he started laughing.

"Y'all sure hit it off fast as fuck, all hugged up and shit What's up with that?"

"Come on cousin, it's all good, you finally did something right."

"Yeah, I just bet! Y'all just do y'alls thing."

"You know we're gonna do that," Aleasha replied. "But where's Lonna?"

"I dropped her off at home, but ain't nothing happening with me and her anyway."

"Why you say that?"

"Because it just ain't. Bee, what's up cousin, are you out here working?"

"You already know, so why ask?"

Mike looked next door, and across the street, and saw no one was out, so he knew it was his time to shine. All three of them sat on the steps and hustled. When Aleasha got sleepy, Mike took her to his room and let her sleep in his bed.

Mike went back outside with Bee, and they smoked and hustled. Mike looked down at his pager and saw it was 2:20am. He knew it was time to make his move. He got up and told Bee he'd be right back, as he walked to the car. He drove past the house to see if the truck was parked outside. Just like he hoped, it was, and it was parked under a big tree.

Mike parked down the block and he walked back with his

screwdriver in his hand. He walked up to the drivers door, and punched the lock and opened the door. To his surprise, there still wasn't any sound on the block.

Without making a sound, he placed the speaker-box, the amps, along with the six-by-nines, in the street next to the drivers door. He then looked under the drivers-seat, and just like he knew it would be, he found the tape deck to the Alpine Snatch out. That too had to came, along with all the wires he could get his hands on. He put his new find neatly on the speaker-box, as he got out of the truck and closed the door.

He walked back to his car and pulled it up along side of the truck, as he loaded up his new gear. With one last look, he saw a tape case. He had to have that too. With his task complete, he made the ride home with a smile on his face. When he pulled in front of his house and saw Bee's car was gone, he was glad. Without a second thought, he went straight in the house and hit the bed. Sleep was past over-due!

GOING NOWHERE FAST
CHAPTER16

Mike opened his eyes and rolled on his back. He laid there looking up at the ceiling, as he mapped out his moves for the day. With his daily plan in order, he jumped up and got in motion. He put on his Nike's. There was no need to get dressed because he slept in his clothes. He then went into the bathroom and brushed his teeth and washed his face. Before he could walk out of the bathroom, his mom cut him off.

"Look, I would really like to use my car today, for a couple hours, if that's ok with you?"

"You know what mom? I forgot that is your car." Mike joked.

"That don't make no sense, I got to ask permission to use my own car."

"Momma, don't be acting like that, come here and give your baby a hug and kiss."

She gave him what he asked for, but she couldn't leave out, "Boy, you're sick."

"I know I am, but the girls love me."

"Yeah, I bet they do, but look, I'll be back by 12:00, then I will need you to take me to the shop. I told your aunty I would come help her today."

"Don't trip, I'll be here," was his exit statement, as he made his way back to his room.

He sat on his bed and started the task of rolling his morning blunt. Just as he was dumping the blunt in the windowsill, all he could hear was his mom yelling, "Boy, don't be in there dumping that bull in the windowsill."

That's when realized the windowsill was cleaned out.

"Man, I got to put a lock on my door," was all that he thought. He knew some of his work was missing, so to get a little get-back, he dumped the blunt out in the windowsill anyway. Then, he sat back on the bed and finished rolling up. Once he was finished, he put the blunt behind his left ear. He stood up, as he looked down to where his pager should be. The sight of it not being there made him sense something else. He then realized just how light he was. Panic set in fast. He frantically tapped his pockets. What he felt brought terror to his mind. All four of his pockets were empty. All he kept saying over and over again was, "Think, Think, Think Mike!"

He stood there in the middle of his room thinking to himself, "I found the weed and the blunts on the floor next to my bed, so where could the other shit be?" He ran to the bed and lifted up the mattress, and the sight of nothing, intensified his anger. Then it was like a light came on in his mind. He dropped the mattress, and sprinted for the front door. Just as he reached for it, the door came open. He had to take a quick step back to prevent the door from hitting him in the face.

The sight of his mom eased his mind because he feared she would be gone already. If that was the case, he couldn't check her car for his shit. As soon as his mom saw him, she had a mouth full to say.

"Boy, come get that speaker stuff out of my trunk. I'm going shopping for food, so I need all the space I can get."

Mike thought, "Damn, I for got that was even in there."

He smiled, as he said, "Mom, don't even trip, I'm gonna take care of that right now. I'm going around back, so I can take it through the back door. When I'm done, I'll bring the car back around front."

"Boy, just hurry up. I need to get moving."

"Mom, I need your keys because I lost everything, and I mean everything."

She glared at him because she understood what he meant. She didn't want to really cut in to him, but she knew she had to say something. "Boy, you need to slow down and think about what you're doing."

Not in the mood to take it any further, she just handed him the keys.

Once inside the car, the first thing Mike did was look under the drivers seat, nothing! The glove-box, nothing! Under the passenger seat, nothing! His anger shot up to an all time high, and he started banging on the steering wheel. "Fuck, Fuck, Fuck!" was all he said, over and over again.

He looked over to the building and saw his mom standing there shaking her head. Then she walked back in the building.

He started up the car and drove to the back to unload his hot goods. By the time he made it back to the front, his mom was sitting on the steps. When he she saw him, she got up and walked to the car. Mike put the car in park, in the middle of the street, and he got out. As his mom got in the car, she said, "Boy, look under your pillow with your blind self."

Realizing what she said, Mike broke in to a dash, as he headed for his room. He did what she told him, and just like he hoped, everything was there. "Man, I must of put it there last night before I went to bed," is what he said out loud, as if someone else was in the room with him.

With everything back in its proper place, he was feeling a little heavier, so he made his way back outside. Mike found his spot on the steps and sat down. He grabbed the blunt from behind his ear. Surprised that it was still there, he gave it a little kiss before he put it in the air.

He smoked his blunt, and made a couple of sales.
When he got done, he realized how hungry he was. Without
a car, he knew the only quick trip he could make was to SA
to grab a snack. He didn't waist any time on walking the
two-and-a-half blocks to the gas-station. Once there, he
figured four M&M cookies, slightly micro waved, with a
small thing of milk, would do the trick. With the milk in
hand and the cookies in the microwave, his pager went off.
He looked down at the number, and said to himself, "My
car got to be ready."

Now he had to decided on how he was going to get to the
paint shop. He thought, "It ain't that far, I could walk or
should I call a cab?"

A block away from S.A, he looked behind him to see a bus
was coming. Mike threw the last bit of milk, and stuffed the
last cookie in his mouth, as he dashed for the bus-stop.
Once on the bus, he quickly found a seat up front, instead
of the known cool spot in the back.

Mike couldn't believe, he of all people, was on the bus. He
was literally praying that no one that he knew got on. He
was in such a hurry to get off, he rang the bell a block early.
Too proud to say he made a mistake, he got off anyway and
walked the rest of the way.

At the paint shop, there was little to discuss. Mike like
what he saw and he let it be known. As he opened the car
door to get in, the clerk told him not to was his car for two
days. Without a reply, Mike started it up and drove off. All
the way home, Mike was thinking about how he had to get
one more thing done to his car. Getting his windows tinted
was the last thing on his list. He figured he could take care
of that when his mom made it back.

Instead of parking in front of the building, he parked in
back. Then he retrieved his hot goods from the back hall of
his apartment. With everything seated nicely by the drivers

door, he sat down and rolled up another blunt. He smoked half, as he hooked up his new sounds, then he put the blunt out. When he got done with the sounds and he liked what he heard, he closed the door. Then he re-lit the blunt. Satisfied that everything was hooked up right, Mike knew he had to break in his new ride with a proper smoke session. So, he sat there with all of the windows rolled up, and smoked, as he listened to his beats. After he finished the blunt, he sat there vibing with the music. Mike rocked to the beat, as if he was in a trance.

Lost in his own world, he went through almost every tape in the tape case. It was the tap on the window that brought him back. If it wasn't for the song going off, he might not have heard the tap at all. He looked up to see his mom standing there, so he rolled down the window.

"Boy, I thought I heard you back here."

Right then, the next song came on and all it took was for her to hear the bass one time and she snapped. "Boy if you don't turn that mess down!"

Mike just bobbed his head to the beat, while he looked at her with that smile on his face.

Fed up with his bull, she popped him over the head one good time to get him focused. "Boy, I know you heard me with your crazy butt....."

Satisfied with such attention, he started laughing, and he did what he was told.

"Now that don't make no sense," his mom stated.

"Dang ma' how did you get back so fast?"

"Boy how long have you been sitting back here? You know it's after twelve right?"

Realizing just how stuck he was, Mike cut his car off, and said, "Are you ready to go?"

"Boy I been waiting on you."

"Well I need you to follow me first so I can drop my car off. "

"Well meet in the front, and boy, don't be driving fast."

"Now come on ma' do I do that for real?"

"Boy I ain't even bout to answer that.... But I'll meet you in the front."

" I'll beat you there," said Mike, as he put the car in motion.

After Mike dropped his car off, along with his mom, he went back to the building. He sat out there hustling and just like he hoped, Bee pulled up. Mike was somewhat surprised to see that Aleasha was still with him. Before they could get out, Mike walked up to the car. He stuck his head through the passenger window, which Aleasha had down. He then said, "What's up girl, what's wit your cousin?"

Aleasha bit down on her bottom lip and mean mugged Mike, then said, "Boy don't say nothing!"

"Girl, I ain't trippin' on you two. But what's really goin' on Bee?"

"The same old shit, you know, but have you ate yet?"

"Not really, why you wonna go somewhere and eat?"

It was Aleasha that answered, "Hell yeah, I'm starving."

Mike said, "Girl, wasn't no one talking to you."

"Whatever Mike, but are you coming or not? A bitch needs to eat."

"Well, I'm glad you know what you are."

Bee shook his head and in a low voice, he said, "Come on cousin, don't go there with her, be cool and kick back."

Mike took a step back and threw his hands in the air. Then he said, "Damn, this shit's getting serious I see. I don't want no trouble."

"Boy, get in this car, and let's go get something to eat," was all Aleasha had to say.

Mike walked to the back door and climbed in.

As they finished up their Texas Toast and 6 oz. Steaks, Mike's pager went off. He looked down at the number and saw it was one he wasn't familiar with. Mike checked on the time and saw it was now 2:35. He quickly calculated how long he thought it would take the tint shop to tint his five windows. He figured, due to the fact that the clerk at the tint shop said they would get right to his car, two hours was more than enough time for them to get done.

A smile appeared on his face after he accepted that's who was paging him. Without a word said, he stood up and walked to the pay phone by the door. Just like he hoped, it was the tint shop, and the man on the phone said his car was ready.

As he hung up the phone, Bee and Aleasha were walking up. He looked at Bee, and said, "Cousin, I need you to take me to get my car."

"At the same spot we took it yesterday?"

"Naw, I slid through there this morning and picked it up.

"It's at the tint shop."

"Cool, come on let's roll."

As soon as Bee put the car in motion, Mike rolled his window down. He then cracked open is last blunt. To Mike, a good meal wasn't complete without a blunt for dessert. On the ride to the tint shop, the main focus was the blunt, so there was little said. As they pulled up in the parking lot, Mike was the first one to spot his car. It was parked right under the sun, like it was on a showroom floor.

All Mike could do was smile, as the sight of his car made him feel so proud. He figured Bee didn't even recognize his it, because he said, "Mike, they ain't done with your car yet?"

Mike just laughed, as he got out and ran into the tint shop. With his bill paid, and his key's in hand, he walked back outside to see Bee still in his car. With his head held high,

and the biggest smile on his face, Mike walked to his car. As he opened his door, he made sure he looked over to see the look on Bee's face. Just like he hoped, Bee's jaws dropped. With a little laugh to himself, Mike got in and started it up. To add to the moment, Mike just sat there, and turned his new sounds up. The sound of the bass shot chills up Mike's spine, and he knew Bee was feeling it too.
Just when he saw that Bee was about to get out of his car, he pulled off. He stopped on the side of Bee's car and cracked the door, as he turned the music down. He then told Bee to meet him back at the building. With this music turned back up, he got in traffic.

The ride back home was made in slow motion for Mike. He rode past all of the hot spots that were on the route to the building. He knew the young hustlers would be out doing what they do. It was their reaction that he was after, and he got what he was looking for, as he turned heads.

Satisfied that his presence was felt, he got focused on getting back. Mike made a stop at the corner store to pick up a box of blunts first. At the corner of his block, Mike saw Bee's car. They were parked across the street from the building. Mike pulled up on the side of them, and got out. He told Bee to meet him around back. Then Mike got back in his car and pulled off.

Once in the back, he turned his car off, but kept the music playing. As he closed his eyes and bobbed his head to the bass. As the song went off, the sound of the passenger door opening startled him. As he flinched, and made a move to where his gun was at.

"Damn cousin, what's with you, nigga?" Bee asked. " That don't make no sense."

"Boy, you better be cool! I already told you about moving too fast around this bitch," Mike replied.

"Boy, you need some help," Aleasha expressed.

"Yeah I know, that's why I don't fuck with your cousin no more. I need some of her good help, but she ain't on it!"

As he said the last word he realized they were still standing outside, "Damn, why are y'all still standing out there?"

"Shit cousin, is it safe to get in yet?"

As they got in and closed the door, Mike then realized there was no music playing. Just that fast, panic set in. "Damn, I blew something out that fucking fast?" Was all Mike said, as he played with the volume.

Aleasha said, "Boy, move!"

She simply pushed eject, and flipped the tape over. Sure enough, that is all it took, as the music started playing once again.

With a smile on his face, as he bobbed his head to the beat, he said, "I knew that's what was wrong with it. I just wanted to see if y'all could catch it."

"Yeah, I bet," was Bee's reply, and they all started laughing.

Mike then handed Bee a blunt, and Aleasha, a bag of weed. Bee understood what that meant, so he cracked the door and dumped the blunt out. When he finished, he looked over to see Mike doing the same ting.

Bee told Aleasha to hold the bag open, as he dipped his hand in what they called the "Cookie Jar," and came out with a nice amount of buds. He then sprinkled the buds evenly throughout the blunt, and on the other side of Aleasha, Mike matched Bee's moves, stride-for-stride.

Aleasha looked at Bee, then at Mike, and the sight of them so focused on such a task, along with smiles they both were wearing, sent her to tears, as she laughed so hard.

Both of their eyes went straight to the bag, which Aleasha still held open, and Mike was the first to speak. "Girl, give me that before your silly ass spills something."

161

"Here, take this shit! That don't make no sense, you two need some help for real."

Without a comeback, Mike took the bag and put it up. Then he went back to the task at hand. By the time he got done, Bee had his blunt lit already, and they sat in the car and smoked both blunts, as they all rocked to the music.

GOING NOWHERE FAST
CHAPTER 17

As the weeks went by, everything seemed to be falling into place for Mike. Now that he had two spots to hustle from, he figured there was no reason for him to leave the Hood. Mike believed the saying, gang-banging and hustling, don't mix. At that point in his life, he was trying to live by that saying, as he got his money on.

While he was at his sister's house hustling hard, Bee was at the building, doing the same. Mike also made sure he gave Jackie's a hundred or two hundred dollars worth of crack, to sell to her family.

Even though the flame between him and Jackie was at an all time low, Mike still spent time with her and their daughter. The time away from the madness, to Mike, was the closet thing he figured he would get to having a normal family. The one thing that he truly dreaded was growing up to be like his dad. To Mike, he wasn't a dad at all, he was more like an unreliable friend. A friend that Mike didn't want to be anything like.

The road for Mike, so far, was a very smooth one. He had no clue about the pothole which he was about to fall into. Soon, he would be consumed by the coldest darkness, and the trip back to the light would truly be a long one.

With close to everything invested, Mike still didn't slow down on his daily spending. He wired Big Cie the forty five hundred, and paid another five hundred for some rims for his car; which he knew he shouldn't have done. Where the rims came from never was an issue for Mike. He only worried about his bankroll being nearly depleted.

Sure enough, the first day he put the rims on his car, he ran into trouble. With his fresh finger-waves, and new outfit, he found himself in the County Jail, for receiving stolen property.

As Mike slid through the city flossing his ride, the fool who's rim's they really were, spotted him. He followed Mike all the way from over south, to over north. Mike decided to go by Lucky's, and that's where he stopped. By this time, the fool was already on his cell phone talking to the police dispatch. He was giving them updates on where they were at, so hopefully, a police car which was in the area, could pull Mike over.

Mike never saw it coming. He was too busy putting on a show for those around him. When the police pulled up, Mike was sitting on the hood of his car. He was loud talking, and bobbing his head to Scar face; just lost in his own fantasy. The sudden long faces and silence of those around him got his attention. Mike followed the eyes of everyone else and looked behind him.

Down the street, he found the source behind such a mood change in the atmosphere. It was a police car, stopped in the middle of the street, and a man was talking to them through their window. With one smooth move, Mike ducked in his car, and turned down the music. Such a beautiful dream turned into a nightmare, right before his eyes.

Mike got back out of his car, only to find a police officer and the man he saw talking to the police, standing right there. The officer was the first to speak; he started off real respectful. "How are you doing today sir?" He asked Mike.

"Fine, is there a problem?"

"Well, I'm gonna get to that, but first, let me ask you, is

this your car?"

"Yeah, you can say that. Why, what's up?"
Mike's heart was pounding, as he tried to remember if he was dirty in any way. Mike knew he left his gun at the building, then he remembered Jackie and Bee had the little work that was left, that eased his mind. Now, he just had to deal with why the police and this fool, he didn't know, were at his door, asking questions.

Then it came out of the officer's mouth, "Those rims there, where did you get them from?"

"Damn! Not the rims," was all Mike could think. He knew it was over, but he kept his cool. He was thinking there was no way the fool could prove they were his rims. Mike then answered, "I bought them out of town."

"Well, this young man here thinks those are his rims, and there's only one way to prove they're not."

"Well, how's that?" Mike asked, with his arms crossed in a defensive posture.

"I engraved my name on the back of each rim," the fool replied.

As the words came off the fool's tongue, Mike unconsciously shook his head. He knew it was a wrap.

The officer then looked at Mike, and said, "So what I'm gonna need you to do is get your jack out and take off one of those rims, then we can take a quick look and get this over with."

Mike did what he was told, and sure enough, the fool's name was right where he said it would be.

Two hours in the County Jail was all it cost Mike, along with the five hundred dollars that he spent on the rims. As soon as Mike got out, he and Bee went down to the impound lot, to try to get his car. He was told that it had a hold on it. The clerk behind the window, gave Mike a number to call, to get the hold removed. Mike took the number and walked straight to the pay phone and called it. On the fourth ring, an officer picked up. He asked for Mike's information, so he could find his case. Mike gave him what he asked for, and he was put on hold. A few minutes later the officer got back on the phone and asked one last thing, "Did you give the hubcaps back?"

With no second thought, Mike said, "Yep."

"Well, I'm gonna make the call and you should be good to go."

"I'm at the impound right now, so how long do you think I should wait?"

"Give me ten minutes, then you should be able to get your car."

"Thank you," Mike replied, with his most sincere voice, then he hung up.

All Mike had to do was smile and Bee knew it came together. As they stood by the phone talking, the clerk called out Mike's name. When Mike walked to the window, the clerk told him he could go back and get his car. When Bee saw Mike walk to the side door leading to the holding lot for the cars, he walked out to his car.

As soon as Mike walked out of the side door, he saw his car, and it still had the rims on it. He broke into a speed walkers stride, as he smiled from ear to ear. Once Mike got inside, he kissed the steering wheel, then he turned it on. Before he pulled off, he found the song with the most bass. Then he turned it up, just right to where the bass sounded the deepest. He pulled up to the security-arm, and rolled down his window to punch in his number. As the arm went up, Mike once again put on a show. With the bass vibrating his trunk, Mike did a brake stand. Burning the rubber off the back tires. The front brakes kept the car from moving, but the back tires were spinning, because he held his foot on the brake and tapped the gas with his other foot. This gave birth to a cloud of smoke.

When he was sure he had everyone's attention, he pulled off. Mike stopped behind Bee's car and did another brake stand, then sped off. A block away, he waited for Bee. With both arms hanging out of the window, Mike had the dirtiest smirk on his face.

When Bee pulled up and rolled down his passenger window, Mike said, "What's really good?"

"Damn Mike! I thought you said they got the rims?"

"Shit, I thought they did, well fuck em!"

"Yeah, I feel you on that, now where are you headed?"

"Back to the building, I need to make some paper, forreal!"

"Well, I'll meet you there," was all Bee said, as he pulled off.

Mike cracked a smile, and put the car in motion. The race was on and Mike was not the one to lose a race for nothing.

Just like always, Mike was the first to make it back to the building. Bee never had a chance, because Mike was more of a risk taker. Through red lights, sidewalks, through parks, down the wrong side of the street, was all fair game when it came to Mike. His whole life was a chance, a gamble. He was uncomfortable if he wasn't on the edge, but survival was a must for Mike.

Back at the building, it was the same old routine. They found their spots on the steps, and they smoked while they got their hustle on. When Mike felt they'd done enough hustling, he told Bee, "Come on, let's roll."

They got in Mike's car and pulled off. Mike made a stop at his favorite two spots, the corner store, and the weed house. Completely prepared, Mike headed for the park where all of the homies hung out.

Like always, Mike had to make a grand entrance. Instead of coming up the alley closet to the park, he came around the long way. This way, they would hear him coming before they saw him. Mike then made his way up the alley real slow. Just like he planned, all eyes were on him. The park was packed, just like he figured it would be.

At first, everyone was tense. When they realized who it was, the gang-signs flew up, as a handful of the homies started bobbing their heads, as if they were in the car too, listening to music.

To ice his entrance off, Mike sped up, then stopped, as he did a brake-stand. With one hand out of the window, Mike threw up the gang-sign, which they all shared. All of the homies cheered him on, feeding his greed for power.

Instead of parking in a parking spot, Mike shut down the alley. He parked in the middle of the alley, and he and Bee got out of the car, to love from everyone. The hand shakes and hand daps came flying. Mike was the man of the hour, and he loved the attention.

"Smoke on Cuz," was what Blast had to say to Mike, and it was on.

Mike said, "Cuz, you already know what time it is when I show up. Shit, you know I got to smoke."

All of the weed heads in the crowd were paying close attention to Mike and Blast. They all knew with them two, in due time, something was getting smoked.

Mike saw a group of his home girls doing their own thing, off to the side. He said, "Hold on Cuz, I'll be right back," and he walked over to the home girls.

He showed the girls some love and they showed love back. Mike then pulled out a box of blunts and handed two blunts to one of the girls. After he put the box up, Mike pulled out a fat bag of buds. To another home girl, Mike told her to hold her hand out, and he gave her a handful of bud.

"Good looking out, Cuz," was all the home girls kept saying over and over again.

Mike just cracked a smile, and said, "Y'all enjoy y'all self," and he walked back to his car.

Back at his car, Mike sat on the hood, just enjoying the scene. He watched as Blast was looking his car over.

"Cuz, them chrome and gold ones are looking real nice on here," Blast complemented.

Hearing those words from Blast felt good, and Mike's pride was higher than ever.

Feeling like a king, Mike handed out four blunts to four different homies. He then handed Bee the bag of weed and told him to hold it open. After Mike handed Blast a blunt, he opened up a blunt of his own. The other four understood, so they showed their respect, as they sat back until Mike and Blast were done rolling theirs. Mike rolled up two, and handed one to Bee.

After the four homies got the weed they needed, Mike, Blast, and Bee got in Mike's car. With the windows rolled up, Mike was the first to put his blunt in the air. Before he knew it, all three blunts had fire to them.

As Mike smoked, he looked out to the crowd and he liked what he saw, everyone was enjoying themselves. Out of nowhere, Mike started up the car and pulled off. No one said a word, they just kept on smoking. In the zone that Mike was in, he did his best driving. He shot in and out of traffic, and from lane to lane, like he was in an action movie. Still, Bee and Blast didn't say a word, they just kept on smoking. When the liquor store came into view, Bee and Blast knew where they were headed.

With two bags full of gin, orange juice, ice, and cups, Mike made his way back to the park. This time, Mike took the quick way to the park, and parked his car next to Blast's. Before Mike got out of the car, he told Blast to hand him the two bags. With the two bags in hand, Mike made his way to the nearest picnic table. Then he pulled out the two gallons of gin, and said, "Who's trying to get their drink on?"

As soon as Mike knew everyone got the message, he sat that gin on the table, and walked back to the car.

Blast and Bee were standing outside of the car, talking to some of the home girls waiting for Mike.

Mike didn't even make it completely to the car, when Blast said, "Damn Cuz! I almost forgot to tell you, I talked to Cuz, and that should be here any day now, so keep your eyes open, ya dig?"

Right away, Mike understood, and he went right into action. Mike looked at Blast, and said, "Well Cuz, let me get on my business. I got to get moving so I can get back to this spot. I'll slide through tomorrow, so be cool."

"Alright Cuz, take care," is what the home girl that Mike gave the blunt to said.

Mike smiled at her, and said, "I can dig that, what do they call you Cuz?"

"Lady Shot, Cuz."

"Yeah, I can see that," was all Mike said, as he thought about who Big Shot was. He could tell she had a good heart, just like Big Shot, and they were both loyal. Not to mention, they both had a lot going for themselves. Mike said, "Well Cuz, y'all ce cool, and if y'all ever need anything, if I got it, you got it."

With that said, Mike got in the car. He looked over at Bee, who was already laid back in the passenger seat waiting, and shook his head. Mike backed out and pulled off real slow. He stuck his head out of the window and threw up his gang sign. Mike then rocked his head back and fourth, bobbing his head to the beat. Every hand in the park shot up, as they represented their Hood.

A block away, Mike turned the music down, and said, "Bee, I want you to hold the car overnight, because I'm about to go spend the night over Jackie's. Look, I need you to pick me up early, forreal."

Bee said, "Man, why don't you just take me to my car?"

"Cuz, can you just do what I asked? Damn!"

"Don't trip Mike, I got you."

"Look Bee, I got to go over here and make sure everything's everything. I also got to make sure baby's keeping her eye open for the package."

"I'm already knowing, you don't go to say no more."

"Well, if you knew, then why was you acting stuck?"

All Bee said was, "Cousin, I'll be here to get you in the morning."

"Thank you."

GOING NOWHERE FAST
CHAPTER 18

For the next two days, Mike stayed at Jackie's all day and all night. The package still didn't show up, and Jackie's mom started asking questions like, "Mike, what are you up to?"

"Why you say that?"

"Because you've been here for the past two days, and every time there's a knock on the door, you go running to the window. I'm tellin' you, something's up."

Without a reply, Mike walked to the phone and called Bee. As soon as Bee picked up, all Mike said was, "Come pick me up," then he hung up.

He then gave Jackie that look they both understood, and he walked to the back room. Just like he knew, Jackie was right behind him. They both walked in the room and Jackie closed the door behind her. Mike walked straight to the bed and laid on his back, as he watched Jackie standing by the door, in her big T-shirt and pants.

With a sexy smile on her face, she looked deep into Mike's eyes, as she pulled off her pants with one smooth move. She walked over to the bed and climbed on top of Mike and rode him until he couldn't hold on any longer. Just as he let himself go, there was a knock on the door.

"Boy, someone is out there honking for you, so let's go," was all Jackie's mom said.

Jackie rolled off of him, unto her back, and Mike pulled up his pants, sticky and all.

He stood up and bent down and gave her kiss on the forehead, then he said, "Look, keep your eye out for the package, and I'll be back."

"I'll be here, I ain't going nowhere."

"Well look, you need to go up front, so you can hear the door," was the last thing Mike told Jackie before he walked out of the room.

As soon as Mike got in the car, Bee was the first to talk, "What's up cousin, is it on or what?"

"Shit's still stuck, but I ain't trippin' it a be here."

"Man, I hope so, because you know we're on our last leg."

"I'm not worried, but right now, take me to the house so I can get dressed, and we can hustle up on something real quick. Shit, I don't even got no weed, so you know shit's bad."

"Here, I came up last night at the building," Bee replied, handing him a bag.

Mike cracked a smile as he took it, and said, "Shit, about time you came through."

"I ain't about to feed off into that bullshit, so you can pull that car over, because I ain't getting in."

"You funny ass nigga, kick back. Damn!"

"I ain't trippin', I'm not about to go there with you today."

"Well stop at the store, so I can get some blunts."

"I already got a boxe in the glove box."

"Damn, I see you on yo' shit today."

"And I see you're still going to keep the shit coming."

"Man, just drive. Damn, you'll fuck up a nigga's whole day wit' that sensitive shit."

"Yeah, whatever."

With their feelings expressed, and the tension at an all time high, the rest of the ride to the building was made in silence. Once at the building, Bee found a spot on the stairs, while Mike went straight to the back, to check on his car.

There was no doubt in Mike's mind that his car was all right, due to precautions he took. He removed one rim, the battery, along with the speaker box. Besides some dirt, everything was like he left it. Content with his find, Mike made his way through the back door to retrieve his missing goods.

With everything back in it's proper place, Mike drove around front, and parked. As he walked up the stairs, Bee said, "Are we rolling in you car today?"

"Yeah, I thought we would take it to the car wash, then hit some comers."

"That sound like a plan to me, I'm with that."

"Let me get dressed real quick."

"I'll be out here, grinding."

Mike walked in the house, to see Rolanda's mom Tanya, and her best friend Shell, sitting at the table with his mom. All eyes were on Mike, and his mom was the first to say something, "Boy, I thought I heard you out there with that music."

As if he didn't hear his mom, Mike looked at Tanya, and said, "What up stranger, where you been hiding at?"

"For real Mike, it ain't like you really care."

"Look, I ain't going there with you," Mike replied. "But look, where's Rolanda?"

"At the house with my sister."

"Hi to you too, Mike," Shell cut in, begging for some attention.

"Shell, don't be acting like that, I see you."

"Well, you could have said hi, or something."

"Yeah I know, but I'm trippin' right now, how did y'all know where I stayed at?"

"We seen your mom at the shop, and she told us to stop by," Tanya replied.

"I'm glad y'all was in the right place at the right time."

" See there you go, just know shell had to talk me into coming."

" Oh, so you're still acting up!"

"Boy, don't try to turn it around on me. You're the one that left us, me and your daughter, so don't go there."

"Look, why don't you come in the back with me so I can talk to you while I get dressed."

"You go right ahead, I'll wait out here for you."

"Girl, you better go back there with my baby, and quit acting like that. Y'all need to sit down and get things right," Mike's mom instructed.

"That's what I'm talking about, mom."

Tanya looked at Mike's mom, then she stood up with her hands on her hips. "Boy, you better be glad your mom said what she said, so let's go shoot!"

"All girl, don't be acting like that, you know I'm still that deal."

"Boy look, let's go," Tanya replied.

As they walked away, Mike's mom said, "I don't want to hear no funny noises coming from back there."

"Don't worry about it mom, you will," Mike joked.

"The only funny noises will be coming from you. I'm telling you Mike I ain't on that."

"We'll see about that," was Mike 's reply, as he smiled and led the way.

When they got in the room, Tanya sat on the bed, while Mike went to the closet, to find something to wear. Still trying to stand her ground, Tanya stood up, as if she was about to leave. Then with her hands on her hips, she looked at Mike, and said, "If you don't got nothing to talk about, I'm going back up front."

Mike just stood there with his outfit in hand, looking at her. She understood what that meant, so she still tried to put up a fight. "Boy, don't even start."

Mike walked up to her and kissed her aggressively, and just like he knew, the fight in her gave way.

It turned into a confession, as she said over and over again, "Mike, I missed you so much, you just don't know."

Mike then laid his outfit on the bed. Then he laid next to it. He extended his hand, and she looked at it as if it was a snake. Not buying it, he gave her that look of his, and took it.

Mike guided her on top of him, and all of her built up tension was released, as she melted into his arms.

"Mike, I can't stand to be hurt again."

"Baby, don't worry. Just enjoy yourself and let me please you."

That line was the icing on the cake. Like always, she was under his spell, and they both knew it.

As the hot water rolled down his back, he thought to himself, "Man, I'm good! Damn, I forgot just how good her pussy was. I might have to make more time for her. Shit, I might have to hit that one more time before I let her go."

Unfortunately such pleasant thoughts were interrupted by the bathroom door closing behind her.

Within moments Mike found himself getting mad, because she left after washing up, without saying by. He didn't understand why she didn't wan to get in the shower with him, but as long as she washed up was all that counted.

When he made it back to the room, he was surprised to see she wasn't there, waiting for him. He quickly got dressed, and was even more shocked when he made it to the front room to find only his mom.

"Boy, what are you looking like that for?"

Realizing it was written on his face, he tried to play it off.

"What are you talking about?"

"Well whatever, anyway she left her number and she said give her a call."

"That's cool mom, just hold onto it for me."

Embarrassed that his mom read him like a book, he made his way to the door. Just as he grabbed the door knob, his mom had one last thing to say, "Boy, I told you about wearing your heart on your sleeve!"

Mike stopped in his tracks, and just looked at his mom with them big baby eyes, waiting to hear more.

"That's all, now go do what you was about to do."

As Mike closed the door behind him, he heard his mom say, "Watch yourself out there."

With out a reply, Mike walked outside to see Bee hitting a stang, and he was no longer alone. Dave was with him, and a fool named Ce Ce was with Dave.

Dave was an old friend that Mike ran into while he was at his sister's house, standing outside hustling. Ever since the reunion, they'd bee hanging out from time to time. "What's up Cuz, smoke one?"

Was the first thing Dave said when he saw Mike.

"Cuz, it's all good, I see you got Ce Ce with you. What's up with y'all?"

"Cuz, we're trying to see what's up with you, and hopefull we can get our hands into something."

"Well Cuz, y'all can roll with me and Bee; we really ain't on shit right now."

"Cuz, I'm with that."

"Damn Ce Ce, you could of spoke to a mutha fucker, or something."

"Come on Cuz, you know it ain't like that."

"I know, I'm just fucking with you."

"So, what's up cousin, what are we about get into?"

"First off, Bee take the keys, you're driving."

"Well, where are we headed?"

"First, we need to go to the car wash, then we'll go from there. So come on, let's roll."

As soon as they got in the car, Mike handed the bag of weed he got from Bee to Dave, and told him to roll up some blunts. Just when they were pulling off, Bee said, "Mike, did you get the blunts out of the glove box?"

"Damn, I sho' forgot. I'm glad you said something when you did. Damn Dave, Cuz, how was you gonna roll up with the blunts?"

Right then the logic in that hit everyone, and they all started laughing.

"Shit Cuz, I don't know, I was waiting for you to give me the blunts, like you always do."

"Shit, you was going to be waiting for a long ass time."

"Shit, I see that now."

"I bet you do. Well look cousin, let me get your keys so I can go get the blunts real quick."

As soon as he made it back in the car, he handed Dave a box, and told him to roll up them all up. Without a word said, Dave went right to work.

After the task of getting the car washed was complete, they rolled around the city, vibing to the music, just smoking away. Without saying a word, Bee pulled into a gas station and stopped at the pay phone. Without giving it a second thought, when he felt the vibration of his pager going off, he knew who it was, so he had to call back right away.

The thought of not seeing Aleasha for a third straight day, was too much for him to take. She had to be paging him to let him know he could come pick her up. As soon as he reached for the knob to let down the window, Mike had a fit.

"Cuz, you better get out and use the phone! And when you get out, make it quick because I don't want no smoke to seep out."

No one said anything, because they knew he was for real.

While Bee was on the phone, they kept smoking. Bee's phone call wasn't long at all. He heard what he was looking for, and that was all that he needed.

Without a word said, Bee put the car in motion, and headed straight for the highway. Out the corner of his eye, he saw how Mike was looking at him crazy. Knowing it was coming, Bee said,

"Man, Aleasha and her friend want to come kick it. So I'm going to get 'em."

He knew as long as she had a friend with her, Mike wouldn't trip. Just like he figured, Mike didn't say a word, he just passed him the blunt.

When they pulled into Aleasha's parking lot, Mike started feeling uneasy because they were back over north, by where he bumped into the fool over the rims. He made sure, this time, that he didn't leave his gun at home. So, to ease himself, he placed his hand on it. Bee read Mike's face, so he parked between two cars, and as he was getting out of the car, Mike said, "Man, hurry up, don't be on no bullshit!"

Not wanting to get into with Mike, Bee didn't say a word, he just got out and ran up to the buzzer. Mike sat there looking at Bee talking into the speaker, thinking to himself, "Man, I hope Aleasha friend is cool."

His train of thought was broken when Bee got back in the car and slammed the door. Mike turned the music down because for the first time, he didn't want to cause a scene.

"Damn cousin, you ain't got to slam my door like that, Shit!"

"Don't even trip, it won't happen again."

"Well, I hope not."

Mike looked in the back at Dave and told him to blaze up. As he was turning around, he saw Aleasha walking up to the car, and just like Bee said, she had someone with her. He then stepped out of the car to get a better look, and what

179

he saw he couldn't believe. Aleasha's friend was a fine, long haired, short red bone, like he liked.

Before the girls could make it to the car, Mike looked in the back at Dave and CeCe, and said, "Cuz, where y'all need to be dropped off at? "

Seeing threw the bullshit that Mike was on, everyone started laughing.

Aleasha and her friend walked up, and Aleasha said, "Damn, what's so funny?"

"Girl, quit trippin' and get in the car, y'all two sit up front, I'll sit in back," Mike replied.

"Damn, look who's actin' nice for a change," Aleasha joked.

"Yea, enjoy it while it last," Mike replied, making his way to the back.

GOING NO WHERE FAST
CHAPTER 19

They pulled up in front of Dave's building, and Mike looked at him and CeCe, "Well look y'all, I'm gonna get up wit' y'all a little later."

Before the last word rolled off Mike's tongue, everyone started laughing, because they knew he was on bullshit about coming back.

"Yea whatever Cuz," Mike replyed. Well Shit, you should let us get a blunt or something?"

"Well Cuz, I told you to roll up five, but we only smoked four, so y'all can have the last one; now get out."

"You're so full of shit Cuz."

"I know Cuz, but I still love me, so it's all good."

As soon as Dave and CeCe exited the car, Mike closed the door, while Bee pulled off.

Bee then asked, "What's up cousin, where are we headed?"

"Look, stop at Tony's house real quick."

"Don't even trip, I got you. Should I got through the back?"

"Yeah, park in the back."

It didn't take any time to make it to Tony's, because she lived less than a block away. As they drove past Blast's building, Mike saw him and his girlfriend coming down the back steps. Before the car came to a complete stop, Mike was getting out. "Y'all go right on in cousin, I'll be there in a minute."

Without waiting for a reply, Mike started walking over to

181

where Blast was standing by his car.

"What's cracking Cuz?"

"Shit Cuz, you know that shit still ain't showed up."

"Damn Cuz, shit, I just talked to the homie, and he told me to tell you, you should of got it by now."

"Shiiit, I been posted up at the spot, so I don't know what's going on. I know I didn't miss it."

"Well Cuz, you know if some funny shit jumps off, don't go down to the post office to try to pick it up."

"Shit Cuz, I'm already knowing, but check this out, what is y'all about to get into."

"Shit Cuz, I got to make a few runs, that's about it."

"I can dig that. Well, I got this fresh work in the house, that I got my eye on. I go to see if I can make her my next victim. Shit, you know I got to have her."

"Cuz, you're a fool."

"Yeah, I'm already knowing."

"Well shit Cuz, you should let me roll on the gold ones, and you can roll in my Monte."

"Cuz, you don't got to say another word, I got you, so let me run in real quick and get the keys for you. So come pull your car up in my sister's back yard, next to mine."

That was right on time for Mike. He was sure this move of switching cars would win him the fine red bone's panties, for the night. On the ride form Aleasha's, Mike lost count on how many comments he made to let it be known that they were in his car.

Mike walked in his sister's and all eyes were on him. Tony and her baby's dad were watching TV, "Brother, I need to talk to you real quick."

"I bet you do, but give me a minute, I'm on one." He kept walking to the back room where he knew they were waiting. He opened up the door and stood in the doorway, and said, "Bee, let me talk to you real quick."

Without a word said, Bee walked out to the hallway, where Mike was waiting.

"What's up cousin?" Bee asked, a bit confused.

"Look, I need the car keys, and give Tony a pill. She might not have no money, but still give her one."

Mike took the keys, and sprinted back outside. Before his sister could say anything, he said, "Bee got something for you," and he kept on moving.

By the time Mike made it back outside, Blast and his girlfriend were already sitting in Mike's car with the windows down. As he walked up to the drivers window, Blast handed him his keys and Mike gave him his.

Once Blast got what he needed, he started the car. "Alright Cuz, I'll see you tonight."

"It's on," was all Blast said, as he put the car in motion, with a big smile on his face.

Back In the house, Mike told his company it was time to roll, and he led the way back outside.

As they left, Mike realized his sister was nowhere to be found, so he figured she was locked up in the bathroom, doing what she does.

Once outside, he walked straight to the car and got behind the wheel. When Bee saw Blast's car, he knew Mike was going to be doing the driving. He thought to himself, "This nigga's always putting on a show."

The girls got in the back and Bee sat up front. Mike didn't like this arrangement, but he wasn't tripping. He told himself on the way back, he would make sure shit got right.

Mike started up the car, and before the music could really start playing, he turned it all the way down. Mike knew he had the red bone's attention, and he told himself he was going to do all he could to keep it.

Mike jumped right on the highway, and Bee already knew where they were headed; to their favorite spot, Go-cart racing.

They spent an hour or so out there, Go-carting and playing video games. Then they went to get a bite to eat. As they were eating, Bee said, "Cousin, I need to get my hustle on."

Mike understood just what Bee was saying; his money was at an all time low. Without a word said, Mike got up and walked to the counter and paid for everything. When he got done paying, he saw that his stash too, was at an all time low. With everything paid for, Mike looked at the table and saw everyone was watching him. He then waved at them and headed for the door.

Mike pulled the car up to the curb of the food spot, and waited. When Bee and the two girls walked out, Mike was all they saw. Bee opened the door and was holding the seat, to let the girls get in the back, when Mike said, "Cousin, let Rachel sit up front with me."

"Damn! All shit," both Aleasha and Bee joked, as Rachel just smiled.

With everyone in their proper place, Mike headed for Tony's house. He pulled up in the back, and the first thing he did was look around for his car, which was not there. He figured Blast was still handling his business, so he wasn't tripping. Rachel was about to get out of the car, when Mike said, "Rachel, why don't you come roll with me, and let them go in the house and do what they do."

Without a word said, she let Bee and Aleasha out and she got back in. Mike pulled off, not knowing where they were headed, then it hit him, "it's time to take a trip to the lake."

Once at the lake, they sat in the car and smoked a blunt. Then they got out and walked a little, kissed a little, and Mike figured he would leave it at that.

They then got back in the car, and headed back to Tony's. Mike was feeling good about the vibe he was getting from Rachel. On the ride back, that was all he could think about. Mike pulled up in the back, and once again, his car wasn't there. He was really starting to worry now.

As soon as he got out, his worries became reality. Mike heard someone calling his name, and looked over to Blast's stairs, to see Blast's mom. He looked at Rachel, and said, "Go on in, I'll be in, in a minute."

Rachel did what she was told, while Mike walked over to Blast's mom.

Blast's mom didn't give Mike a chance to say a word, she just dropped it on him. "I just got off the phone with my son, and he told me to tell you to come get him out of the County."

"Why is he in the County?"

"He said the police pulled him over, and some fool was with them talking about them was his rim's on your car."

Before she could get the first line out, Mike already knew what happened. Mike closed his eyes and shook his head slowly, as he said, "You don't have to say another word. When he calls back, tell him I'm on my way. Do he got bail or something?"

"Yeah, he said it's only two-fifty."

"Well, I'm gonna take care of that right now."

"Alright then."

Mike didn't even have to count his bankroll to know he had a little over $300 left, and now $250 of that was gone. Out loud, he said, "Fuck!"

He knew shit was getting real bad. Now all he could think about was the package. Mike thought to himself, "Man, if the package still ain't make it, I got to hit some kind of lick!"

Mike walked in the house, and like always, his sister was sitting on the couch. Before she could speak, Mike said, "I don't got shit for you, so don't ask."

She quickly read his face, and realized it wasn't a good time. She could tell he had something on his mind, so she let him be.

On the ride to Bee's car, not a word was said. From the way Mike stepped in the room, and said it was time to roll, everyone saw something was bothering him, so they gave him his space.

When Mike pulled up to Bee's car, he broke the silence, "Look cousin, you got to take them home, I got to go get the homie out of County."

"Don't trip cousin, it's all good."

Mike then looked at Rachel, and said, "Baby girl you gonna be with Aleasha tomorrow?"

"Yeah."

"Well, I'll see you then, but page me you got the number."

"That sounds like a winner."

"Alright y'all, I got to roll."

Mike went down to the County Jail, and paid to get Blast out. He didn't wait at the desk. Mike walked back to the car. There, he rolled up his last blunt. As he did what he loved to do, he thought about where he was doing it at. Due to the fact that he was in his "I don't give a fuck" mode, he brushed it off. Mike didn't care about the cop cars rolling up and down the street, or even about those walking up and down the street, he kept rolling.

When Blast got in the car, no one spoke. Mike just pulled off. They spent so much time going in and out of County, it was a regular thing for them. Before Blast could say it, Mike handed him the last blunt. Blast took it, and said, "Damn Cuz, how did you know what I was thinking?"

"Come on Cuz, I know you better than you know yourself."

Blast said, "I can see that," as he let his seat back. Then he lit the blunt.

Before Mike realized it, he was pulling up in front of Jackie's house. He put the car in park, and they sat there and finished up the blunt. While Mike hit the blunt one last time, he looked up at Jackie's window, to see her looking down at him. Mike then turned down the music, and looked at Blast, and said, "Cuz, I'm gonna get up with you."

"Cuz, if you need anything, just let me know."

"Don't trip Cuz, it's all good," and with that said, Mike got out of the car.

As Mike walked up to the door, Jackie was standing right there, with the door open. He prayed she had some good news for him. Without saying hi first, Mike said, "Did it get here?"

She just shook her head no. Mike pushed his way past her, and said, "Fuck!"

Jackie hated seeing him like this. She wished she could do something to help out, then it hit her! She ran up the stairs, and Mike was sitting on the couch holding his baby girl. Jackie looked him in the eyes, and said, "Mike, come in the room, I really need to talk to you."

Reluctantly, Mike made his way to the room. He hoped she wasn't on no fucking shit, because he wasn't in the mood. When he made it to the room, Jackie was sitting on the bed.

Mike stood there in the doorway looking at her, and then he said, "What's up?"

"Come in and close the door, Damn!"

Mike just shook his head, as he thought, "Here we go." Thinking he knew what she wanted, Mike laid back on the bed and grabbed her hand. Jackie pulled away, know what he was on.

She said, "That's what you thought I was on? Shit, I ain't on that."

Somewhat stunned, Mike asked, "Well what's up?"

"You need a lick, don't you?"

"Hell yeah, what's up?"

Smiling, Jackie said, "Yeah, I thought that would get your attention."

"It sure did, now what are you talking about?"

"Look, this fool parks his Blazer in the first garage downstairs, and the locks don't work on the garage."

A smile appeared on Mike's face, as he asked, "Do it got rims and beats?"

Proud of herself for corning up with such a plan to help out, Jackie replied, "Hell yeah, it got all that shit!"

That was all Mike needed to hear. He went straight to the phone and called up Dave.

When he picked up, all Mike said was, "Cuz, get over here! I'm at Jackie's, and bring a screwdriver."

Dave didn't have to think twice about it, he always knew the deal. So Dave didn't have to ask any questions, he already knew the deal, and he was more then ready to get in to something. So, as he slipped his shoes on he was like, "Cuz, don't even trip. I'm on my way."

He then hung up the phone, and quickly gathered up his things.

It didn't take Dave no time to make it to Jackie's. Once there, him and Mike went right to work. Just like Jackie said, there was rims and beast in the truck. Behind Mike's sister Tony's house is where the tag team stripped the truck. Mike took the beats, while Dave got the rims.

Feeling a lot better, Mike made his way back to Jackie's. Now that he had something to fall back on, he was in the mood for some true love making. Prouder then ever, that his girl came through for him, he blessed her time and time again that night.

GOING NOWHERE FAST
CHAPTER 20

When Mike woke up the next morning, he was feeling a lot better now that he had something to fall back on. He knew someone always wanted some nice sounds for their car, so he could quickly get a sale for his new hot goods. Everything was starting off just right, he figured. Jackie had a nice plate of cheese eggs, with toast and jelly, along with his favorite drink, which was orange Hi-C.

Just like always, his happiness was short lived. He heard someone calling his name outside, so he looked out the window to see two fools, and one had a big furry dog standing on the side of him.

Mike looked down at the two fools, with a frown on his face, as he thought, "What's up wit this two clowns?" "What's up homie, do I know you?" Mike asked, trying to get to the bottom of things.

"Nigga, where's my truck?" The fool holding the dog asked.

"Homie, I don't know what you're talking about," Mike fired back in disbelief. "So you need to move around."

"Is that right, don't even trip, I got something for your ass."

By then, Jackie walked to the window to see who Mike was talking to. As soon as she made it to the window, Mike was head to the couch, where he had his gun between the pillows.

When she saw the two fools, she then realized where

189

Mike was headed. She ran over to stop him, before he did something he couldn't take back. "Boy, don't go there please just chill."

"Baby, these niggas got me fucked up, who the fuck is that nigga anyway?"

"That's who's truck that was. Shit, he must of found out his truck was missing."

"Damn, here we go again with this bullshit!"

Mike then realized how quiet it got outside, so he went back to the window to see what was up. What he saw made a bad situation turn into a shitty one. The fool was bent over in the window of a police car, talking to the police.

Mike said, "Fuck!"

Then he walked to the rocking chair and sat down. There was only one way in, and one way out, so he knew he was trapped. He knew it was over, and sure enough, there was a knock on the door.

Jackie walked to the door, but they both knew who it was. She opened it, and the police walked in. They looked right at Mike and asked, "Is your name Mike?"

"Yep, that's me."

"Well, could you stand up, because you're under arrest, for receiving stolen property."

As they handcuffed Mike, Jackie's mom came out of the back room, and just watched as the police walked Mike out of the house.

Mike wasn't tripping, he knew they didn't have anything on him, so they would have to let him go. He figured he would spend four hours in the bull pen, then they would have to cut him loose.

Everything was going just like he knew it would. They took him straight to the bull pen. Once in there, he found him a roll of toilet paper, to use as a pillow, and he stretched out on the hard wood bench. He laid there resting his eyes, waiting for his number to come up to use the phone.

He figured he'd been in the bull pen for an hour and a half, so he sat up knowing it should have been time for him to get his phone call. Just as he sat up, he heard a lady's voice say, "Mike! You motha fucka you better get you a lawyer!"

He turned just in time to see Jackie's mom getting escorted to a back cell.

Mike sat down and racked his brain, trying to put it all together. Within the next five minutes the police called him to use the phone. He jumped right up, and walked to the cell door, "Yeah, I need to make a call."

Once at he phone, he gave the police Jackie's number. On the first ring, Jackie picked up and she was crying.

"Jackie, what's up?" Mike asked, worried sick.

"Mom tried to steal the package. She went to the post office, trying to pick it up. The police raided the house and found the gun. They said they been watching the house for like five days."

"Shit, I don't know what you're talking about," was all Mike said, then he hung up.

As quick as he sat down, was as quick as he stood up, and walked back to the bull pen door. The police officer that opened the bull pen door, for Mike to use the phone, told Mike to follow him.

Under his breath, Mike said, "Fuck," as he stood there looking at the officer walking down the hallway. The officer stopped and turned around, realizing Mike wasn't behind him.

He then said, "If you don't want to go home, I could place you back in there."

The words, "go home," were all Mike needed to hear to get him moving. He damn near ran past the officer, as he ran to catch up. "I got to put you in this other holding cell.

It's a phone in there, if you need to make a call. I'll be back in no longer than ten minutes, then I'll take you to the front window to get released."

Once in the holding tank, Mike ran right to the phone and called Bee. The phone rang four times, and Bee picked up.

" Cousin, you got to come get me right now, I'm in the County!"

"Damn, what's up?"

"Man, it's some bullshit, but fuck that, just come get me right now, alright?"

"Don't trip, I'm on my way."

Mike hung up the phone, and started pacing back and forth. The waiting was killing him, as his thoughts went wild. Everything came to a stop as soon as Mike heard the keys. His heart was beating fast, as he waited to hear the fucked up news that it was a mix up, and he was now being charged with something. The officer held the door open, and said, "Come on, I'm ready to take you up to Releasing now.

Out loud, Mike said, "Thank you Lord."

As the last word left his mouth, he and the officer started laughing.

Once outside, Mike walked to the corner to wait for Bee, and he also needed some time to reflect on what just happened.

Ten to fifteen minutes had passed, and Mike started getting irritated. Then he heard a horn. He walked in the middle of the street, and waved form side to side when he saw it was Bee.

Bee spotted Mike down the street, so he pulled up and Mike got in the car. They drove in silence for quite some time. Then out of nowhere, Mike said, "Jackie's mom tried to steal the package. Her dumb ass went down to the post office to try to pick it up."

Bee didn't say a word, he just listened, as Mike talked. "Yeah man, Jackie said the Fed's told her they been watching the house for like five days, so shit's hot. We need to lay low for a week or two, you know?"

"Yeah cousin, I feel you."

"Well, how much money do you got?"

"Shit, close to two hundred, that's all, but I got another two in work."

"Well, let's go to the building, so I can get dressed, and you can try to get that off, real quick."

" I'm with that," Bee replied.

"Then we can get up with Aleasha and Baby girl."

"Yeah, Rachel spent the night over Aleasha's last night."

"So it's on then?" Mike asked, praying for some kind of good news.

Bee smiled, and said, "And you know this, man!"

Once at the building, Bee got right down to business. He found his spot on the steps, while Mike went inside to change.

Like always, business was good at the building, and Bee enjoyed every bit of it. When Mike made it back outside from changing, he was glad to see Bee bent over in a car window, making what he knew was a sell. Instead of breaking Bee's focus, Mike just walked to his mom's car. Once he saw Bee stand up , and the car pulled off, Mike shouted, "Bee!"

Bee turned to see Mike stand by his passenger door.

Mike said, "You ready to roll?"

"Yep," Bee replied, more than ready to get to Aleasha.

Mike was feeling like a king after they dropped the girls back off. He made sure Rachel was feeling oh so good. The time alone at his sister's house paid off, like he knew it would. On the way back over south, Bee got a page, so he pulled into the gas station on the corner of Broadway and Lyndale to use the phone.

Mike figure this would be a good time to feed the engine some oil. He got the hood fixed in place, bent over and began poring. That's about as fare as he had a chance to get. Moments later, the first blow knocked him out. As soon as the beat down started, it was over, and Mike didn't a chance to see no one.

When Mike woke up the next morning, he found himself in the hospital. All he could remember, was trying to stand up, and falling back down.

When he looked around the room, he saw his mom was there, along with Jackie, and he was surprised to see Big Cie, and Blast.

When Cie looked down at him, he said, "Damn Cuz, they tried to stump you to death!"

First there was a moment of awkward silence, and then everyone in the room started laughing.

"Fuck you Cuz!"

Blast then bent down and handed Mike a pair of Loc glasses. "Here Cuz, you're gonna need these for awhile."

"Cuz, it's that bad, for real?" Mike asked.

"Hell yeah Cuz, they fucked you up!"

Right then the phone rang, and the room got quiet. Jackie picked it up, then handed it to Mike.

"Hello."

"I heard what happened. Are you alright?" Rachel asked.

"Yeah, I'm cool, but look, why don't you page me in a hour, and I should be out of here."

"Ok, just make sure you call me back."

"Don't trip, I got you."

Mike hung the phone up, and just laid there and blanked out everyone, but the thoughts of Rachel.

Ready to get things moving, his mom looked over ay him and said,"Mike, Mike, boy you hear me?"

"Yeah mom, what's up?"

"Here, take these clothe and go in the bathroom and get dressed."

Mike got out of the bed, and sat the glasses Blast gave him on the bed, as he grabbed his outfit from his mom. As soon as he made it in the bathroom, he went straight to the mirror. The sight of two black eyes almost brought tears to his eyes.

" Yeah Cuz, you was right," said Mike, as he walked straight to the bed, and picked up the glasses. "I'm a be needin' these," he added as he put them on.

Just like he figure, the room went up in gutt busting laughter.

"When y'all are done getting a good laugh off me, we can leave?"

"Don't get mad at us because you let someone get the best of you," said his mom. "And your cousin didn't help."

"Mom are you done?"

"Anyway, where was your little toy? You usually keep it with you."

"Mom, for one last time, the police took it when they raided Jackie's house."

Blast asked, "Yeah Cuz, what's up with that?"

"Whats up wit' what?"

"Yo' cousin!"

"I told him he was scary, Jackie chimed in pissed.

"Jackie, leave it alone. Come on Cuz, let's roll. Mom, I'm a need to use the car, a little later, so I'll be home after while."

"Well, I'm going down to the County building to fill out for a gun license, so I can get you new toy. Then I'll be home."

Mike was the only one in the room that wasn't surprised by what his mom just said. She spoiled him like no other mom would. It wasn't a typical way a mom would show her

195

love, but it worked for them.

"Mom, that sounds like a winner, for real."

"Oh yeah, before I forget, take your money. They found it in your pocket when they cut your pants off."

Just the word money took Mike to his happy place, and a little smile came over his face. Cheerfully he grabbed the few buck, and just by one look he knew she put some more with it. He figured she was up to date on things thanks to Jackie.

With a bit more pep in his step, Mike lead the way out to the elevator. As they waited, he gazed at the ground, as he tried to get his thoughts together. It was apparent things were moving too fast, and he knew it was time to pull back, and rethink things.

First it was his car, then it was the package, now this. The doors opened and everyone stepped in the elevator, but Mike. He stood there in his own world.

"Mike, are you coming baby, or should momma tell the doctor you're staying?"

Mike just shook his head as he walked to the elevator.

"Man, I zoned out!"

"Yeah Cuz, we see that," Blast replied.

"Blast Cuz, who's driving?"

"You know I go the Monte out there, why, what's up?"

"I wanna slide by the impound to see what's up with my car."

"Don't even trip Cuz, I got you."

Once in the parking lot, Jackie got in the car with Mike's mom, and he got in the car with Blast and Cie.

They rolled up to the impound. The clerk told Mike all he needed was some rims, then he could get his car out.

Mike looked at the clerk, thinking, "If it ain't one thing, it's another." He told the clerk he'll be back, then he walked out.

Cie saw Mike walking out of the door, so he got out of the car, and held the seat back to let Mike get in. Without saying a word, Mike just got in, and Cie got back in and closed the door.

Blast turned the music down, and he and Cie looked in the back at Mike. "Cuz, what's up, if you need something, I told you I got you."

"I'm cool Blast. Cuz, they just said I need some rims. I'll put something together by tomorrow, so I ain't trippin'."

The only thing he really wanted to do was get to Rachel. Everything else could wait.

Blast heard all he needed to hear, so he turned the music back, up and put he car in motion.

Once they made it to the freeway, it was Cie's turn to turn the music down, and this time, instead of looking back at Mike, he stayed looking straight ahead. "Cuz, what's the deal with the package I put together for you?"

"Shit Cuz, Jackie's mom tried to steal it."

"What you mean by that?"

"She went down to the post office to try to pick it up, and the Fed's was waiting for her."

"Well, did you tell her to get it?"

"Fuck No!"

Mike figured that was all Cie wanted to hear, because he turned the music back up, and didn't say another word.

GOING NOWHERE FAST
CHAPTER 21

Mike spent the next hour or so rolling around with Blast and Cie just smoking, as they made their rounds through the hood. Mike was trying to time it just right, because he wanted to be there when his mom pulled up.

His words of "drop me off at the house," and the vibration of his pager going off, were in sink with each other. As he said the last word, he look down at his pager and the sight of Rachel's number put a smile on his face.

"Damn Cuz, what you got to get into all of a sudden?" Blast asked.

"Blast, where are you trying to go with this, Cuz?"

"Cuz, all I'm saying is why can't you kick it with the homies?"

"Cuz, don't even start that, I just got something I need to take care of."

Cie turned around and looked at Mike, and said, "Well look Cuz, real soon, I'm gonna take another trip, and when I make it back I should have something for you."

"Shit Cuz, I was surprised to see you now."

"Yeah homie, I had to come back real quick, to track down some of my chips I got in these streets."

"Well Cuz, you know it's whatever with me, I guess. I'll see you when you make it back."

"Yeah Cuz, be ready."

Mike heard all he needed to hear, so he just closed his eyes and let his mind rest. He didn't know if he fell asleep, or what, but all he knew was he felt someone shaking him.

When he finally opened up his eyes, he saw Cie and Blast both looking back at him, and he could tell Cie was the one that was shaking him. He didn't say anything, and he didn't move, he just sat there on stuck mode. Cie started shaking him again, and this time he heard him calling his name.

Mike just sat there thinking,"Don't they see me looking at them?" Then he noticed, "Damn, it got dark quick." That's when he remembered he still had the dark glasses on. He started laughing, as he took them off.

"Cuz, you didn't feel me shaking you, and calling your name?" Cie asked.

"Cuz, I'm stuck as hell! I was sitting here looking at y'all, thinking, why is Cuz still shaking me? Shit, I'm looking right at him, and then, that's when I remembered these damn glasses."

Blast looked at Cie after he heard what Mike had to say, and they all started laughing.

"Yeah Cuz, you 're stuck as hell," was all Cie could say.

Mike then realized they were at the building, after he surveyed the scene. The first thing he looked for was his mom's car, and he was somewhat glad to see, it was no where in sight. He figured she should be pulling up any minute now, so everything was falling in place like he planned it.

Cie opened the door and got out, to let Mike out of the back. Before Mike got out, he put his glasses back on. Once he got out, and Cie got back in the car, Mike leaned in the window.

"Cie, make sure you get at me when you get back."

"Cuz, I got you."

"Blast, I'm gonna get up with you, Cuz."

"Well Cuz, you do that."

"Alright Cuz."

Mike then stepped back and watched, as Blast pulled off.

Mike turned around, and was glad to see that for the first time, there wasn't anyone out and about hustling. Instead of finding a spot on the steps, he figured it was best to wait in the house. He wasn't in the mood to deal with anyone at this hour.

Just like always, the door was unlocked when Mike turned the knob and gave it a little push. Right off, he knew that meant someone was sitting at the table. This irritated him because he knew he was walking into a questionnaire, and he didn't feel like being bothered.

Like he thought, Tony and his little brother Sam, were at the table, and as he walked in, all eyes were on him.

Tony couldn't help but ask, "Little bra, are you alright?"

Still trying to keep his cool, Mike only said two words, "I'm good."

Then, without another word said, Mike walked to the window and stared up into the clouds, and faced his thoughts. "Man I hate for my little brother to see me like this! When Tasha see me, what is she gonna think? They both deserve better than the madness that's around them right now. It's time for me to really pull myself together, and get things right."

Mike been entertaining thoughts like those for quite some time and he was out to make a difference for his family. Only if he knew the right way to go about it, he would then have a chance.

Tony and Sam sat at the table just watching Mike. They both knew he wanted to be left alone. If you knew Mike, you knew if he wanted to be left alone, it was best to do just that, so that's what they did.

His next move caught them by surprise. He turned around and walked out of the door, without saying a word. Together they watched, as the door closed behind him.

Sam said,"Someone's gonna get it good!"

"Yeah, you're right about that, he's pissed," Tony replied.

The sight of his mom pulling up snapped him out of his daze, and brought the thoughts of Rachel back into prospective. Once he made it outside, he was glad to see his mom no longer had Jackie with her.

"Mom, I need to use the car."

"You usually just take it, so why are you telling me now?"

"I was just letting you know."

"Well, make sure you put some more gas in it, because I filled it up. And call that girl."

Mike knew she was talking about Jackie, so he said, "I will."

He figured his, "I will," didn't sound to convincing, because his mom replied, "Boy, you know God don't like ugly."

He had no comeback for that; he knew he was playing a dirty game, but he didn't care. Just as he was getting into the car, his mom called out to him, "Mike, you be careful out there, and we should be able to go get you a new toy in a couple of days."

"Mom, I'm good don't worry, I'll be alright."

"Just watch yourself out there."

The trip to Rachel's didn't seem to take long at all. Once Mike parked, he cut the car off and just sat there. He took his glasses off and looked at himself in the rear-view. The sight of his blood shot eyes, and the black ring around each one, disgusted him. He put the glasses back on, and got out of the car.

He walked up to the door of Rachel's building, and gave it a little push. Just like he'd hoped, it was open. He walked in and took the three flights of stairs to Rachel's floor. When he made it to her door, he just stood there for a minute, and gave himself a once over. he knew first impression was everything, and he also knew there was a good chance that her mom was home. Now he hated the fact he always waited downstairs, when he came to pick her up. From foot to shoulder he felt all right, but when it came to the most important, he was a mess. He knew he couldn't take off the glasses, so he kept them on, and knocked.

He realized how nervous he was, and he cursed his heart for beating so fast.

The first time he only knocked twice and he got no answer, so he figured he should knock one more time. This time, he heard someone unlocking the door. Mike then closed his eyes, and said a little prayer, "Lord, please let it be Rachel, please let it be her."

When he heard someone answer, he opened his eyes and his prayer was answered. Rachel came to him and hugged him tight.

Mike felt himself getting hard, and he was happy she was glad to see him. Rachel then stepped back, and took his glasses off. She gave him a once over, and put them back on. "It's not that bad," she added.

"Yeah, if you say so. It's a woman's job to tell her man nice shit."

"I wouldn't lie to you. But look, are you coming in, or are you staying out there?"

Once Mike stepped in, the only thing that caught his eye, was the two little boys standing side by side, looking at him. Right away Mike knew they were twins. A quick read, and all indications pointed to trouble.

To test the water, Mike walked up to them and stuck out his hand, to give the first one a cool dap of his fist. He hoped that his read of the boys was wrong. What he got in return, gave merit to his read of them being trouble. As soon as first one kicked him in the shin, the second one was following up with a punch to Mike's two best friends. Out of instinct, Mike stepped back after he felt the sharp pain of the kick. That took away most of the force behind the punch.

As fast as it started, it was over. Rachel struck the two little boys with her own sneak attack. The sight of them scrambling to get back on their feet, as they ran off to the back room screaming, eased the pain in Mike's stomach.

"You have to excuse my two nephews, they're bad as hell!" Rachel explained.

"Yeah, I felt that in more then one place," Mike joked.

Without another word said, Rachel walked up to him and kissed him. She knew that was the cure to any man's hurt pride. She then took his hand and led the way to the couch, where they sat and watched TV until Rachel's sister came home.

From time to time, Mike felt someone watching him. When he looked, there they were, staring at him from around the comer of the hallway wall. Mike closed his eyes behind his dark glasses, as he tried to get mentally ready for the attack he knew they were planning.

"Are you ready to go, or are you staying here?" Rachel asked.

Oh, was he happy to hear her voice. When he opened his eyes, she was standing at the door, with her night bag hanging form her shoulder.

"Baby, I thought you got lost back there, so I was about to take a nap."

"Boy, let's go, I wasn't even back there that long."

Mike stood up and walked to the door, then he stopped and looked at the boys. With a big smile on his face, he said, "Bye now, I'll see you two later."

Rachel grabbed his hand, and said, "Boy, come on here, and leave them alone."

They spent the rest of the day together, just the two of them. First, they got a bite to eat, then Mike felt it would be nice to see a movie. After that, Mike made a few stops through the neighborhood, and then he felt it was time to get back to the spot.

A few blocks from the building, the flashing high beams of a car behind them caught Mike's eye. He couldn't tell who it was because the car was riding so close to his bumper. Mike knew an SA gas station was on the corner of the next block, so he told himself he would pull up in there to see who this was following him.

Everyone knew the police stayed posted up in the SA parking lot, like it was another police station. Mike was trying to use that to his advantage. He knew Rachel was watching him with a worried look on her face, but he kept on driving like there wasn't anything wrong.

He pulled in and his thoughts were flying. "Here it is, less than 24 hours ago I got attacked in a gas station, and this time I know something bad might happen."

Mike parked and went to open the door, but had to quickly close it back. The car that was following him pulled up so close, Mike thought they would rip the door clean off, if he opened it.

When Mike saw who it was, at first he was surprised, then he was enraged. Mike opened his door as much as he could and squeezed out, and then his mom's drunken boyfriend got out of his car.

"Boy, where is your mom at?"

"Look man, you better go lay your drunk ass down and sober the fuck up!"

"Boy, I said, where is your momma at? She's at your sister's ain't she?"

"You need to stop looking for my mom, and I mean that," Mike fired back, pissed.

His mom's boyfriend looked at him one last time, shook his head, and got back in is car and drove off.

Mike turned to see what he already knew; his mom's boyfriend was headed in the direction of his sister's house. As he turned to get back in the car, he realized just how deserted the gas station was; there was no one else in sight. He laughed to himself, as he thought, "Yeah, that's just my luck, if it was trouble, I was on my own like always."

With his mind focused back on the issue at hand, he got in the car and pulled off. Rachel still didn't say a word, she just watched him.

Mike appreciated the silence. He knew he had to get his thoughts together, when it came to what he was about to do, when he found, what he knew he would find.

He felt his anger rush over him, as he pulled up to his sister's house. There it was, his mom's boyfriend's car. Without a second thought, he put his car in park, in the middle of the street, and got out. He walked up to the brick wall next to his sister's front steps, and found what he was looking for. He then made his way to the door. He didn't bother to knock, he just walked right in, and as soon as he saw who was looking for, " Bam! Bam! Bam!" Was the sound brick to flesh made, as Mike smacked his mom's boyfriend in the mouth with his weapon of choice .

Ron dropped to his knees, holding his mouth, and Mike then turned to see his sister's baby's dad. Mike looked at him with the face of a mad man, and he held his stare until he was sure he got is message across. He then let the brick fall to the floor, as he walked back out. His job there was done.

Back in the car, he put both hands on the wheel, and just sat there to let this hear slow down, from beating so fast. Rachel looked at his face, then at his hands, and saw one of them bleeding. "Baby, your hand is bleeding," was the only thing she thought to say. She saw him pick up that brick, but she dared not to ask him what he did with it.

Trying to remain cool, all Mike said, even though he started feeling the stinging in his hand was, "Are you staying with me tonight?"

"Yea," Rachel replied, and she couldn't believe how fast she said it. She hoped she didn't sound desperate. She had to face it, the way she felt every time she was around him was something she wasn't used to. She'd been around a handful of niggas before, but it was something about Mike that kept her hot and wet, in all of the right places, and she loved it.

Mike heard all he needed to hear, and he picked up how fast she said it. He cracked a little smirk to himself, as he thought, "I got her."

He then pulled off, and made two stops, the weed house, and the store to get some blunts. Before he got out of the car to go in the store, he asked Rachel if she wanted anything. She said no, and Mike got out of the car and walked in.

liked the answer she gave, not because she didn't want to buy her anything, but because it let him know that she wasn't one of them girls that just had to get something because it was offered.

Once he got back in the car, he just looked at Rachel, and she was looking back at him, looking fine as ever. He then leaned over and she met him half way , and they kissed in the most passionate way. Mike reluctantly pulled away, knowing if they kept that up they would end up getting it on right there, not that, that was a bad idea.

"Damn girl," was all Mike said, as he broke their eye contact, and pulled off. She just smiled, because she knew that was a good "Damn girl," and she also liked how he seemed to now be in more of a hurry to get to where they were headed, so they could hopefully be alone.

For time like this, Mike knew there was only one place to go, so he jumped on the freeway, and headed to Motel 6. Once on the freeway, Mike looked at his hand for the first time, and then he placed it on the arm rest.

Rachel sat there in silence, watching Mike's every move. When she saw him place his hand on the arm rest, she went right to work. She looked in her night bag, and came out with a napkin and dampened it with her tongue. When she was sure it was wet enough, she grabbed his hand and gently wiped away the dry blood. When she was satisfied that she did her best, she let the window down and tossed out the used napkin.

Not once did Mike look down at his hand, but out of the corner of his eye, he saw her every move. At first, he didn't have a clue to what she was doing, but when she came out of her bag with the napkin and licked it, he understood. How many times has he become a victim of his mom's same actions? It wasn't the same, he told him self because his mom used to do it in all of the wrong places, like in school, or that time she did it on the bus when they were sitting in the back with all of them girls. He was so into the girls, he didn't even see his mom lick her thumb, until it was to late, she was already working him over. Chin in the most tightest grip ever, to make sure he couldn't move, as she licked her thumb, and went to work on the side of his mouth. All he could say was, "Mom!"

And all she said back was, "Boy, be still."

Watching Rachel do the same thing made Mike like her even more. He told himself, "This got to be the one."

Then still looking straight ahead, he said, "Thank you baby."

GOING NOWHERE FAST
CHAPTER 22

The next morning, Mike opened his eyes and was captivated by the sexually powerful, awaiting eyes of Rachel. They both laid there, looking deep into the soul of the other, just waiting for what they both knew was about to happen next. Mike felt it, and he was pretty sure Rachel felt it too, as if she wasn't the one behind the passion built up in one spot of his body.

Even thought he woke up every morning in the same state, this morning he thought he felt fingers leading it on, not that he was complaining. At first he thought it was all a dream, the exotic time they had last night, going at it for hours, then the fingers he thought he felt, but when he opened his eyes and saw her lovely eyes wide awake, he understood.

He could feel he was still naked, and he was pretty sure that she was too. So, without a word said, he climbed in between her awaiting, wide open legs. Before he could complete his move, her hand was guiding him into the spot of her body that yearned to be complete.

She laid there awake for quite some time, just watching him sleep, listening to the sounds of life as he breathed.

"Oh, how complete did he make me feel last night," she thought to herself. " And now I yearn to feel it again, and again. The way he moved, the way he touched me and kissed me, in all the right places, as if he was my body. I cant stop touching him, and all of a sudden, I cant stop touching myself. Oh, how I want to wake him up so bad!

I made sure a part of him was wide awake already, now all he needs to do is open his eyes." Just as she thought it, it happened.

He opened his eyes, and she thought to herself, "There is a God." As soon as she saw his eyes open up, she realized she was opening up her legs, getting more than ready. As they laid there, she started getting worried, when he didn't say anything.

"What's wrong with him?" she thought. "I know he's hard already, so what is he waiting for?"

Right then she realized he was moving, and it was in the directions she needed him to be moving in. There was only one thing she was looking for, and she found it as he got in position. As soon as she felt the tip of his joystick touch the spot of her body that needed to be cooling off, she heard herself say, "Yes." She then bit her bottom lip, and closed her eyes, as he slipped deep inside of her.

Once Mike took her to a stage where her body shook, like an old washing machine on spin, and the only words she could say were, "I can't take it!" Ready, he let himself go, with three more quick strokes. With the last one, he melted into Rachel's arms, as she hugged him with all of her might. Mike broke her grip, as he kissed her on the cheek, and rolled off of her, unto his back, next to her. For the next minute or so, they both remained on their backs, with their eyes closed, as they let their breathing slowed down.

Once Mike felt Rachel was back in control of herself, with his smoothest voice, he said, "Baby, go get the shower ready."

Without a word said, she jumped up and headed for the bathroom. Mike just watched his pride and joy slide across the floor, taking in the beauty of her backside. Just when she reached the bathroom door, Mike called to her, "Rachel!"

She turned around facing him, and gave him what she knew he wanted. With her hands on her hips, and her back arched so her already firm breast could stick out even more, she said, "Yes."

Her actions caught Mike off guard, and the sight of her in such a way, was too much for him to take in. he lost his train of thought, and all he could think about was the work of art standing before his very eyes. The rising of his joystick refocused his thoughts, then he asked it, "Baby, do you fuck me?"

She looked deep into his eyes, and said, "Yes." She then turned and walked into the bathroom.

Mike wasn't surprised by her answer. He knew what she would say, he just wanted to hear her say it. With that out of the way, he cracked a smile, and headed for the bathroom, right behind her.

Showered up, feeling good, and loved, they checked the room one last time before they headed to the car. Once inside the car, Mike looked at Rachel longer than usual.

"What's up Ba?" She asked.

"Rachel, baby you know you don't have to go home."

The way he was looking at her, she knew something was on his mind, and when he said what it was, she understood what he was saying. It sounded good to her; she would love to live with the man that made her feel so alive.

"Well, later you can take me by my house so I can get some of my clothes."

"I got you, don't even trip, we'll do that."

Only if Rachel knew she wasn't the only feeling so alive. Mike felt like a king, and at that moment, he didn't have a worry in the world. To him, his day was starting off just right, and he figured a time like this called for a nice breakfast.

Once they ate, all it took was the sight of the bill, for the darkness to once again take over Mike's bright day. After he paid, he knew it was time to regroup, when he saw how short he was on cash, so that meant it was time to get back to the building.

The trip to the building didn't take any time, he drove straight there. When he pulled up, he saw all of the regulars out and about, doing what they do. To his surprise, Lucky, Brandon, and Dave were sitting on the steps in front of his building.

Before Mike could get out of the car, his awaiting party were at the door. Brandon even opened it , to let him out. Rachel didn't know if this was good or bad, and she had no clue what to do. She hadn't been with him long enough to know his friends, so she didn't know if they were friend or foe.

As Mike went to get out of the car, he looked over at Rachel to see a worried look on her face. Right away, he understood. "Baby, everything's cool, don't be worried, they're friends of mine."

Rachel didn't say a thing, she just got out of the car, and stood by the passenger door, and watched Mike talked to his friends, in the street.

Mike walked over to where Rachel was standing, and took her hand as he lead the way into the building. With Rachel behind him, and the rest of the party behind her, Mike walked into his house. As he walked in the door, he saw everyone was sitting at the table, and like always, all eyes were on him. This time, he knew it was for a different reason.

His mom looked at him and smiled. When it came to her boyfriend Ron, he had a few things he needed to say as he held an ice pack to his lip. "Son, you knocked out your step dad's gold tooth! Man, you didn't have to go do all that!" "Man I told you to stop looking for my mom," Mike replied.

But you didn't want to listen," Mike added, sizing up his work. you just kept looking for her."

Rachel and the others just looked at Mike in disbelief.

Rachel then replayed the scene in her head. "So that's what he did with that brick. Damn, my man's crazy," she thought.

"I bet you'll listen next time, won't you!" Tony questioned, which caused them all to laugh.

"Come on y'all. Mom, I'll be in the back for a while, so if someone comes looking for me, send them back there."

"Boy, before y'all go back there, get you one of them paper bags on the side of the icebox, to dump that blunt stuff in."

"Be cool mom, I already know."

"Yeah, I bet you do."

Instead of stopping in the kitchen to get the bags, Mike walked his company back to the room first, then he doubled back to the kitchen. When he made it to the room, with the bag, he saw everyone had a blunt in their hand, with a crack down the middle, just waiting to empty out the tobacco.

"Yeah, we're about to get it crackin' around this bitch!" He thought, as he stepped in and closed the door behind him.

Mike opened his eyes and looked around the room, only to find Rachel looking up at him as she laid next to him, and Dave was on his other side out cold. When he didn't see Lucky and Brandon, he already knew he fucked around and passed out while they were smoking.

"Damn!" He thought.

"I was wondering how long you was gonna sleep," Rachel stated.

"Damn baby, how long was I out?"

"That's a shame, you don't remember a thing, do you?"

"Hell naw," Mike replied.

"Well, you was sleep for like a half hour."

"Is that right? Did anyone come looking for me?"

"Not that I know of, and your friends said they'll see you later."

Mike then reached over and gave Dave a shove, and said, "Cuz, get up."

As if he wasn't sleep, Dave set up, and said, "Cuz, I'm up. Shit, you're the one that passed out."

"Yeah I did that," Mike agreed. "But dig this Cuz, we got to make some moves. I need some bread."

"Cuz, you know I'm wit' whatever."

The first thing Mike did was find someone to buy his hot goods he had over at his sister's. Back on, after the sell, he and Dave, along with Rachel, sat outside of the building, hustling.

When night fell, Mike gave the rest of his crack to Rachel, and told her to go in the house and kick it with his mom. Then he and Dave jumped in the car and rolled around, until Mike found what he was looking for. All it took was thirty minutes worth of work, and Mike was on his way to get his car out of the impound; now that the had the four new rims in the back.

Surprisingly, everything went smooth at the impound. They let him get his car even though all he had was his permit papers. Once they got the rims on, Mike dropped Dave off at his mom's car, in the parking lot. He then told him he would lead the way back to the south side.

On the way back to the building, Mike stopped to pick up some weed, then to the store to get some blunts. As soon as Mike pulled up in front of the building, he saw Rachel sitting in the window. As soon as Rachel saw Mike, she jumped up and ran to the door to meet him.

He saw how fast she moved out of the window, when she saw him, so he started getting worried. He hurried up and parked. He didn't even look to see if Dave was behind him still, or what. All he cared about was seeing what was wrong with Rachel. As soon as Mike walked in the building, Rachel was standing in the hallway, with her hand out. Mike looked at her hand and saw she was holding some money.

"What's this?"

"Well, why you was gone, one of them ladies kept coming back, and me and your sister took care of her."

"Well baby, what's left?"

"We sold it all, but there was one left, and your sister asked for it. She said you wouldn't trip cause we sold everything else."

Mike took the money an then counted it; $280 dollars on the dot. "It should have been three, but Tony talked her out of one," Mike thought. He then put the money in his pocket, cracked a smile and gave Rachel a big, wet kiss. He looked at her, and thought to himself, "I'm really starting to like this girl."

As the weeks went by, things were going real good for Mike. Besides the three or four times Jackie would come to the building, and run Rachel off. Every time Mike would be driving up the street, just in time to see Rachel walking to the bus stop, with her head down. Mike would have to literally beg her to get in the car, and come back home with him, and every time she did.

Mike knew Jackie would keep coming over to the building, and he also knew Rachel was no match for Jackie. Mike like having his cake, and eating it too. Even though he was with Rachel, and she stayed with him, he still spent time with Jackie, on the side. He and Jackie had been through so much; there was no way he would ever turn his back completely on her. He loved them both in their own special way. Together, they made the perfect woman, and he had no plans on letting one, or the other go.

Then it was the 9mm, his mom bought him, that everyone that were regulars at the building, got to know. Like one night, while he and Rachel were watching TV, there was some of the regulars hanging out in front of the building, being loud. Mike looked out of the window and told them it was time for them to move around, after he looked and saw it was close to two in the morning.

They all said, "Alright Cuz, it's all good."

Mike then went back to the couch, and Rachel laid her head back on his lap. Just like he knew, five minutes later, they were still outside making noise. "Watch out baby," was all he said, as he reached under the pillow and pulled out his gun.

Use to Mike's actions, Rachel laid back down and watched him walk out of the door. With in moments all she heard was a series of gun shots, then it was the door opening and closing.

Mike didn't say a word, all he did was open the building door, and fired six shots in the air, and everyone went running. He then walked back in the house, and to the couch, where Rachel sat up to let him put the gun up, and sit back down.

Just as fast as Mike got things back on the right track, he soon realized just as fast things could once again fall apart.

It all started when Rachel asked Mike if Tony could take her to the store in his car. Mike wanted to say no so bad, but after Rachel gave him her sad baby face, he gave in, like always. He figured, since the store was only four blocks away, they should make it there and back, with no problem. On top of that, it shouldn't take them long at all.

As they pulled off, he thought to himself, "The store's only four blocks away, so why did they need to take my car in the first place?"

He then told himself, he wasn't tripping, "They'll be right back."

215

Mike made a couple sells, and that took his mind off of the issue of Tony and Rachel. When things slowed down, and he figured close to ten minutes had passed, he started getting worried. Just then, he heard some music, and when he looked down the block, he saw his car. His worries were over, so he thought. Instead of stopping, they rolled right by. Still trying to keep his cool, all he said to himself was, "I see they got jokes."

Mike was so thankful that a man walked up, asking him for something nice, for $50. That was just enough to take his mind off of the games Tony was playing with his car. So, Mike walked the man in the building hallway, to make the sell.

When he came back outside, he was just in time to see Tony and Rachel pulling up to the stop sign at the corner. As they made the turn on to the block, Mike's heart just dropped. All he said was, "Damn!"

The police car behind Tony turn their lights on, pulling them over.

Tony pulled over and parked right in front of the building. Just like that, his car was gone because Tony didn't have any license. When it came to Rachel, she too was gone, because her mom put out a missing persons report on her, after she was gone for a week.

Mike just sat there and watched, as they put his car on the flatbed of the tow truck. Then Tony was let out of the police car, while the cop pulled off with Rachel still in the back.

With one smooth swoop, his pride and joy were both gone, and once again he felt all alone. He didn't give Tony a chance to make it to the building; he met her halfway.

"Tony, what's up with Rachel, what did they say?"

"Boy, that girl's only 16."

"I don't give a fuck, I'm only 17," Mike snapped.

"So what the fuck!"

"Well, they said she ran away, so they're on their way to take her home."

That was all Mike needed to hear. He walked straight to his mom's car, got in and drove off. He knew if that was the case, she would be back at his side, by the end of the night.

GOING NOWHERE FAST
CHAPTER 23

When Mike pulled up in front of Bee's house, he was glad to see him standing on his steps, talking on his cordless. That was one thing Mike loved about himself; he was a very forgiving person. He knew most of the people that he knew wouldn't have anything else to with Bee after he sat there and watch him get attacked.

With Mike, he looked at everything as a lesson, and then he would say it was his fault for not being more aware. He knew Bee was scary, but he still hung out with him, so he chose to blame himself for what took place.

Like always, he kept the car in drive, with his gun on his lap, as he seemed to watch everything around him.

Bee was somewhat surprised to see Mike pull up, but he didn't let it show on his face. He quickly walked up to the passenger door and got in.

"What's up cousin, what are you up to?"

"I'm cool, what's up with you, are you rolling or what?"

"Well, let me take this phone in and lock up."

"Don't be bullshitting, because I would like to keep your block a peaceful place."

Bee got the message loud and clear. He didn't really care about his block staying peaceful, it was his well being that he hoped could stay peaceful. Ever since the attack at the gas station, Bee hated being around Mike and his new found friend, Mr. 9mm.

Everyone that knew Mike, and was around him most of the time, knew he was getting more and more reckless.

218

When it came to Mike, he found himself feeling deeply depressed, and the confusing part was he also found himself feeling lost. He didn't understand how that could be, when he had Rachel and Jackie. What he did realize, was when he got high, that washed away all of those feelings.

So, with that understanding, he made it his business to stay high from sun up, to sun down. Believe it or not, he was able to do this for quite some time.

Once again, Mike and Bee were a team, and things were back to normal. Mike invested all of his money in the package, and they both hustled, while Rachel and Aleasha kept them company.

Mike felt, since he was the one that paid for the package, he would let Bee do most of the hustling. Mike soon realized that wasn't good idea, because night after night, Bee would go home with the money he made for the day. So, when it was time to buy a new package, once again, Mike invested close to everything he had.

This time around, after everything was bagged up, Mike split things down the middle, and gave Bee half, as he put the other half in his pocket.

Bee handed his half to Aleasha, and she made it vanish after a dip and a tuck. Bee then let his departure be known, "Well look, I got to make a run, we'll be back a little later."

Mike was glad to hear those words from Bee, because he didn't really feel like being bother anyway. It was one of those days for Mike, where he didn't like how he started out the day, feeling. It was like everything around him was dark; the sun was covered by dark gray clouds, his mom and Tony were at it again. It just seemed his whole surroundings was trying to bring him down.

It was close to 1:00 pm, and Mike figured he already smoked four blunts by himself, not counting what he smoked with Bee.

He and Rachel sat in silence, for quite some time, and then out of no where, Mike stood up.

"Come on baby, let's roll."

As fast as he could move, he made his way to the front door and out he went. He didn't look back to see if Rachel was behind him, until he made it outside. Like always, she was behind her man, following his every move.

Once inside the car, Mike handed Rachel the package, and started up the car. He didn't have to tell her what to do with it, she already knew. She loved having some kind of purpose, when it came to her man. Whether it was holding his package, his gun, or rolling up a blunt, or washing him up after sex, it was all for the cause of love, and she loved doing it all for her man.

Mike put the car in motion, and headed for the freeway. Rachel looked over, and said, "Ba, where are we headed?"

"I need to make one stop, then I was thinking we could go out to your place and hang out, because I need to get away."

"Yeah, we can do that."

"Do you feel like cooking? And I'm not talking about no hamburger helper, neither."

"Real funny. Yeah, why?"

"I was thinking, after I make my stop we could stop at the store and pick up something for you to cook."

"How about spaghetti and fish?"

"That sounds like a winner to me, if you really know how to cook it."

"You know what? I ain't even going there with you."

"Baby, I lover you sweet ass too; now come give me a kiss."

"Nope, because all you're gonna say is I can't kiss, like I can't cook."

"Come on baby, we both know you can cook, so quit trippin'."

Like always, she gave in and gave him a big fat, wet kiss, and like always, he had something slick to say after wards, "Yeah, I knew you couldn't resist me."

She knew it was coming, so when he said it, she just smiled, and thought to herself, "He's a sweet asshole, and I love him for that."

When mike pulled up in front of his uncle Bob's house, he cut the car off and just sat there in silence. For the past week, Mike found himself feeling some what guilty for not spending more time with the only true father figure that he ever had in his life, his Uncle Bob.

Rachel didn't know what to think, as Mike at there in silence. Over the months that they been together, she learned how to accept his ways as normal, so she gave him his space. She just sat there, and waited for him to get his thoughts together.

Mike looked at the house door, and smiled at what he saw. The screen door closed, and the house door open, like always.

"Come on baby, I want you to meet someone."

Rachel looked towards the house she saw him looking at, and thought to herself, "I wonder who lives here?"

As they walked up to the house, Rachel found herself feeling a bit nervous. Before they could make it to the door, Rachel heard a man calling Mike from inside.

"Mike, is that you nephew! Bout time you came and seen your old Uncle Bob."

Right then, Rachel was able to put a face with the voice, as Uncle Bob opened the screen door, to let them in.

"What's up unc? I want you to meet someone. Rachel, this is Uncle Bob, Uncle Bob, this is Rachel."

"Hi," was all Rachel could think to say.

"Now what is a beautiful young lady like yourself doing with this maniac?"

"Well, he's a sweet maniac, so I guess that makes him special."

"I see you're as crazy as he is, so you're gonna fit right in with this family," Uncle Bob replied, laughing to himself.

"Come on baby, don't mind Uncle Bob, he's a fool," Mike stated, as he did his best to comfort her.

"Well, I'm starting to see where you get it from."

"Oh, I see everyone's got jokes now," Mike replied, as he closed the door behind him.

They spent the next hour, or so hanging out with Uncle Bob, watching TV, and sipping on a cocktail. When Uncle Bob's wife made it home from work, Mike rolled up a blunt, and they all reluctantly took their turns hitting it. Once it was gone, Mike felt it was time for him and Rachel to head out.

"Here's a little something for y'all for later, me and Rachel got to get moving."

"Well nephew, you make sure you and Rachel stop back through, and Rachel, take good care of my nephew for me, Ok?"

"I will."

"Y'all be careful out there, it's suppose to storm real bad later."

On the way to the store, Mike was praying that due to the weather, the store wouldn't be packed. Every time he would make such a trip with a woman, he would replay them long, stressful outings he would go on with his grandma. The two things he hated the most, waiting in a long line, and being in one place for a long time. The two things seemed to come with going out with his grandma, and he hated it.

His prayer was answered; they were in and out with no time wasted. Back on the road, heading for their destination, Mike found himself in a place he hated to be caught up in. He was stuck in thought, replaying one of the

worst moments of his life. When he and his best friend
Low, were playing with guns, pointing them at each other,
Low pointed his gun at Mike pointed his at Low, but
something in Mike's mind told him to pull the trigger. The
boom, then the flash, followed up by the smoke, gave birth
to confusion.
Mike then looked down at the ground to see his best friend
laying there, bleeding severely from the shoulder. Later,
they learned that if the shot would have been an inch closer
to the right, he would have died. Mike felt so bad, he
couldn't face going to the hospital, only but one time. Even
when Low as back up, and moving around, Mike couldn't
find the courage to tell Low how sorry he was, so he stayed
away from his close friend.

Ever since the horrible accident, Mike made sure no one
around him played with guns, even if they knew what they
were doing. Mike would tell them, "I thought I knew what
1 was doing when I accidentally shot my best friend, I
didn't think the gun was loaded, but now 1 know things can
happen, so no one should play with guns, not even a
gunsmith."

"Ba, don't miss the exit, you know it's coming up."

Mike was glad Rachel said something, because he knew
he would have missed it, in the daze he was in.

"Rachel, roll me up a blunt, real quick."

"Shit, it don't look like you need another one."

"I'm good, I was just in deep thought about something."

"That ain't nothing new, now give me the weed if you
want me to roll up."

"Here baby, roll up a good one too."

When they made it to Rachel's, they sat outside in the car,
while Mike smoked half of the blunt. When he was done,
he grabbed the bag out of the back, and followed Rachel up
to her apartment. Once they walked in the door, Mike

quickly looked around to see if he could spot the terrible two. He was somewhat surprised that they were nowhere in sight. From the looks of it, no one was home but them.

"Baby, where do you want me to put this bag?"

"You can put it on the table."

Rachel then walked down the hall to where the rooms were. She opened each door to see if anyone was there besides them, and what she found pleased her. They were there all alone, and she was in the mood to be touched in more than one place.

"Ba, hurry up, come here."

Not thinking anything of it, Mike followed the path she took, and he found her standing in a room doorway. When she saw him, she took a step back, forcing him to walk into the room. Once he was in the room, she walked up to him and kissed him. She broke away from the kiss, and when

Mike opened his eyes, he found her on her knees, looking up at him. She worked his belt and button, then she pulled h is pants down to his ankles. With her hand inside the slot of his boxers, she found his joystick fully alert. The finding of her prize, put a big smile on her face, and she did all of this while she kept eye contact with Mike. Such a connection slowly slipped away, as she brought Mike's joystick out for some fresh air.

The fresh air didn't last long, as it was put up once again. Instead of inside some cotton, Mike's joystick found a new home inside ofRachel's mouth. Even though Mike loved what he was feeling, he didn't want it to end like that, so he grabbed her by the chin, and lead her back to her feet. Back on her feet, she knew what was about to happen next, so with a smile on her face, she slid her pants off, while she looked deep into Mike's eyes.

The tapping on Mike's leg woke him up. At first, he didn't know where he was, then he realized, he was looking at the faces of the terrible two. At the same time, they both said, "Come on, it's time to eat."

Mike looked at the table and saw everything was set up, and Rachel's older sister and her mom, were sitting at the table.

"Man, how long was I asleep?" He thought. "I don't even remember sitting here. How did I get here anyway? The last thing I remember, me and Rachel was going at it, damn was I dreaming?"

Mike then looked at the button on his pants, and found his belt undone. Right then, he knew it wasn't a dream; he figured he must have passed out. When he looked up, he saw Rachel walking his way with a plate, and a cup of orange Hi-C, which was is favorite.

"It's cool, I can eat at the table."

"No here, you're alright."

"Thanks baby, I'm starving."

Rachel stood over Mike, as he took his first bite.

"Is it good?"

"Hell yeah!"

"Well, I told you I could cook."

"Yes you can."

Rachel then walked to the table and ate with her mom and sister and nephews. Once Mike got done eating, he was ready to get to the other half of the blunt, but he didn't say anything.

It was like Rachel was reading his mind or something, because she told her sister she was going to have to wash the dishes, because they were about to leave. When Mike heard those words, all he could do was smile, as he stood up and walked to the door, where Rachel was standing with her night bag.

"I'll see you, mom."

Even though Mike hadn't really said anything to her mom before, he felt he had to say something. So, he simply said, "Y'all take car."

"And you take care of my sister."

"I will always do that."

"Well, you can bring her home sometimes."

"I will Ms. James."

"Boy come on, alright y'all, we got to go."

Grateful that Rachel saved him once again, because he was starting to get nervous about what to say next, he just walked out. When they got in the car, Mike leaned over and gave her a kiss. It was his way of showing his gratitude for the little things she does for him. Before he started the car, he first put some fire to the half of a blunt he had waiting for him. Satisfied, he started the car and pulled out.

"Rachel, do you want to hit this?"

"Boy, no."

"Damn, it got dark quick."

"You was just asleep for a long time, and it's about to really storm. That's why it looks so dark out."

"Well, let me get us to the building."

The straight trip to the building didn't take any time. With a fresh box of blunts in the glove box, and a nice bag of wed left, Mike felt there was no need to make any stops.

"Baby, reach in the glove box, and get them blunts."

When Mike got out of the car, he was surprised to see that no one was out and about, doing what they do. Something didn't seem right. Things were too quiet for Mike. He was starting to get worried.

Right when they made it to the building door, Mike told Rachel to give him the package. She did what she was told, without thinking twice. Mike then told her to go on in the house.

Mike took hundred dollars worth of work out, and put the

five pills in his mouth. He then walked on the side of the building, and tossed the bag, with the rest of his work in it, behind the first little bush he saw.

As he walked back to the door, he realized he forgot his gun in the car. Without a second thought, he ran and got in. Before he could step inside of the building, a raindrop landed on his forehead.

For the rest of the night, Mike smoked on his bag of weed, as he listened to the storm, and watched TV with his family. As the rain came pouring down, and the wind kept blowing, everyone slowly went to their rooms to go to sleep. When it came to Rachel, she fell asleep on the couch.

Once Mike realized it was only him left, he walked to the window and sat there for quite some time, watching the storm. The pounding of the rain, the sound of the golf ball sized hail striking the cars. Then, the power of the wind, that seemed to be testing the strength of the roots of the strongest trees.

Such a sight called for one thing, and Mike had the answer. He rolled up one more blunt and smoked, as he took in the destruction of the storm.

"This is what I call peace," so he thought.

GOING NOWHERE FAST
CHAPTER 24

Like every morning, Mike woke up around the same time, but this time, there was a surprise waiting for him. As soon as they saw him open his eyes, his mom, little sister, and little brother, along with Rachel, started singing, "Happy Birthday, Happy Birthday, to you!"

As they were singing, Mike thought to himself, "How could I have forgot all about my birthday. Damn it's August 25th already, man time is flying."

"How does it feel to be a big old 18."

"Mon, don't start."

Just like he knew they would, they all rushed him punching away. Mike saw that even Rachel was in on the action, and then he realized that every now and then, the punches would get a little bit harder. He understood what was taking place, everyone was getting him back for all of the frustration that he caused everyone. He played along, as he did his best to deflect each blow.

The first sign of Mike's counter attack sent everyone running.

"y'all can run now, but I will get all of y'all, one by one, later."

Satisfied with their actions of retreating, Mike got up from the couch, and gave the spot where he was sleeping, a once over. Right away, he saw four of the five pills that he put in his mouth last night. Once he lifted up the pillow, and still didn't find the fifth one, he figured he'd swallowed it, or his mom or Tony got him for it, but either way, he wasn't tripping.

With a smile on his face, he made the trip outside to get his work. What he found quickly turned his smile into a frown. There was no longer a first, second nor third bush. The whole side of the building was a muddy mess. It was like someone snatched up everything. Along with that, he quickly realized his work was also gone. Right away, he replayed his time in the window, last night, looking at the mighty storm.

"Fuck, what the hell was I thinking?"

He kicked at the wet dirt, where the bush was once at, hoping his package would appear, which it didn't. His mind was filled with rage, and the most intense depression washed over him. He knew he had to escape the realm of such feelings, and he need to do it quick. Without a second thought, he ran to the car, started it up and pulled off.

The first stop was the corner store, then he stopped by the weed house. He kept the car running while he ran in; but before he got out, he put his fifteen dollar budget together. As he got out, he realized his gun was about to fall out of his pants. After what happened to his package, he forgot that he even grabbed his gun from under the pillow of the couch. With his gun tucked back away, he made his way to the back door of the weed house. After two knocks, the door came open and the Medicine man waved Mike in.

"What's up my man, what do you need?"

"I need two for fifteen."

"Man, I can't do it. I need twenty for two, or I can give you one for ten. Look, there fat as hell!"

Mike didn't even look at the bags the fool had in his hand. He just looked at the floor in disbelief, from what he'd just heard. Mike slide his hand under his shirt and came up with his gun. He then placed it on the kitchen counter aggressively, as he kept his finger on the trigger.

"Look my man, I spend good money with you, and now you're telling me I cant get a deal!" Mike snapped.

"You're right my man," the medicine replied, scared as fuck. "Well look man, you can have these two on me, I don't want nothing no trouble."

Mike took the tow bags and put them in his pocket, highly satisfied.

"Man I ain't on no bullshit, but you know I spend good money, so just work with me from time to time."

"You're right."

"Alright man, I'm gonna get up with you a little later."

Mike walked out to his car with his gun in hand. Before he pulled off, he sat there and rolled up. He was hoping the Medicine man would try something, so he could have a reason to release some of his frustration. When he saw that he didn't even peek out the window, Mike figured there wasn't anything going on his way. Once he got the blunt lit, he pulled off madder then when he pulled up.

Getting two free dime bags wasn't good enough; someone had to pay for his pain. He rode up and down Franklin Avenue, smoking his blunt, and looking for some new prey. It didn't take him long at all to spot who was out there selling bud. All he had to do was spot the older Mexican, standing off to the side, by himself, and watch as he would make a sell from time to time.

Mike put the blunt out, and parked a few blocks away from where he saw the man standing. Before he got out of the car, he gave himself a once over, by checking his gun, to make sure he had one in the chamber, then he tucked it back in his pants, under his shirt. Satisfied, he got out of the car and made the walk to where the man was standing.

Mike found him in a nice spot, standing at the edge of a building. This was a perfect set up for Mike, because the alley was right there, next to the building. Mike figured he would walk him down the alley, then take whatever he had.

"What's up my man, who got the fat bags around here?" Mike asked.

"You're looking at him. What are you trying to get?"

"Something real nice for eighty."

"Come on, follow me, I got something real nice for that."

Mike didn't say another word, he just followed the man down the alley, into a back yard, and up some back steps.

Mike thought to himself, "Man, this might turn out better than I planned."

Once they walked into the back door, they walked right into a kitchen. Mike closed the door behind him, but he left it cracked just a little for a quick get away. Everything in the house was quiet, and Mike was sure they were there alone. Like a hawk, he watched the man walk to a nice round, plastic trash can. After he pushed aside some old newspapers, he came out with a nice brown paper bag. Right away, Mike knew what it was filled with. He felt himself getting anxious, but he knew he had to take his time and do it right.

What happened next was too much for Mike to take. The man turned his back on HIM and put the bag on the table. Then he started looking in it.

"Now, you say you wanted something for?"

The man was unable to finish his sentence, once he felt what he knew was the barrel of a gun, pressed against the back of his head.

"Slowly, put everything in your pockets, in the bag," Mike ordered.

The man did what he was told, without any questions.

"Now, I want you to walk towards the bathroom."

Before the man knew it, Mike struck him in the back of the head with the gun. The man slumped to his knees, then he completely fell to the ground, like a sack of potatoes.

"Damn, that shit do work."

Glad, and somewhat surprised, Mike looked down at the man, to make sure he wasn't faking. Satisfied that the man was out cold, Mike picked up the bag, and made the trip back to the car. Instead of going the way he came, he took the long way to where he parked. He didn't want any of the Mexican's friends to see him walking down the street with the brown paper bag, that they all knew about.

Back in the car, he put the brown paper bag on the passenger seat, then he lit up the little blunt that was left. He sat there and smoked on the blunt to calm himself down, because his heart was still racing.

Back under control, he started up the car and made a U turn. At the cornyer, he turned down Franklin, once again, the opposite way from where he saw the Mexican standing. Thanks to the red light, Mike had time to look down at the bag on the seat. Still not sure what his prize was, because he had yet to look inside, he found himself feeling a little bit better.

His focus on his prize was interrupted by the sound of a car system. Mike looked over to his left to see a group of familiar faces, that he didn't like, at the gas station, standing around two cars. When the light turned green, instead of going straight like he had planned, he took a quick right. In between puffs he started talking to himself out loud, getting his mind set on what he was about to do.

"Cuz, who the fuck do these fools think they are. They think they can just go and do what the fuck they want! Well, I got something for they ass."

A block away, he found a parking lot for a high rise, and he figured that would be a good places to park. With the car parked between two cars, he got out and left it running. He then sprinted back to the corner, across the street form the

gas station, where he saw the fools at. As he got closer to the corner, he could tell they were still there, because he could hear their music faintly. Sure that no one was watching him, he stood close to the wall of the building on the corner, and stalked his prey form across the street.
As soon as he saw them giving each other dap of the hand, as if they were about to leave, he got at it. He waited for a car to pass, then he began walking towards them, as he gave them everything he had in his clip.

As soon as his last bullet exploded, he too was gone. The ride back to the building was made as fast as possible, by nothing but back streets, where he felt he was somewhat safe from the police.

The pounding of his heart caught his attention, and he found himself wondering why it wa beating so fast?

"Shit, I got to hurry up and make it back to the building, so I can sit my ass down, because that blunt got me fucked up."

Then he heard another voice in his mind tell him, "Nigga, it ain't the weed, it's because you're nervous as a bitch in heat."

He couldn't help but laugh, as he embraced those last thoughts, which were filled with nothing but the truth.

As he pulled up in his alley, he grabbed the brown paper bag, and placed his gun, which he had on his lap, in it. Instead of parking in front, he felt it would be best to park in back. With the paper bag in hand, he let himself in through the back door. He made sure he was as quiet as possible, he was in no mood to be questioned in any way.

It was just his luck, it wasn't quiet enough, as soon as he locked the door, his mom called out to him, "Mike, is that you?"

" Fuck," Mike whispered. "Yeah mom?"

"Come here, real quick."

He could tell from how close her voice was, that she was in her room. That was a good thing, because he couldn't let her see the bag.

"Alright, here I come mom, hold on."

Oh how happy was he too see Rachel's face, when she opened up the door, coming out of his room.

"Here baby, take this, and wait for me in the room."

Rachel looked down at the bag. She then grabbed it as she walked back in the room and closed the door.

"Mom, what's up?"

"Come on in here, I got something for you."

All it took was for Mike to walk in the room, and her taking one good look at him , for her to know something was up.

"Boy, why do you got that silly look on your face, what did you go out there and do?"

"I don't know what you are talking about."

"Boy, I know you, you can play dumb if you want to. You didn't park in the back for nothing, and where is your toy at?"

"It's in the room, I don't know why you're trippin'."

"Boy, take this money, and go have a good time and stay out of shit, it's only a hundred dollars."

"That a work, thanks. I need all of the help I can get. I lost my package last night, so I got to start all over again."

"Boy, I keep telling you to slow your ass down. Boy, here. I know I can't tell you nothing."

Mike took the money and walked out of her room, mad at himself for getting her started. When he walked in the room, Rachel was sitting on the edge of the bed with the bag between her legs. Mike grabbed it, and sat next to her on the bed. He dipped his hand in the bag, and the first thing he came out with was his gun.

"Baby, go look in the closet on the shelf, and grab me the

box of bullets and grab me a sock too."

She looked at him somewhat shocked at his requests, for the first time, but she still got up and did what she was asked.

Mike saw how she looked at him, and he didn't like it one bit.

"Baby, what's up, what's on your mind?"

"It ain't nothing, I'm alright."

But it was something, she was trying to put the puzzle together. The parking in the back, which she saw out of the bedroom window, then the worried look he had on his face when he got out of the car, with the bag in his hand. Then, it was what she saw in the bag. To top it all off, was his request for the bullets and the sock. How many times had she saw him go through that same routine. Putting bullets in his gun by using a glove, and when he didn't have a glove, he would use a sock.

The first time she saw him go through this routine, he was using a sock, and she didn't know what to think, but after the second and third time, she quickly caught on. So the one she knew for a fact, from his request, was he need to put some more bullets in his gun.

Before she left the closet, she had one last thing to do. While she was by herself, with her eyes closed, her prayer went something like this: "Dear Lord, I pray that he didn't do nothing too crazy, and I pray that he didn't hurt no one. I do thank you for bringing him safely home to me. Thank you Lord."

Feeling a lot better, her smile returned. She handed Mike the two things he requested.

"That's what I'm talking about. Smile for me baby, cause I need all the love I can get."

"And I'm the only one to give it to you."

"Well, can I have a kiss? Damn, you ain't kissed me all morning."

"If you didn't run out and do whatever it was you did, and was here with me, you could have had all the kisses you wanted."

Hearing the truth coming from someone other than him, about his actions, it was like taking a dagger to his heart. That alone caused the atmosphere in the room to change, and for the first time, Rachel saw something in Mike's eyes that she found troubling.

Mike didn't bother to reply verbally, he let his body language express just how he was feeling about her remark. He turned and looked her in the eyes, as he slid the sock on. He then gave her the most sinister smirk he could muster.

Nervous, but not sure what to do, or say, Rachel just stood there and watched him put the bullets into the clip of is gun. When she saw him put the last bullet into the clip, and he put the clip into the gun, and cocked it, she unconsciously took a step back from the spot where she was had been standing. His next move really caught her off guard, but somewhat pleased her. He put his gun in the waist band of his pants, picked up the bag, and walked out. Once she heard the back door slam, she knew he was gone.

GOING NO WHERE FAST
CHAPTER 25

As the days went by, Mike placed himself in the confines of his neighborhood. It was this thirty block radius, running east and west, and another fifteen blocks, running north and south, that became his prison.

The only venturing out he did, was when he made the trip to see Rachel, now that she was living back with her mom. When it cam to the relationships of those sharing Mike's self made prison, they seldom got neglected. It was another story when it came to those relationships with his kids and all, that didn't breath the same air as he did in his small little world.

Such segregation only caused Mike's heart to grow colder, while his views on life, grew darker. Blind to the sever change that was taking place within, he only pushed to medicate himself further with his weed smoking, and reckless actions.

Instead of hustling, while he sat on the front steps of his building, he found himself on a corner with six or seven of his homies from the hood. Dave was always one of them. He and Mike became real close. When you saw Mike, nine out of ten times, you would also see him.

Then you had Lucky and Brandon. They would stop by the corner and hang out, now that they were living back over south. Most times it wasn't a good idea, but now I give it more thought, it was never a good idea. Lucky was still enemy #1, with KeKe, and the rest of his crew, which happened to be mostly childhood friends of Mike's.

KeKe and his crew were more then welcome to come hang out in the neighborhood that Mike and his crew called their stomping grounds, and they did at times. This meant they had to stay on their toes when they hung out. Lucky didn't want to bump into the wrong person, and Mike didn't want to be caught in the middle of it, if he did.

It wasn't that Mike didn't have Lucky's back, because if he ever needed some help, Mike would be the first to step up. The thing was, Mike knew if he got into it with KeKe and his crew, he would then be forcing some of his friends, in his crew, to choose sides against the friends they all had in KeKe's crew. Mike also knew if Lucky was a part of his crew, which he wasn't officially, the outcome of this madness could come to a peaceful end.

Mike rarely drove these days. He put aside the driving, to walking and riding a bike, that he got from a feen for a pill. This type of transportation had it's up's and down's, in the eyes of Mike. Unlike driving, and being vulnerable to the cops pulling him over, and finding the heat he always kept, along with his work, he felt he could dodge the cops a lot easier, getting around this way. The down side to this, was he had limited protection against those wishing to do him harm. This gave birth to the highest level of paranoia, that Mike had ever felt before.

With every screech of a tire heard, and the speed of an oncoming car change, or even the slamming of an unseen car door, they would all cause Mike's hear to start pounding, as his hands got sweaty. He would then jerk his head in the direction of such a sound, or movements, while his right wet hand, found a resting spot on his life saver, tucked away in his waistband.

Even without such warnings, his thoughts of such encounters kept him uneasy. It was like a voice of someone else lived in the mind of Mike. With every step or pedal he took, came the taunting voice in Mike's head.

"Mike, what are you gonna do if that car coming this way is them fools that would love to kill you? If I was you, I would duck behind that parked car right there, and when they get closer, I would let them have it. Well, you better make up your mind Mike, because they're getting closer!"

There were times when the voice would get the best of Mike, and he would do what the voice suggested. It was a good thing that he would always wait to see who it was, approaching, before he finished the act. He would then stand up from behind the car, or sometimes it was a tree, and say to himself, "Fuck, this shit is crazy!"

The taunting voice would really have a good time with Mike if he found himself in a crowd of people.

"Watch out Mike, there behind you!"

Mike quickly accepted the taunting voice as being a part of him now, but to top off the chaos which became his life, came one more hurdle. Just when Mike felt his life couldn't get any more unstable, he was proved wrong. All it took was for him to take one step inside of his house, for him to realize a change was coming. The sight of boxes, along with the pictures, and the nick knacks, throughout the front room missing, he knew that could only mean one thing, his mom was packing up to move.

"Mike, is that you?"

"Yeah mom, what's up?"

"Well, if you didn't come up missing for three days, you would've known I decided to move back home with momma."

"Move back home with momma where?"

"Boy, where is momma at? Yes Cleveland, and I'm glad you're her because I need you to ride with me to get a U-haul."

"Hold on mom, let me get this right, you're moving back to Cleveland?" "That's what I said, I got to get away from this madness."

"Well, how are y'all getting there?"

"How else? By driving. And by the way, you're gonna be driving the U-haul, while me and the kids follow you in my car."

"I see you got everything figured out."

"Boy, come on here, ain't nothing else to talk about. Let's go get this U-haul, and get that out of the way."

Once they made it to the car, Mike walked to the passenger door and got in. through the front window, his mom looked at him sitting there, with that silly frown on his face. She shook her head, and walked to the drivers door and got in. Before she started up the car, she looked over at Mike still sitting there with that long face, she hated to see.

"What's up, you ain't driving today?"

"I'm cool, go head and drive ma'."

She knew her moving back to Cleveland would bother him, and she saw it was. One thing she hated, just like any other mother, was hurting her baby. For this reason, it made her decision to move back to Cleveland, a hard one to make.

She hoped Mike would like the idea of moving back home, and he would stay down there with her, but she had to face the fact of who she was talking about. She knew it wasn't going to happen. For two days, she prayed that Mike would understand this was the best move for her to make. She knew he hated seeing her using. So, she felt if she got away form those that kept pulling her down, she would have a better chance of getting her life back together. So, for Mike's future happiness, along with the rest of the kids, and her own, she felt moving away was the best move to make. "Hurt now, but be proud later," is how she looked at it when it came to Mike, and his feelings.

Hearing such news was like someone taking a dagger to Mike's heart. He knew, the fact that she was packing up to move was bad in itself, but hearing where she was moving to, was a whole other story. The thought of loosing the little structure he had left in his life, place him in a state of disbelief.

"Man, I can't believe this shit is happening. What the fuck am I suppose to do? She knows damn well, I'm not trying to move to fucking Cleveland. Shit, if Jackie would of got her own spot, like I told her, shit will be cool. I ain't fucking with Rachel and her mom. I could go to Aunt Rhonda's, but fuck that, ain't no fucking going on over there, so that ain't the move. Damn! I got to come up with something quick. Then I got to deal with the fact that once mom's gone, who's gonna be my backbone then? Damn, this shit is fucked up!"

After driving for ten minutes in complete silence, while they allowed the other to embrace the many thoughts that were running through their minds, Mike's mom said something she knew he'd love to hear.

"Well I talked to your uncle Bob and he said he would loved for you to come stay with him. Now that's if you don't plan on staying in Cleveland with us."

Hearing those words was like sweet music to his ears. The thought of a proper reply wasn't needed. There was only one right answer on his mind.

"Well, I guess I'm gonna have to take my clothes over there tonight then." With that said, Mike had one last thought, as he smiled. " Man, I love that woman!"

GOING NOWHERE FAST
CHAPTER 26

Instead of making the trip to Cleveland to drop off the U-haul, and coming back on the Greyhound, the trip turned into a three week vacation for Mike. He found that by being away from the madness back home, gave birth to a peace of mind was truly needed.

Day in and day out, he would find himself sitting on the front steps of his grandma's house. He would sit there watching the unfamiliar faces of the kids that lived on the block, playing in the street. The more he watched the kids play, the more he started to admire their focus and dedication, when it came to them achieving their goal of having fun. It was this display of such actions that refueled Mike's drive to dust himself off, and fight back.

"If I was that focused and dedicated to my hustle, I know I could get my money right."

He entertained the thought, over and over again, while he took in the beauty of seeing the kids enjoying themselves. All it took was for Mike to think that same thought for the tenth time. He stood up and dusted himself off, as he said, "Who's to say shorties can't be inspirational." With that said, he walked in the house with only one thing on his mind.

As soon as he saw his mom, he let his mission be know, "Mom, take me to the bus station, I'm ready."

She couldn't help but ask, "Boy ready for what?"

"I'm ready to go back home."

"Why all of a sudden?"

"Look mom, I'm really not trying to go through all of this."

"Well, boy let me get myself together, and I'll take you, but I waqnt you to know, I don't want you to leave."

"I know you don't, but I got to go."

Know she was going to tum up the pressure to get him to stay, Mike didn't say another word, he just walked away. He was in no mood to fall victim to that motherly wisdom that she always seemed to have when he had his mind set on doing something.

As he walked into the back room, he thought about the many times she tired to get him to stay home. She would always end up saying, "Baby, please stay home tonight. I got a bad feeling that if you go out, something bad is gonna happen to you."

Then he was forced to think about how he would brush her warning off, by saying, "Mom, you're trippin', I'll be alright."

It was the end result that he really hated to think about. The night would end by him making that dreadful call home. It never seemed to surprise him, how she would pick up on the first ring, already knowing it was him.

All she would say was, "Mike, where are you?"

After he swallowed his pride, his reply would be, "You already know where I'm at, now would you please come and get me? You was right, I'm down in Juvenile."

Mike had no room in his plans for that "mother, you was right" curse, so he figured, the less they talk, the less chance she would have to lay it on him.

far, so good, he thought, as he walked into the room to pack. As he gathered up this things, his mind was racing with thoughts, "Now all I go to worry about is the ride to the bus station. Fuck! I don't know how I'm gonna survive that. Well, now's a good time for me to step up my game, when it comes to staying on my toes. Lord knows if I can master the task of preventing mom from hitting me with that motherly curse, I can master the task of getting my money right. This shit's really eating me up inside, and I'm sick of feeling this way. I got to be there for Rachel, now that she's pregnant, and I'm gonna make sure this baby has the very best, from start to finish. I got a job to do, and I'm gonna make sure I do it right. Most likely, Cie will be back in town, when I touch down, so I got to hook up with him right away."

"Mike, Mike, Michael! Boy, I know you hear me calling you." His mom snapped.

Mike just happened to glance over at the door. He was surprised to see his mom standing there, staring at him.

"Mom, what's up, was you calling me?"

"Boy, that don't make no sense, you didn't hear me calling you? I was standing right there."

"I didn't hear nothing. You know how I get when I'm thinking about something."

"Well, I'm ready to take you to the bus station. Are you ready or what?"

Mike looked down at his bag. He was surprised to see that his things were packed away already. He took it as a good sign that everything was falling into place for him. A big smile appeared on his face, and his mom zoomed in on it.

"Boy, what's that big smile on you face all about?"

"Mom, I'm feeling good, and I know better days are coming."

Feeling better than he had in months, he snatched up his bag. He then brushed past his mom, as he made his way out of the room. She took a step back, and watched, as Mike headed for the front door. She just had to ask, "Mike, ain't you forgetting something? You ain't gonna say bye to your grandma?"

"Damn!" He thought. "I'm speeding like a motha fucka. How could I forget about grandma?"

To play it off, he simply said, "Mom, I'm just taking my bag to the car. You know I can't forget about grandma."

His mom didn't care to respond to such B.S, she just watched, as he walked out of the front door. With her hands on her hips, she shook her head, as she thought, "Yeah right, I bet you didn't forget about her."

When Mike walked out of the door, his little sister and brother stopped playing. From a friends yard, across the street, they both watched Mike's walked to the car with his bag in his hand. Together, they watched Mike's every move.

Still not knowing he was under surveillance, Mike placed his bag in the car. He then headed back inside. As soon as he stepped in, he saw his mom and grandma sitting at the dinning room table, talking.

When Mike's mom and grandma heard the house door close, they looked up to see Mike standing there. It was his grandma that spoke first.

"Baby, come over here and give your grandma a hug a kiss. Your mom told me you're going back to Minnesota today. Well, be careful, and here take this. Me and your mom put a couple of dollars together for you."

Mike walked over to the table and gave her a hug, as he took the money. With the money in hand, he looked over at his mom. She was giving him that look, and he knew what she was thinking, "Boy just think, you forgot all about her."

He was right, because that's just what was on her mind. Ready to get moving, Mike's mom said, "Momma look, if anyone calls me while I'm gone, let them know I had to take my son to the bus station. Let them know I'll be back in an hour and a half. So boy come on here, let's get this over with. I got a date tonight, and I'm not about to miss it."

Before Mike headed for the door, he put the money in his

pocket, and said, "Alright grandma, take care."
She replied, "Now you be safe, and you call if you ever
need something."

"I will," was all Mike said, he then followed his mom, as
she walked out of the front door. As soon as he made it
outside, he looked and saw his little brother and sister
sitting in the back of the car. They were both looking his
way.

Together, the sat there thinking, "I know my big brother
didn't think he was getting away without saying bye to me."

Wearing a smile, which was a reflection of embarrassment,
Mike walked to the car. All the while, in his mind he did his
best to justify his actions. "My grandma's one thing, but to
forget about them, is something else. I guess I'm just
focused on getting my money right."

The ride to the bus station was going just like he hoped it
would. No one was really talking. The only action going on
in the car was from his brother and sister taking turns
playing with his ears. Then playfully, they pulled his hair,
and pinched his neck. From time to time, they would find a
way to hug him the best way they could.

It was his sweet little sister that changed the temperature
in the car. She leaned in between the driver's seat and
passenger seat, and asked, "Mike, do you have to go? Why
cant you stay here with us?"

All of the sudden, Mike felt like he was placed on the hot
seat. He felt the sweat building up under his shirt. His mind
started racing with thoughts, "Man, I got to put out this fire,
quick, before my mom starts throwing her wood into the
flames. Lord knows I wont be able to put it out if that
happens."

He saw the answer to the burning fire coming up on the
next corner. As calm as he possible could, he said, "I wont
be gone that long. I'll be back before you know it. A mom,

stop at that store on the next corner, I need to grab
something, real quick."

His mom looked over at him with a smirk on her face, and
said, "Yeah, I bet you do, all of sudden. You know I know
you better then you know yourself. Anyway, grab your
mom a root beer why you're in there."

"Do y'all want something?" Mike asked to the two in the
back.

"Yeah, I want some gum," Tasha replied.

When it came to Sam, he had other plans. He said, "I'm
going in with you, so I can pick out what I want."

Knowing what was coming next, Mike beat Tasha to it.
He opened the door, and said, "Y'all both come in."

Mike listened to one of the three tapes that he had, in his
new Walkman, that he bought. Mike's plan was, tune
everyone out for the rest of the ride to the bus station. This
way, he was sure to be safe from the motherly curse.

While Mike was bobbing his head to the beat, the two in
the back were confused about something. They were
wondering why Mike was wasting his batteries, when he
could listen to the same tape in the car tape deck.

His mom understood such a tactic could only mean one
thing, he was trying to sound someone out. She knew she
was the intended target, and she was fine with that. It was
knowing that his silent act was making the little ones in the
back suffer, that was eating at her. She drove for quite some
time, sucking it up. She was doing her best to keep her
cool, but she couldn't take it any longer. She let her
disapproval of such actions be known, by saying over and
over again, "That don't make no sense, that's real selfish!"

The little ones in the back just looked at each other. They
both knew that trouble was coming. "Mom and Mike are at
it again, but why?" they thought.

Out of the corner of his eye, Mike saw her lips moving,

but he didn't care to know what she was saying. He knew it wasn't good, and whatever she was saying, was meant for only one person, him.

Focused straight ahead, like an airplane navigator, Mike fixed his sight on the bus station, which was coming into view, two blocks away. The closer they got, the more confident he got, when it came to him dodging the motherly curse. So, he couldn't help but think, "Yes! I beat her, now I know, can't nothing stop me!"

He then closed his eyes, and rocked his head to the beat. Once he felt the car slowing down, he opened up his eyes, thinking they were there. He soon realized the only reason they were stopping, was because of the light turning red. His disappointment was quickly washed away by him realizing the bus station was only across the street.

Just as Mike closed his eyes again, he felt someone removing his headphones. Right away, he knew it was someone in the back. Then he heard her sweet little voice, which after he heard what she had to say, he wished he didn't hear it at all.

"Mike, do you really have to go? I'm scared that if you go to far, my prayers wont be able to keep you safe, and something bad might happen to you. Like that time you had to wear them dark glasses."

The car went silent, as she said what was on her precious little mind. Instead of being inside of a car, it was more like a ghost town. Everything seemed to be moving in slow motion, in the eyes of Mike.

"How could she, of all people, hit me with such a message?" he thought.

Hearing such words from her daughter, made Mike's mom oh so proud. With a smile on her face, she turned around and looked at her daughter. She then said, "I couldn't of said it no better."

The light turned green, and she pulled off. It didn't take her long to spot the open parking spot in front of the bus station.

Mike still didn't say a word, he didn't even put his head phones back on. He just sat there, stunned. "Please, not like this," is all he thought. His mom looked over at him, and she saw that look of defeat in his eyes.

"Oh, that's what it was, he was trying to prevent me form talking him out of leaving, by saying if he leaves, I feel something bad is gonna happen to him. Well, he did that , but he had no clue his little sister would do it for me. Now I just hope he does the right thing," she thought.

With a full understanding of things, she couldn't help but laugh. Feeling the need to rub it in, she felt she had to ask one or two questions. "Mike, what's up, you don't have nothing to say to your sister? Now are you sure you still want to leave? Because you know, just like your little sister said, not me, something bad might happen to you."

She did good at first, but she couldn't hold it any longer, she started laughing so hard, she couldn't hold back the tears.

Mike looked at her, and right away he knew she figured out what he was trying to do. He then turned and looked at his sister, and said, "I'll be back soon, just keep praying for me."

"I will."

"Sam, you take care of your little sister while I'm gone, and I mean that."

"I know."

As Mike squeezed between the drivers and passengers seat, to get his bag, they both gave him a big hug. Before he got out, he gave his mom a hug and a kiss. She had only three words to say, "Mike, be careful."

Mike got out of the car and watched, as they drove off.

Out of the back window, the two waved at Mike.
 As he did his best to keep sight of the car, he thought,
" There's no way Tasha knows what she's talkin' bout....
Hell naw!"

GOING NOWHERE FAST
CHAPTER 27

Mike laid there, awake in his bed at his Uncle Bob's house. He was replaying everything that happened in the last two month, since he'd been back in town.

He made it his business to come back in October, which was always a good month for him, ever since his daughter Shonna was born. This year, her birthday didn't bring Mike enough joy to wash away the pain and guilt he was dealing with, which came from the death of his very close friend, Lucky.

Mike thought about the last conversation he had with Lucky. It was the same day Lucky officially joined Mike's crew, and chose to be Lil' Kaos?

" Cuz, why lil Kaos?" Mike asked.

"When I die Cuz, I want it to be chaos at my funeral, homie," Lucky's replied.

Somewhat confused, Mike said, "Well Cuz look, do what you do. I got to make a move. I'll see you when I see you."

At first, such an answer didn't make sense to Mike. Two days later, when he found out Lucky got killed, he was still trying to make sense of it.

Next, came the part Mike hated the most, how he beat himself up for five days straight, until Lucky's funeral. He told himself over and over again, "If only I would have been there. I know if I was there, there's no way I would of let him go into that crack head's house by himself, to try and save his girlfriend. Man! His mom told him to leave that bitch alone! Cuz why didn't you listen?"

The only part of this madness Mike didn't mind going over in his head, was how he was able to find peace, when it came to this matter. He remembered how he found a seat in the back of the funeral home, and watched as all of the familiar faces cried and hugged each other. Mike figured he would let everyone walk up to the casket, and pay their respects to Lucky first. Then he would get in line last.

Mike slouched back in his chair, and closed his eyes. He let his mind drift off into a world of his very own.

Mike was quickly forced back into the world of madness. First by the sound of women screaming, and chairs being knocked over. Then, once Mike opened his eyes, it was the sight of more then four people fighting. Mike didn't budge, he remained seated, as he looked straight ahead at the casket. He cracked a smile, as he thought, "Well Cuz, you got your wish homie. It all makes sense now."

Mike realized how it seemed someone was tugging at the loose thread, that held his frail little life together. First, it was his mom moving back to Cleveland, then it was the death of Lucky, and soon after that, he found out just how unstable Rachel could be.

There was no way he could remain laying down. Mike had to sit up, as he thought about what happened between him and Rachel.

Mike woke up that morning feeling like a king. Rachel woke him up with her good morning special, like she did every morning. Under the mattress, was the package he got before he went to bed. The keys to the car, he bought two days prior, were also under there. Mike felt like he felt so many other times, proud of himself, because he was making progress. He knew he was on the path to the top, and this time, "Wasn't nothing going to stop him."

After Mike and Rachel pleased each other, Mike rolled out of the bed. He then stood up, and said, "Come on baby, you're rolling with me today."

Rachel didn't say anything in return. She just smiled, because she was more than happy to hear those words.

Showered up and dressed, Mike rolled up, as he waited for Rachel to get herself together. By the time Rachel came out of the bathroom, Mike smoked the first blunt, and he was rolling up a second one.

Rachel stood in the door way of their room, looking at Mike, and said, "Ba, do you want me to cook something real quick, or are you ready to go now?"

"Shit, I thought something bad happened to you in there."

"Yeah whatever, I wasn't in there that long."

"Baby, yes you was. But anyway, don't even trip, we'll stop somewhere while we're out."

"Alright, well I'm ready."

Mike then gathered up his paraphernalia, which helped him live the life he was trying to live. Before he walked out of the house, he remembered to turn on his pager. Within ten seconds, it went off. He looked down to see who it was, and the sight of the code behind the number, put a smile on his face.

Rachel zoomed in on such a smile. Needing some answers, she said, "Well, who is that, that got you smiling?"

"Girl, don't start that shit, it's a feen over south."

"And?"

"He must got some money for me. I'm got to slide over there real quick."

"Well, you know your baby needs to eat."

"Be cool, we're gonna eat, and don't start stressing. I don't want little man in you stomach stressing with you."

"Well, how do you know it's a boy?"

"It it, trust me."

"If you say so."

"I do, and push that lighter in for me."

Mike sat there on his bed, and remembered just how high he got that day. It was due to the fact that he spent the whole day with Rachel. Every blunt he had her roll up for him while he kept driving, he had the luxury of smoking each one by himself.

Halfway through the nigh, when Mike's high was at it's peak, he looked in the rear view. What he saw almost made him lose his breakfast, lunch, and the little dinner that he had. It was cop car coming up behind him fast. In a low whisper, he said, "Ba, when I turn this corner, I want you to crack your door, like I taught you, and slowly drop that shit."

"Why?"

"Because, the haters are on my dick, but don't look back."

Mike was glad that he disconnected the interior light, when he first got the car. If he didn't, he knew such a move wouldn't work.

Rachel did what she was told, and she did it as smooth as a pro. Mike didn't have time to show any signs of appreciation. His mind was racing with the thoughts of what his next move should be. He turned, and the police turned with him, like he knew they would. It was only a matter of time, before they would hit their lights, and he knew it.

Mike frantically looked from side to side, trying to figure out just were they were at. That's when he was blessed with a beautiful sight. He realized just where they were. He could see his Aunt Rhonda's apartment building, coming up on his right. Mike quickly pulled into the open parking spot, in front of her building, and cut his car off. He and Rachel both got out and slowly, as the cops crept past.

Before Mike took a step, he had to let his heart find it's normal rhythm. He then had to steady himself, because he didn't trust his ability to walk.

Once he felt somewhat comfortable, Mike walked to the building. At the door, he buzzed his aunties apartment number, and like always, Rachel was right by his side.

"Ba, do you think we should walk down there, and grab that before someone finds it?" Rachel asked.

"I don't trust them bitches. They're probably in the cut right now watching us, just waiting for us to make a move. So we're gonna go up in here and chill at my aunts."

Once they got inside, and Mike had a chance to sit down and relax, he realized just how high and tired he was. He glance at Rachel, and said, "Baby, look, I'm gonna take a quick nap to clear my head, then we're gonna hit the highway to get out to the house."

"Whatever," she replied.

Mike figured, he was only asleep for no more than ten minutes before the shaking of his shoulder started. Rachel was behind such action, and she kept saying, "Mike, get up, I'm ready go home. Mike, come on get up."

With his eyes closed, he said, "Damn Rachel, be cool, shit!"

After he brushed her off, he quickly went back to sleep. But again, that didn't last long. This time it was the sound of the apartment door closing, that woke him. Right away, he knew it was Rachel leaving. He entertained the thought of jumping and running after her, but he decided if she wanted to act stuck and leave, so be it. That decision too, was short lived because his aunty stepped in to refocus his plans.

"Boy, get up, and take that girl home!"

It didn't take him no time to fall in line with her orders. His only words were, "Alright aunty, I got her. Man, I told her all I needed was a little rest."

"Well, you shouldn't of been smoking all of that stuff you

love so much."

Mike got himself together, and as he stood up, he started feeling a lot better. He even felt like smoking the last blunt he had rolled up.

"Well aunty, let me take his girl home. I'll slide back through sometime this week."

"Alright baby, I love, and be safe out there."

"I love you too aunty, and I'll be alright."

"Ok now."

Once he tapped his pockets, and looked on the table where he knew he put his keys and they weren't there, he felt like his whole world was lost. Without another word said, he ran out of the door, and he didn't stop until he made it outside, only to see his car still parked. "Thank God," he said, "I don't know what I would have done if she took my car."

Like every other time in his life, such peace of mind didn't last that long. "If my car is here, then where the fuck is Rachel and my keys?" He thought. " Fuck, her crazy ass is about to get on the bus with my keys."

He then looked down at his pager to see what time it was. The sight of 12:30 am, sent him running again. This time he was headed for the bus stop. He knew Rachel was there.

"Lord, please let the last bus be late. Fuck, do it come at 12:35 or 12:40? Fuck! I got to hurry up and get there before the bus do."

As the bus stop stared to come into view, right away he saw Rachel standing there looking at him.

"Girl, come on, let me take you home."

Rachel didn't say anything until he finished crossing the street.

"You didn't want to take me home when I wanted to go, so now I'm getting on the bus."

"Then where's my keys? Shit, why don't you just bring

your ass on, and let me take you home?"

"You didn't care a little while ago, so why do you care now?"

"Look, I'm not trying to go through this with you."

"Well, I'm about to get on the bus, and here it comes."

"Rachel, stop playing, you're not getting on the bus with my keys."

When the bus pulled up, the bus driver opened the door, and Mike said, "We're not waiting."

The bus driver then closed the door, and pulled off. Mike then looked at Rachel, and said, "Now, are you ready to walk back to the car, so I can take you home? You know that was the last bus."

"I don't care, you're still not getting your keys."

Hearing that, sent Mike to his boiling point. He couldn't face her any longer because he knew he was one step from losing control. So, he turned his back on her, and said, "Rachel, why the fuck are you playing these fucking games? You're about to make me fuck you up. Damn!"

When she didn't respond, Mike turned around, only to see her running down the street. The last thing he remembered, before he blacked out, was Rachel falling to the ground, and him standing over her. When he came to, he found himself in the back of a police car, on his way to the County Jail.

"Officer, what am I being charged with?" Mike asked, beyond confused.

"Right now, it's for a family court warrant, I guess you owe some child support, or something. Yeah, that's what it is. Most likely you'll go to court in the morning, and I see you've got the money on you, so you should be able to handle whatever you owe, if it's not that bad."

Right then, Mike remembered about his package. "Fuck!" Is all he said.

The family court worked out just like the officer predicted. Mike paid, and the warrant was dropped. What Mike soon found out, when he was escorted out of the court room by a guard, was he had another court appearance to make on the third floor. He didn't understand at first, and that quickly changed when he walked in the courtroom, and saw Rachel. She was sitting at the table with what looked like a prosecutor. Like so many other days of his, this day quickly went from sugar to shit.

Mike spent the next two days on the phone, in County Jail, convincing Rachel he was sorry, and he still loved her. After the 59th call, he got through to her, and she went down to the County, and dropped the charge.

Mike was brought back to present by the sound of his Uncle Bob's voice.

"Mike, come out here and smoke one with you Uncle Bob."

Mike sat there on his bed for a minute or two, in silence. He was still reflecting on his ordeal with Rachel.
He then shook his head slowly from side to side, as he thought, "Man, I can't believe I'm still fucking with her crazy ass."

GOING NOWHERE FAST
CHAPTER 28

With every aspect of his life in shambles, and the taunting voice in his head, back singing a new tune, Mike knew there was only one cure for such a sickness, Smoke until you numb the pain, was the only answer. And that's just what he did.

To act fast on such an antidote was a must, because Mike found himself starting to believe what the taunting voice was saying, over and over again to him.

"Mike, you fucked up again. Damn, you will never get it right, so face it, you're a true fuck up!"

Mike quickly teamed up with Dave, and together, they marched through the sticky snow in search of their prey. After ten block on their cold journey, they spotted what they was looking for.

"I know he's got good weed," Dave stated firmly.

Mike took one look, and smiled when he saw the old Mexican man looking his way.

"Cuz, I hope this fool ain't at the same spot I hit awhile back, but shit, fuck it if he is."

"Mike, where we gonna hit him at? Right here?"

"Cuz, just follow my lead, he's gonna take us to his spot. Fuck that, because what I need, he ain't got on him. Feel me?"

Oh, Dave felt it, and the Mexican soon felt something too. He felt the butt of both guns, as they slapped him in the chicken wing, before running his pockets.

Mike laid there for a moment watching Rachel as she gazed

out of their bedroom window.

"I wonder what she's looking at," he thought.

Feeling like some one was watching her, Rachel turned around with her lil belly poking out. Right away she locked eyes with Mike and smiled.

"How long have you been up?" She asked.

"Not that long," Mike replied, as he focused in on her lil tummy.

"Damn, your stomach is getting big as fuck!" Mike stated.

"This is how big it pose to be at five months. It's the same size it was two days ago when you was rubbing it."

"It's been five months, for real?" Mike asked.

"Yea, crazy," Rachel replied, now smiling from ear to ear.

"Damn! It seems like you was just two months yesterday."

"Yea time is flying," Rachel agreed.

" A baby, did someone drop me off last night?"

"Yeah, I think it was your homie that just got up here from California. I think his name is Stone, or something like that."

"Is that right?"

"Yep. We was suppose to go out to eat, and to a movie last night, because you're suppose to be going out of town to see your mom. The only reason we didn't go is because you was so fuckin' high. Shit, like you been for the last three months."

"Hold on. You say I'm pose to go see my mom today, for real?"

"Yeah, I got your bus ticket right here in my purse. Boy, you need to lay off the weed for awhile, because you cant remember shit."

"Look, fuck all that. When do my bus leave? Damn!"

"Don't be getting no attitude with me because you can't remember what you did last week, let alone yesterday."

Mike felt his temperature rising, so before he snapped on

her, he walked out of the room. He figured a nice hot shower would do the trick of relaxing him, so he headed for the bathroom. He soon found out a hot shower wasn't always the best way to go. Instead of clearing his mind, it gave birth to a mighty storm of questions, which he had no answers to. The longer Mike kept his head under the water, the more he racked his brain trying to put together the pieces to the puzzle.

Like every other unpleasant situation Mike got himself in, he made sure this situation too, ended quickly. His means of escape, this time around, wasn't weed, sex, or even a drink, it was achieved by him simply getting out of the shower. As he dried off, he couldn't believe how he was feeling worse off then when he first got in.

"Man, why the fuck am I feeling like this?"

"Ba, I didn't hear you, what did you say?"

So caught up in the whirlwind of his own madness, he didn't even realize he had spoken out loud.

"Man oh man, I'm really tripping. Shit! I need a blunt."

No sooner did he think it, Rachel was walking in the bathroom with a lit blunt. As she handed it to him, she said, "Ba, take this and relax."

Firmly gripping the blunt, Mike said, "Baby, you must of read my mind. Damn! Where did you get this from?"

"I knew one of these days you'd be stressing, so I put a little something up for you. I took I out of that big bag you had awhile back."

"Girl, you truly are a life a life saver." "Yeah, I love you too."

Back in his comfort zone, with his lungs filled with smoke, Mike took his time, and got dressed. As he did so, Rachel sat on the bed and watched.

"Baby, you still didn't tell me when my busleaves?"

"Well, I just called when you was in the shower, and one leaves at 1:30, 5:30, 7:00, 9:00, and 12:00 midnight; it's up to you."

"What time is it now?"

"Let me see, it's close to 11:00."

"Well look, call me a cab. I'm gonna try to make the 1:30 bus."

"Ba, why do you got to leave so soon? Why can't you take one of the later ones?"

"Baby, let's not go through this, please!"

"Alright, alright, how long are you gonna be gone?"

"No more than a weeks. That's not gonna kill you. Is it?"

"Yep, but I ain't gonna say nothing."

Once Mike finished getting dressed, he told Rachel to stand up. He had to get under the mattress to get the little money that he had, along with his gun. When he lifted it up, he was shocked to see what he knew was two ounces of weed.

"Damn baby, I thought I didn't have no more weed."

"I didn't think so either."

"Where did I get this?" Mike asked, showing her. "Don't ask me, you must of put it there last night when you came in."

"Well, shit, I ain't complaining, this should hold me while I'm gone."

It did hold him for a little over a week. When it was all gone, he took his frustration out on the dirty streets of Cleveland. He woke up every morning around 5:30 a.m, got dressed, jumped in his mom's car, and got on the search for his daily prey.

His mind was once again so clouded, he had no clue just how reckless his actions had become. Mike didn't care what the situation was. If he had the impulse to lash out, there was no stopping him. His older sister Tony had the chance to see his madness, first hand.

It started out as a typical ride to the store. While Mike drove, Tony rocked her head to the beat of the song that was playing on the radio. The ride was going just fine until the light quickly turned red, and Mike had to slam on the brakes before he ran into the back of the car in front of him.

"Damn! Why didn't he just go through the fucking light?"

"Boy!"

Before Tony could say another word, Mike looked over at her with that look she hated to see. Instead of matching his stare, she turned her head and looked out of the window, as if to say, "What are you looking at?"

Before she knew it, she heard the door slam, then she saw Mike walking up to a young man. She then stuck her head out of the window to get a better look. That's when she saw Mike pulling out his gun. In shock, she watched as the young man lay face down. Mike then went through his pockets, socks, shoes, and he even made the young man spit something out of his mouth.

Mike didn't care about them being on a busy street, or it being broad daylight out. When he saw the transaction, it was time to act. With no hesitation, or second thought, he put the car in park, got out, and pulled it. Not only did he take all of the young man's money, he also took the four pills he had in his mouth. On top of that, he found a glass tube, of what he knew was "Wet."

The honking horns of the cars that were forced to drive around his car didn't stop him, nor did the few people standing on the comer, watching in disbelief. It wasn't until he was satisfied with his search, that he then calmly walked back to his car and drove off.

Tony's reaction did nothing but feed his ego even more.

"Boy, you are crazy, but can we do that again?"

"Girl, quit trippin'."

"Well, how much did we get?"

"We, Hell! I'm about to take my ass back to Minnesota with his little change."

"At least let me get a dub."

"Here, take these four pills, and don't ask for shit else."

"Why are they so wet?"

"He had them in his mouth. Now please leave me alone so I can think."

"That's what I'm talking about, cut me in, or cut it out."

"Keep talking shit and you'll be walking home."

"Boy, don't play."

"Well, be cool then, shit."

"Alright, I'm done, but look, you're about to go back home for real?"

"Yeah, I'm about to turn the hood out with his wet."

"Boy, I heard about that shit. Don't no one in Minnesota want that."

"I bet the homies go crazy when they hear, I got it."

"If they like it, then what are you gonna do?"

Mike simply replied," I'm gonna come back an get some more. Then I'm gonna open up shop and get my money on!"

GOING NOWHERE FAST
CHAPTER 29

Mike spent the first two days back in town with Rachel, but all the while, he was thinking about Jackie.
While he was out of town, he talked to Jackie almost everyday, now that she had her own spot. When she told him about her new apartment, he was shocked at first. Once it set in, hearing those words were like sweet music to his ears. The part he like the most, was the fact she moved into the heart of the hood.

When the two days were up, and Mike figured he'd pacified Rachel enough, he called a cab. The destination: Jackie's.

Once inside the cab, Mike gave the cab driver the address and $30 dollars up front, for the ride across town. He then laid back and closed his eyes, as he did his best to get comfortable. The longer he was in the cab, the safer he found himself feeling. It was like a big load was lifted off of his back, and he liked this new feeling.

"Man, I'm gonna have to start taking cabs more often," he thought.

Mike inhaled deeply, and before he could exhale, his eyes shot open. Frantically looking from side to side, he tried to find the source of the familiar smell of his dad's aftershave. He quickly found it, after putting two and two together. He looked up front and saw the cab driver was freshly shaved, and he had his window slightly cracked open. Mike knew there was no question about it, this cab driver and his dad wore the same aftershave.

Mike thought about the few times he had the chance to

wake up under the same roof as his dad. Every morning started out the same, with Mike in the bathroom, drenching himself in his dad's aftershave. He never knew if that would be his last time seeing his dad, for God knew how long. Mike figured if he could keep his dad's smell with him, he wouldn't miss his dad as much.

Every time Mike replayed those few fond memories, he found himself smiling from ear to ear. This time was no different. It even delivered a drop of peace to his heart.

In such a state, Mike once again closed his eyes, and laid back on the seat. It didn't take long to drift off.

"Sir! Sir! Excuse me Sir! We're here."

Still half asleep, Mike opened his eyes and looked at the cab driver.

"You said we're here?"

"Yes, Sir."

Still in somewhat of a daze, Mike looked out of the window to his right, and saw Jackie's building.

"Well, how much more do I owe you?"

"No, I owe you $1.20."

"Look, keep it, and thanks for the ride."

Mike then got out of the cab and stretched, as he looked around to see who he could see. He was glad, once he saw no one was in sight. He didn't want any of his homies to know he was back in town just yet. He wanted to first spend some time with Jackie, and his baby girl.

"So far, so good," he thought, as he walked up the stairs leading to the building door. Right before he could ring Jackie's buzzer, he saw a young lady coming out of the building. Mike grabbed the door as it was closing. Before he walked into the building, he gave the young lady a quick once over. He then said, "I hope to see you more often."

The young lady didn't bother to respond. She just looked back at Mike and smiled, as she kept on walking.

Somewhat satisfied with her reaction, Mike turned around

and headed up the three flights of stairs leading to Jackie's floor. There was on question about it, Mike liked what he saw so far, when it came to the building. By the time he made it to Jackie's door, he already had the building's future mapped out.

"Man, I know there's good feens in this building. I'm about to turn this bitch out!"

Such plans were just another typical reflection of Mike's dysfunctional ways, which were normal in his eyes.

As he stood outside of Jackie's door, he heard some music playing, so he tapped on the door with a little force. By the time he got to his sixth and final tap, he heard someone turn the music down. Satisfied that he got someone's attention, he just waited for someone to open the door.

Jackie was sitting on the couch, finishing her daughter's last braid, when she heard the first tap. Right away she knew who it was. She'd been waiting for such a tap for two days.

"Mommy, someone's at the door."

"I know, watch out, and let mommy get by."

Not wanting to seem to eager, Jackie slowly walked over to the radio, to turn it down. To get a little get back, she put the chain in place before she unlocked the door and opened it.

"Who is it?" She asked.

"Girl, quit playing, you know who it is."

"Two days ago I would have."

"What does that pose to mean?"

"It means, where have you been for the last two days?"
"You make it seem like you know when I got back."

"Well, I do, because your mom been calling here, looking for you."

"Mommy, is that daddy?" Shonna asked.

"Yeah, it's me," Mike replied.

267

"Mommy, let daddy in."

"I see someone still loves me. Now Jackie, what you gonna do?"

"Boy, you make me sick."

"So, you still love me."

"Boy, watch out so I can take this chain off."

Once inside, Mike gave the front room, and the little dining room a quick once over. A nice black leather couch, an entertainment center, and a little round, wooden, dining room table, was a good starter kit, Mike thought. "I like, I like."

"So, it ain't for you to like."

"Yeah, just like that nightgown you still got on."

"Boy, do you know what time it is why you're sitting there talking shit? If you don't, it's 10:30."

"If that's so, then can we get some cheese eggs? You want some cheese eggs, don't you baby?" Mike asked his daughter.

"Yeah mommy, can I have some toast too?"

"Yeah, mommy, can we have some toast too?" Mike joked, really pushing it now.

Jackie couldn't help it, she had to laugh because she knew just like Mike knew, he had her.

"Boy, you're too much."

"Yes, I am," Mike agreed.

After they ate their breakfast, Mike chased his daughter around the apartment, tickling her. They played and just enjoyed each others company until Shonna climbed up on the couch and took a nap.

"That don't make no sense. Y'all sat there, and ran around this apartment for two hours straight. Now look at my baby."

"I'm ready to put someone else to sleep now."

"And who is that? Because it sure ain't me."

"Is that right? Well, come here, and let's see."

After they went at it for a hard twenty minutes, Jackie was still awake, and her mind was oh so clear. For some strange reason, her memory always seemed to come to life after she had sex, and today was no different.

"Ba, I almost forgot, I seen Big Mike, and he gave me his number to give to you."

"Is that right, I was just thinking about my dad earlier today."

"I was gonna give him your pager number, but I didn't know if you wanted him to have it."

"Shit, I can't find it no way. I think I lost it."

"Is that why you wouldn't call me back?"

"Yeah, why else wouldn't I?"

"Well, I got a new one for you, if you want it."

"Yeah, I'm gonna need that."

"It's on the dresser."

"Baby, you don't got no phone in here?"

"I got a cordless in the kitchen. Hold on, I'll get it."

"Yeah, grab the number too."

Mike didn't waste any time on calling his dad, once Jackie came back in the room with the phone and number. As he was dialing the number, he found himself feeling excited.

"Man! I really want to talk to my dad," he thought.

On the second ring, Mike tensed up, when he heard someone answer. It was the sound of his dad's voice that relaxed him once again.

"Hello!"

"What's up old man?"

"What's going on son? How you been?"

"I been cool."

"So, I see your wife gave you the number."

"That's where I'm at right now."

"Is that right? Well, where is she?"

"Right here, ear hustling'."

"Tell her I said hi."

"Jackie, pops said what's up."

"Pop's what up."

"I heard her, and where's the baby?"

"She's up front, asleep. A pop's, I got a new pager number for you, so go get a pen."

"Yea, I was gonna ask you if you had a number I could reach you, at all times, because I know you're still cooking it up, and I stay around fools trying to eat."

"That's what I'm talking about. I sure need to feed 'em."

"Feed who? What are you and your dad talking about?"

"Girl, there you go, tripping."

"Ha, ha, ha!"

"Pop's, what you laughing at? This shit ain't funny. This girl's crazy."

"If I am, you made me this way."

"Anyway pops, you ready for this number?"

"Yeah, I been ready. I was just waiting for you and your wife to stop driving each other crazy!"

"Jackie, what's the number?"

"Oh, now you need me, right. Well, when are you gonna feed me?"

"Shit, I just fed you. Why you're all on my back? Now, would you please give me the number?"

"You should of thought about that before you started talking shit."

"Boy, y'all two are a mess," Big Mike cut in.

"Yeah pop's, you can say that again, but it ain't me. Hold on pop's. Girl, take this phone, and give him the number. Ba, why you putting me through such madness?"

"Anyway, it's 601-7434."

"Pop's, are you ready for the number?"

"I already got it. I heard her, it's 7434-601, right?"

"Yeah, that's it, but I want you to put 006 behind your
number, so I'll know it's you."

"006, that's cool. Well look, I'm gonna get off this phone,
and let you two love birds do what y'all do. I'll be getting
up with you real soon, so be ready."

"Don't even trip. I will."

"Alright."

"Talk to you later, pop's."

After he got off the phone with his dad, Mike didn't make
his next move until a little after eight. He found it was a lot
easier on his mind to move in the dark when he was
traveling on foot. He thought about calling a cab, but he
figured he could make the twenty, or so, block trip to
Brandon's, by the time the cab finally would make it to
Jackie's.

All the way there he had only one thing on his mind,
getting higher then ever. The fact that he'd been sober for
the last two and a half days, was killing him. He knew if he
waited any linger, he would end up smoking one of the four
"wet sticks" that he had rolled up.

When he made it to the comer of Brandon's block, he
wasn't surprised to see Blast's Monte parked out front.
Every since Lucky died, Brandon's house became the new
hang out spot. He knew he was only steps away from
getting his buzz on, so he put on a little speed walk. The
front door was basically off limits, so Mike walked around
back, only to see C-shot and Dalla Bill's cars parked in the
back yard. Seeing C-shot's car was a very good sign that
some drinking was going down, and Mike was in the mood
to party.

Knowing that the back door was never locked, Mike didn't
bother to knock, he just walked in. As the door opened, the
room went quiet. The smoke that was in the air made it
hard for Mike to see who was in the room. As Mike was

trying to make out a face or two, everyone in the room was trying to see who this was coming through the door. Everyone was tense, not knowing what to expect. It was the sound of Mike's voice that put everyone at ease.

"What's crackin' Cuz, let a young Gee hit something."

C-shot was the first to respond, and Mike quickly read his body language. "Cuz, Cuz ce cool homie."

"Cuz, what's your hand doing under your shirt like that?"

"Homie, you already know I mean business when it comes to pulling this thing out, and letting it ride."

"Well, you can take your hand off. What's that, the seven, or is that the four nickel?"

"Nope, it's their little sister, 3.80."

"Oh, yeah? When you get her?"

"I just got her yesterday."

"That's whats up," Mike replied, looking around the room.

"What's up homie," came from four different directions.

"Dalla' Bill, Blast, Stone, Brandon, what's up Cuz?"

Blast passed Mike the blunt he was smoking on, and said, "Here Cuz, hit this."

"Yea, let me hit that, and you can lit this."

Mike took the blunt from Blast, and he handed him one of the four wet sticks, he'd been dying to smoke.

"Homie, what's this?"

"That's that shit!"

"Oh Yeah! That's what I'm talking about."

C-shot and Dalla' Bill sipped on a cold one, while they watch the other four, chain smoke stick after stick. In the middle of the third stick, Brandon walked out of the room. As he was leaving, he called Mike, as if to say, "Follow me."

Mike looked at the other two, and said, "Let me go see what Cuz is talking about, when I come back, we can smoke this last stick."

Even thought everyone was higher then they had ever been, they really didn't want to smoke anymore, their egos wouldn't let them say so.

Mike stood up, and right away he had to catch himself before he fell, face first. It was like he didn't have any strength in his legs.

After seeing such a sight, there wasn't one person in the room that wasn't damn near crying from laughter.

"Cuz, are you alright?" C-Shot asked.

"Yeah, my leg was just asleep, that's all."

Such an answer didn't call for anything but more laughter, because they all knew he was full of shit. Mike couldn't hold it any longer, he too started laughing, as he tip toed into the next room where Brandon was waiting.

"Brandon, what's up?"

"A Cuz, you know that fool died?"

"What fool?"

"At the weed spot, in the Hood."

"The one that lives on the same block as Cuz?"

"Yeah, so be cool when you're sliding through the hood. The haters already snatched up Dave."

"Is that right? Well what happened to him? And why did they snatch up Cuz?"

"Cuz....Cuz, you're a fool, homie."

"Look homie, you're blowing my high, with this shit. It don't got shit to do with me, so I ain't trying to talk about it."

"Well, I'm gone from it. I just wanted to let you know, so you can stay on your toes."

"I feel you homie. Good looking out, now let's go smoke this last stick."

GOING NOWHERE FAST
CHAPTER 30

After being kicked out, they all decided to head to their home girl, Baby Blue's spot. They were all in the mood for some female company, and everyone knew, that was the spot for such action.

Thanks to Mike, it didn't take them long to wear out their welcome. No one needed to say it, it was known, that once the harsh smell of the wet reached Brandon's grandma, up front, their party would be over.

Before Brandon could hit the wet stick a second time, the door leading to the front of the house, flew open. "Don't just sit there like y'all don't know what's going on, get out, and take Brandon's high ass with you."

With C-shot and Dolla' Bill following in C-shot's car, the zombie train lead the way. Brandon and Stone were in the back, while Mike was in the passenger seat. Blast was doing his best to get them to their destination safely, as he drove.

The four amigo's were so high that they didn't even realize there wasn't any music playing. It was the pounding of their hearts that they were listening to, as they bobbed their heads. No one bothered to speak, and Mike found that troubling. He was in no mood to think, and dwell on the conversation he had with Brandon, but he couldn't help it.

"Man, why did Brandon feel like he had to tell me, of all people, about the weed? I know it don't got shit to do with me, so fuck it. But Damn, I still don't know where those

274

two ounces I found under Rachel's mattress came from. I should of asked him, when did the fool die? The way he was saying it, it was like the fool got killed or something. Then the haters snatched up Dave. I wonder what he did, or is it tied with the weed man? Man, I need to know if I'm in the middle of some bullshit! Man, what the fuck is going on? Fuck it, I'm gone just leave it alone."

"Mike! Cuz, let me out, Damn."

Still caught up in his thoughts, Mike looked from side to side, in a confused state. On his right, he saw Baby Blue's building, and on his left, he saw Brandon getting out behind Blast. "Damn Cuz, we got here quick," Mike noted.

"Mike, just open the door. You're tripping," Stone replied.

"A, we're here for real?" Mike asked, still trying to get it together.

Frustrated by Mike's actions, Stone decided to get out the same way Brandon did. He couldn't stand being back there any longer. He was having hot and cold chills, and his mouth was as dry as Afghanistan sand.

"Mike, Cuz, you're stuck as hell."

By the time Mike made it to the building door, that was held open by Brandon, Mike was out of breath. Once inside of the building, Mike placed his hands on his knees, as he did his best to catch his breath. Everyone else headed up the stairs leading to the second floor, where Baby Blue lived.

"Damn Cuz, it feels like I just ran twenty blocks," Mike stated. "But the fucked up part about it is, everything seems to be moving in slow motion."

When Mike heard the second floor door slam, he knew they left him. He rested a little while longer, as he did his best to pull himself together. Once he realized there was nothing he could do it escape such a high, he climbed the two flights of stairs.

"Was Blast tripping?" she thought. Baby Blue knew she heard him right when he said don't close the door, because Mike was right behind them. At first, she just held the door open and waited. Then, she stepped into the hallway, to take a look, but still no Mike.

"Them high ass nigga's got me tripping now. Mike ain't even in town," she thought. She then walked back into her apartment, and closed the door. Right before she could lock it, she heard someone opening the squeaky hallway door. She snatched her door open, and stuck her head out to take one last look. That's when she saw Mike doing his best to walk.

"Boy, look at you. That don't make no sense."

"What's up Cuz?"

"What the hell you been smoking to make your eyes look like that?"

Mike didn't bother to answer such a question. For the first time in his life, he wished he wasn't high at all. He came to realize, there wasn't any fun in being so high, it felt like you had weights strapped to your ankles and wrists. Not to mention, the tricks your mind starts to play on you.

He was in no mood to chit chat anymore than he had to. He figured he'd paid his respects by saying "What's up," now he needed to find a place to sit his high ass down, so he could rest.

When he finally made it to the front room, there were one set of eyes that caught his attention. He didn't know if he was starting to see things because he was so high, or was that really Kim sitting on the couch, looking at him? Mike was in no mood to make a bigger ass out of himself. So, he figured calling her name was out of the question. He had to get up close and personal, to make sure his eyes weren't playing tricks on him. He did his best to step over Brandon and Stone's legs, because they were both sitting on the floor with their backs to the wall. Even with his best effort, he still ended up stepping on Stone's lower leg, and Brandon's ankle. "Damn Cuz, watch out."

"Sit your ass down."

Such an outburst didn't make it into one ear of Mike's, to go out of the other. The only thing he as trying to pay attention to, was find out if that was really Kim or not. The closer he got, the clearer her face became.

He also realized, for the first time, she had something in her arms. He figured it had to be a baby.

"Why are you looking at me like that?" Kim asked.

No response, just a stare, then his eyes focused on what she was holding. He was right, it was a baby. A baby boy to be exact. "I saw this baby before, but where?" he thought.

Then it hit him, he was thinking about the picture of him when he was six weeks old, hanging over his mom's bed. He couldn't believe how much the baby in her arms looked liked him when he was that age.

"Kim, who's baby is that?"

"Mine, why?"

"Well, who's the dad?"

All at the same time, everyone in the room said, "Cuz, that's all you."

"Y'all tripping," Kim replied. " Mike, you don't know him, he's from out of town."

"How old is he?"

"Six weeks."

Mike was to high to ask anymore questions. There was no doubt in his mind, he knew he was the father. "I'll deal with this another time, but right now, I need to find a place to sit my high ass down," he thought.

Blast and Tone did their best to lay Mike in a comfortable position on Blast's couch. Once they were satisfied, they stood over Mike and watched him sleep like a baby. Such sleep wasn't naturally achieved by Mike. It was the wet that put him in somewhat of a comatose state. Like they always say, "Looks can be deceiving," and in this case, they sure were.

For Mike, there was no peace in the dream world that his surroundings gave birth to. Consumed by so many unanswered questions, Mike found himself fighting a losing battle, once again. Even in his sleep, there was no escaping the conversation he had with Brandon. He was forced to relieve it, over and over again, while he slept.

Instead of someone counting backwards from three to one, then clapping their hands once, it was the vibration of his pager, that brought him out of his trance. Unlike any other time, Mike didn't just open up his eyes, and remain laying there. This time, once he opened his eyes, he jumped right up and stood on his feet. He was glad that he was once again free from such torture. "Lord, Thank You!"

Mike soon realized he wasn't the only person in the room. Stone was on the love seat enjoying his dream when Mike's movements woke him.

"Cuz, what are you on?" Stone asked.

"My bad homie. You know how I be going through a thang."

"Yeah, I sure do. You was trippin' last night."

Mike was in no mood to think about what happened last night. To escape such a conversation, Mike didn't reply, he just looked down at his pager. He wasn't surprised to see his dad's code behind the number. He knew that could only mean one thing, it was time to hustle.

"A stone, you got some work?"

"Yeah. Why what's up?"

"Well, slang me a little something."

"Cuz, I'll tell you what, help me get this little work off that I got, then we can take a trip to the city so I can really get right. Then I can plug you for real."

"Cuz, don't even trip, I got you."

For the next few days, Mike and Stone hit the block hard, hustling. They made most of their sells at Mike's dad, big Mike's house. That's also where they spent most of their time. Mike figured if that was the only way he could spend some time with his dad, he would take it. The face that they both stayed high wasn't an issue. It wasn't like they truly felt comfortable talking to each other anyway.

Once again, things were falling in place for Mike. There was only on thing still bothering him, those unanswered questions which were dwelling in the back of his mind. He did everything in his power to keep them there. From sun up to sun down, he made sure he remained sedated, in one way or another. The only thing he couldn't stop was the homies asking him what happened to Dave. Even when that happened, he did his best to change the conversation.

Mike did his best to keep his mind working. There was no time to relax, let alone rest. He made sure he and stone stayed on the move. The only time he slept was when his body couldn't take anymore running. When that took place, it didn't matter where he was at, he was out.

Living under such pressure started getting the best of Mike. He started feeling like the walls were closing in on him. He no longer knew what to think. He didn't know if he was starting to see things.

It started out as a typical bike ride to the store, to get some blunts. The funny part about it, Mike already had a new box in his flannel pocket. He called himself doing the right thing, by letting Stone and the home girl have some time alone.

He jumped on her little brother's bike, and headed for the store. The ride there went smooth. It was the ride back that became a problem for Mike. Halfway down the block, the store was on, he spotted a suspicious car driving up the block. Right when they were about to pass each other, their eyes connected. Mike looked straight into the silver lenses the white man driving the car had on. At first, he didn't think anything of it, but something told him to take a second look. That's when he saw the suspicious car at the corner, making a U-turn.

Mike didn't give it a second thought, he was out. Once he made it back to the home girl's house, as he ran up the stairs, he thought, "Damn, I ain't never rode a bike that fast before."

With his heart still pounding, he knocked on the door as fast as he could.

"Who the hell is it?" The home girl asked.

"Cuz, hurry up, it's me."

The home girl heard the fear in Mike's voice, and she found herself starting to get worried. She was trying to open the door so fast, that she forgot to take off the chain. "Damn Cuz, hold on."

"Just open up the door please," Mike pleaded.

When she finally got the door open, Stone was standing behind her. He looked at Mike, and said, "Cuz, what's up homie?"

"I just got little haters. I don't know why they was on my dick, but I know they was trying to pull it."

Stone and the home girl both stood there looking at Mike, not knowing what to think.

"Mike, you need to sit your ass down, and chill out. You had me all worried, like you was hurt or something."

"Fuck all of that, I need to smoke. Where can I dump this blunt out?"

For the next hour, they smoked blunt, after blunt. Then they sat in their same spots, stuck for another half hour. If it wasn't for Stone, they could have sat there for another hour or so, doing nothing.

"Cuz, I got a taste for some shrimp fried rice and some egg rolls."

"Stone, you ain't said nothing," Mike replied, loving the idea. " Homie, let's roll."

"Y 'all better bring me back something."

"Girl, don't even trip, we got you."

"A Stone, Cuz, we should call a cab," Mike volunteered.

"It's only six or seven blocks," Stone replied. "We can walk."

Mike knew there was no winning such an argument. Stone had a point. But, when it came down to it, the restaurant was only five blocks away. To Mike, it was five blocks too many, to walk at such a time, when he didn't know what was going on.

Just like Mike thought it would be, it was the longest five blocks he ever walked. His pride was the only thing keeping him from breaking out running. When they finally made it to the block the restaurant was on, Mike broke into a speed walk.

Trying to match Mike's pace, Stone was like, "Damn Cuz, slow down."

"Homie, you can play if you want, I'll see you at the spot."

When Stone finally made it inside the restaurant, he saw Mike was already at the window, ordering.

"Cuz, let me get some shrimp fried rice, and four egg rolls."

"I already know. I ordered enough, trust me," Mike replied.

"Don't even trip, I got it this time. You just get it next time," Mike added.

"That's cool with me," Stone replied.

"I bet it is," Mike fired back.

"Cuz, I'm at the table."

"Well, what kind of pop do you want?" Mike asked.

"Oh yeah. Damn, I forgot all about that. Let me get a orange."

"Yeah, and y'all said I was high."

Mike watched, as Stone walked to a corner table and sat down. Satisfied with Stone's choice, Mike turned around, and watched his food being cooked. Right when his tray of food was being brought to him, his pager went off. He looked at he number, and was shook at first, because it was a weird number, but then he saw his dad's code.

"Pop's got some more money for his son," Mike thought.

Once Mike got his tray, he took it to the table. He then walked to the pay phone right outside. He called the number, and his dad answered on the first ring.

"Hello!"

"Pop's, what's up?"

"Boy, where are you at?"

"Up here on Chicago and Lake, at the Chinese restaurant, eating a little somethin' with my homie. Why, what's up?"

"Can you believe I got pulled over today, and the police said I was little Mike, and I got a warrant for murder?"

"Is that right?" Mike asked, not knowing what to think. "They're on some bullshit, fuck em, I'm good!"

"Well little Mike, watch yourself out there."

"Don't even trip, I will."

"Well alright, just watch yourself, I got to go."

"Alright Pop's."

Mike then hung up the phone, and went back into the restaurant to eat. He did his best to shake the conversation he just had with his dad, but every spoon full of rice he ate, he replayed the phone call.

"Man, I hope, don't know one got me in the middle of no bullshit!"

Mike didn't even realize he said that out loud, until Stone said, "Cuz, it ain't nothing."

Just that fast, Mike lost his appetite, and the sight of the food on his tray disgusted him. Stone knew how Mike could flip out at times, so he didn't think anything of Mike's quick mood change. On some greedy shit, he went right back to eating.

Mike looked over at the two fortune cookies, laying next to his plate. Right away, they had his full attention. He even stopped thinking about the conversation he just had with his dad.

"Cuz, let me see what those lying motha fucka's are talking about."

He wasn't interested in eating them, he wanted to know what the fortune said. Instead of grabbing the closest one to him, Mike grabbed the one that was the farthest away. It was like it was talking to him, saying, "I'm the one you want."

He cracked the cookie in half, and slowly pulled the fortune out. Once he got a firm grip on it, using his thumb and index fingers of both hands, he read it himself,

"Keep Calm, The Big One's Coming."

At first, the substance of such a message was hard for him to grasp. Then, after he read it for the third time, his understanding of such a message became a bit clearer. Without worning, his stomach tightened up in a knot, and he thought he was about to die.

"Fuck!" He cried out, as he noticed the sound of the police in the distance.

As he listened to the screaming sirens grow louder, along with the first pair of screeching tires coming to a halt, all Mike could do was smile. He then looked at the fortune one last time, before he put it in his pocket. Then, Instead of thinking it, he said it out loud,

Keep Calm, The Big One's Coming...

THE FOOTSTEPS OF
<u>GOING NOWHERE FAST</u>

Swallowed Up By The Coldest Darkness
I Can No Longer Tell Day From Night
No Longer Can I See The Sun rays That Provide The Light
In This Domain, The Birds Don't Sing, They Scream For
One Peaceful Thought, I Yearn And I Feen
What Can Intervene, True Love, I Know
But How Much Pain Does It Take For True Love To Show
Up I Look, Mind State Is Shook
I Think It's Up, But Is It Down
Is The Smile On My Face Really A Frown
Right From Wrong, Wrong From Right
How Was I To Know, 8 Years Back Was The Path To The
Light
I Desperately Searched Every Crack and Cranny
And I've Yet To Find One Person Who Truly Understands
Me.....
Love Is The Only Answer,
So Embrace It!

By: Samuel T. Yeager

<u>COMING SOON</u>

- ***THE JOURNEY TO THE LIGHT*, the follow up to (GOING NOWHERE FAST) BY: SAMUEL T. YEAGER**

- ***IT'S AL'IGHT* BY: SAMUEL T. YEAGER**

- ***THE ALTIMATE REFLECTION* BY: SAMUEL T. YEAGER**

GOING NOWHERE FAST

A TALE BY

SAMUEL T. YEAGER

After a dash of Gang Life, two teaspoons of Drug Abuse, a gallon of Unhealthy Love, and six ounces of the Deepest desire, to take your Family away from the Madness in the HOOD, on top of sixty kilos of Failure, then you would only possess, half of the Recipe of
 MIKE'S LIFE...

"GOING NOWHERE FAST" is a reflection of Dis-function in its Rawest Form...

So, if you're looking for Chaos and Confusion in a Tale that's based on a True Story, "GOING NOWHERE FAST" will give you that, and much, much more...

32064264R00162